Praise for Lauren K. Denton

"A Lauren K. Denton novel is like a whispered secret from a dear friend, and her latest lyrical stunner is no exception. *A Place to Land* captures the gray areas of life in all their complexity and questions whether we can ever really move on from the past. In a story of sisterhood and small-town secrets, Denton proves that, in our lives, like our art, there is always a chance to create beauty from the brokenness. Denton is a masterful storyteller who makes magic on every perfect page."

—Kristy Woodson Harvey, *New York Times* bestselling author of *The Wedding Veil*

"Lauren K. Denton is a master at crafting deeply meaningful stories that explore the relationships that give life purpose, beauty, and richness. *A Place to Land* is a touching tribute to sisterhood, first loves, and promises kept."

—Susan Meissner, *USA TODAY* bestselling author of *The Nature of Fragile Things*

"The sweeping romance you need."

—*Frolic* for *The One You're With*

"A family's idyllic home life is disrupted by a stranger in this excellent inspirational drama from Denton . . . [A] powerful, contemplative family saga."

—*Publishers Weekly* for *The One You're With*

"A compelling beach read."

—*Booklist* for *The One You're With*

"*The One You're With* touches on how the choices we make can shape a lifetime, for better or for worse, and serves as a reminder to never take love for granted."

—Heather Webber, *USA TODAY* bestselling author of *Midnight at the Blackbird Café*

"A complex, compelling, powerful story about the roads not taken, the seismic shifts that can happen in an instant, and the way that sometimes, the decisions of the past shape the future in ways we couldn't have imagined."

—Kristin Harmel, *New York Times* bestselling author of *The Forest of Vanishing Stars*, for *The One You're With*

a

place to

land

Also by Lauren K. Denton

The One You're With
The Summer House
Glory Road
Hurricane Season
The Hideaway

a place to land

Lauren K. Denton

HARPER MUSE

A Place to Land

Published by Harper Muse, an imprint of HarperCollins Focus LLC.

This book is a work of fiction. The characters, incidents, and dialogue are drawn from the author's imagination and are not to be construed as real. Any resemblance to actual events or persons, living or dead, is entirely coincidental.

Any internet addresses (websites, blogs, etc.) in this book are offered as a resource. They are not intended in any way to be or imply an endorsement by HarperCollins Focus LLC, nor does HarperCollins Focus LLC vouch for the content of these sites for the life of this book.

Library of Congress Cataloging-in-Publication Data

Names: Denton, Lauren K., author.
Title: A place to land / Lauren K. Denton.
Description: [Nashville] : Harper Muse, [2022] | Summary: "Written in Lauren Denton's signature Southern style, A Place to Land tells a story of sisterhood, healing, and the meaning of home"-- Provided by publisher.
Identifiers: LCCN 2022013212 (print) | LCCN 2022013213 (ebook) | ISBN 9780785232650 (hardcover) | ISBN 9780785232674 (epub) | ISBN 9780785232681
Classification: LCC PS3604.E5956 P53 2022 (print) | LCC PS3604.E5956 (ebook) | DDC 813/.6--dc23
LC record available at https://lccn.loc.gov/2022013212
LC ebook record available at https://lccn.loc.gov/2022013213

Printed in the United States of America
22 23 24 25 26 LSC 5 4 3 2 1

To Meme's Crew, with love

Sugar Bend has always been known as a place of secrets and mystery. In this small town nestled alongside Little River, words spoken in confidence turn to mist, evaporating before anyone else can take notice of them. Fish swim against the current, pushing themselves deeper into the rich river water even as the tide sweeps everything else out into the Gulf. Mourning doves float on the water's early morning surface like ducks, as if the water were a safer place than land. And long-gone memories, thick as the rain-heavy air, tend to come back at the strangest of times, as sharp and clear as if they'd only just happened.

The town of Sugar Bend sprouted in a cozy crook of the river over a century ago, and its people built stores and homes along the thin ribbon of brackish water. Now lazy roads fan out on either side of it, full of candy-colored houses, birds that chirp in the middle of the night, and dogs that crisscross the road in search of the tastiest handouts.

But on the edge of town, the secrets deepen along with the river, and as the water grows shadowy under tree-dappled shade, the mysteries darken as well. For way down deep in the murky blue-green depths, a little boat sleeps. Forty years ago it was laid to rest in its silent, watery burial ground by a pair of strong hands—hands that belonged to a girl whose life was irrevocably changed in the span of one steamy, glass-calm night.

PART ONE

lift

o n e

On a quiet silver morning, before the world—or at least the rest of Sugar Bend—had awoken, Violet Figg took in the spirited birdsong from her back porch overlooking Little River. She wrapped her hands around her mug of tea and closed her eyes to listen. There by the steps was the three-part whistle of a Carolina wren. Up in the scrubby oak along the side of the porch was the soft *coo-oo* of a mourning dove. A great blue heron squawked as it landed at the edge of the grass and lifted its head high atop its skinny neck.

At the quick, squeaky *chit-chit* coming from near the back steps, Violet smiled. She'd started seeing the ruby-throated hummingbirds a few weeks ago, back in town from their yearly jaunt down to Mexico and other parts farther south. She was always happy to see them return.

This morning there were two of them, a male and a female, with wings that beat so fast they all but disappeared. Where the male had iridescent green feathers on his back and the telltale bright red throat, the female's feathers were paler green and she was missing that trademark ruby red. What she did have was a splotch on the underside of her neck that resembled a sun with brilliant rays shooting out from the center. This particular hummingbird had visited Violet's feeders last season, and possibly the one before that too. Trudy didn't believe her, but Violet knew her birds.

"Getting a little breakfast before you start your day, huh?" Violet rose and placed her hand against the screen, and the female turned her head toward Violet's voice. "Well, hello to you too," she murmured. She'd mix up a new batch of nectar for them when she returned from her morning survey. She glanced at her watch. Still had a little time.

At a rustle behind her the birds took one last sip, then flew away, and Violet turned to see her sister lean in through the doorway that led from the kitchen onto the porch. Trudy's blue-striped pajamas were rumpled, and she rubbed a hand over her eyes as she yawned.

At one time in her life, Trudy Figg wouldn't have stepped out of the house without her long blonde hair meticulously brushed and rolled, eyeliner in a perfect cat eye, and lips lined and glossed. She'd sheathed her lovely form in all manner of sparkly gowns and bikinis in her quest to win every beauty pageant she entered, which for the most part she had.

The gowns and bikinis were long gone, along with all traces of makeup, hair products, and her voice, but her face was still beautiful. As much as Trudy tried to run from it, it was hard to hide the still-bright eyes, Cupid's-bow lips, and smooth cheeks, despite her sixty-three years. Today Trudy sported a particularly impressive bedhead, with short gray-brown curls sticking out all over. And knowing Trudy, she wouldn't even try to tame it before shoving a hat on her head and heading out on her daily treasure hunt.

Pausing in the doorway, Trudy tapped her watch and tilted her head in question.

"I'm always up early." Over the years Violet had learned to decipher her sister's unspoken communication, and she often knew what Trudy was thinking even when Trudy didn't reach for the ever-present notepad and pencil she kept in her pocket. Violet nodded toward the bird feeder hanging on the other side of the screen. "I saw Sunshine this morning." It was her nickname for the hummingbird with the sun rays on her neck. "She found her way back."

Trudy had already pulled out her notepad and was scratching out a note. When she finished she held it out for Violet to read. *With all those birds crisscrossing the skies during migrations, what makes you think you have repeat visitors?*

Violet shrugged. "It happens."

Trudy threw out a skeptical glance, but Violet pushed it away. "The birds know a good thing when they see it, and they've been known to go back to the same feeder year after year." She nudged her glasses up on the bridge of her nose. "Regardless, they're here and I like it." Violet faced out toward the river and the wide sky above it. Clear as a bell, light breeze. An osprey swooped over the river, a fish dangling in its talons.

Behind her Trudy began to write again. *I'm going to the*

*island before the tide comes back in. Don't call the coast guard
on me like you did last time.*

"I wish you'd take your phone." Violet wrapped her arms
around herself. Early May in Alabama wasn't cold by any
stretch, but she felt a chill nonetheless. "Those teenagers on the
Jet Skis make me nervous. And the drunk fishermen. You know
how they race each other to get out into the Gulf."

A corner of Trudy's mouth lifted in a grin as she wrote.
*Not too many teenagers out before seven in the morning. And
fishermen won't start drinking until lunchtime.*

Violet opened her mouth to rattle off another reason why it
wasn't safe for Trudy to be out on the water alone, but Trudy
began writing again.

*I'm a big girl, Violet. You don't always have to watch out
for me. I'll be just fine.*

And with that Trudy winked, then ducked back into the
house.

"'Just fine,'" Violet murmured, her gaze still on the spot
where Trudy had been standing. *I do have to watch out for you,*
she thought. *It's my job.*

With Trudy gone the porch seemed more still than usual.
Trudy had been quiet for forty years, but even in her silence,
she could be loud. At least with Violet. Sometimes she seemed
to nearly vibrate with life, but she refused to open her mouth
and let any of it out.

Violet would have been happy with anything—a shout of
anger, a burst of laughter, a single word. There were times, just
after everything had happened, when Violet fought the urge to

grab Trudy by the shoulders and demand she speak. Or at least explain, on that blasted notepad, why she couldn't even say a word to Violet. The rest of the world, okay, but to her own sister? Her only family? But Violet had learned to let that go.

She heaved a lungful of air and slowly let it leak out. Violet loved her sister with every fiber, every shred of her being, and though the past crept back in sometimes, pressing on her shoulders and jabbing her in the stomach with its long, scabby fingers, Violet no longer allowed herself to think about all she'd given up, for love and for obligation. For penance.

Violet settled down in her rocking chair, the floral cushion shaped from years of her back-porch bird-watching, and pushed off gently, setting the rocker into a slow back-and-forth. Before her, the sky over the river brightened by small increments. A splash of mauve here, a streak of pink there. A little while later, Trudy crossed the yard below. Dressed in a pair of black swim shorts and a yellow T-shirt, Trudy—Violet's sole companion for all these years—lugged her kayak under one arm and a bucket for her treasures in the other. The last time she'd gone to Roberts Island, she'd brought home a three-foot piece of gnarly driftwood, now well on its way to becoming a quirky lamp, which their customers would no doubt love and fight each other for. The bucket was too small for wood that large, but it'd be perfect for the shells and dried pods and fronds Trudy was always picking up and toting home.

Violet and Trudy owned and operated Two Sisters Art and Handmade Goods in downtown Sugar Bend. What started as a place for Trudy to make and sell her popular mixed-media art pieces had grown over the years into a shop where patrons could find just-right gifts for any occasion. Trudy's unconventional sculptures were always a big hit, and their inventory also included everything from hand-thrown pottery to small canvas paintings to handmade soap, candles, and door wreaths.

Aside from just an art shop, Two Sisters had become somewhat of a gathering spot for people who needed rest and community—men whose wives were busy shopping, lonely seniors who craved company and conversation, even a few book clubs and knitting circles. Violet and Trudy had bought the shop eight years ago from the previous owners, who'd had to sell quickly, for a song. Trudy had been selling her artwork at the annual art festival for years, but having a brick-and-mortar space allowed her to sell her wares all through the year rather than in one hectic weekend. It also gave her a place to spread out her materials and work without covering their home with sand and splinters of wood. Or at least not as much as she used to.

Downstairs Trudy stepped into the shallow water alongside their dock and slid the kayak in, then carefully sat and picked up the double-bladed paddle. Only when she began paddling, her strong arms pulling the kayak through the glass surface of the river, did Violet stand to ready herself for her morning bird survey.

But just as she reached for her mug, a strange sensation washed through her, like ice water rippling under her skin. She paused, then turned to the screen door and pushed it open. There on the top step, as if someone had laid it there just for her, was a complete set of fish bones.

Violet's breath rushed out and her skin tingled, a chill shooting up her arms and across the back of her neck. The skeleton was about as long as the width of her hand. It had a head with a gaping hole where the eye had once been, a spine with slender ribs sticking out, and at the end, the wispy, fragile bones of a small tail fin.

Despite living mere feet from the river and just a few miles from the Gulf of Mexico, the sight of the bones didn't bring to mind the river teeming with life or the many fish she'd grilled, fried, or baked over the years—instead, she remembered the last day she'd seen *him*. He'd been wearing a crisp navy suit, starched white shirt, shiny wing-tip shoes. And the girl on his arm—Trudy, in a red dress, matching lipstick, and an anxious smile. And his trademark cuff links—tiny silver fish bones winking in the light.

In a quick, angry motion, Violet scraped the bones off the top step with the sole of her slipper, and they landed with a dull clatter in the saw grass growing next to the porch. Dropping to a half crouch—knees aching, heart pounding—she swiveled her head, expecting to see him looming on the dock or in the grass or behind her on the porch. But nothing was there. No one watching. Just a dewy morning stretching out its arms, unconcerned by the warning bells ringing in Violet's ears.

Several years ago when Violet first began taking bird surveys for the Coastal Alabama Audubon Society, she'd wake up ludicrously early on survey days, nervously checking and rechecking her small backpack to make sure she had everything she needed: binoculars and camera, clipboard with plenty of data sheets, three pens in case her first two ran out of ink, visor and official birding T-shirt. It was so important to her—this process of observing, counting, and monitoring the birds she'd loved for so long—that she grew shaky and nauseated. Oftentimes her anxiety was so bad that when she finally made it to the beach and the beginning of her route, her hands would tremble and the data she was supposed to collect would disappear as soon as she'd try to write it down.

It was different now, thank goodness. She'd learned to relax into it, to remember she was dealing with the natural world, where things didn't always go according to plan. It wasn't the plans she cared about anyway—the checklists and routines, the data sheets and computer logs—it was the birds themselves. Their effortless flight through the sky, the ease with which they changed course.

Even as a young child, Violet had watched everything from the tiniest blue-gray gnatcatchers with the squeaky calls to the white ibises and great horned owls that soared over her childhood home. Each species was different—Violet was able to identify most birds in her backyard by the time she was seven or eight years old—but they all had one thing in common: total freedom. Violet loved nothing more than to watch "her" birds, as she thought of them, calling and cackling, foraging and flying, all with the ease and freedom of a creature not bound by anything but the needs of its own little body and brain. Nothing stopped them. Watching them fly was always the balm she didn't know she needed.

Today, after a breakfast of oatmeal and a handful of blueberries, she grabbed her trusty backpack—always stocked with the essentials to prevent the nervous checking of her earlier years—and drove south out of Sugar Bend toward the coast. Though the stretch of white sand fronting the Gulf of Mexico had been virtually empty when she was a girl, it was now lined with overpriced restaurants, trendy boutiques, boat-rental shacks, and tall glittering condos. But despite the constant forward motion of progress, the birds were still there, and it was Violet's duty—and pleasure—to keep her eye on them.

She parked at the resort, as she always did, and passed between the two condo towers. She'd walked the path between these condos so often, she'd worn the grass down to sandy dirt, but the man in the resort's guardhouse always looked the other way when she approached with her binoculars and camera around her neck, her wide green visor shading her face and neck from the unforgiving Alabama sun. A sign proclaimed this portion of beach reserved for "Registered Guests Only," but it had been years since he'd asked for her room number. She'd even taught him a little about identifying the birds he saw flying past his windowed box by the entrance gate.

Poor man, Violet often thought. Stuck inside that cramped little space with frigid air pumped out of the window unit, his only company a tiny TV in the corner and the out-of-towners who pulled through the gate all day. He probably thought similar things about her: *Poor woman, all alone out in the heat, with only some birds to keep her company.*

Today he tipped his cap in greeting as she slid through the gap in the gate and continued to the path between towers A and B. It was still early, only seven fifteen, but the sun was already hot, the sky a clear stretch of pale blue all the way to the horizon. She pulled the brim of her visor a little lower as she came out of the shade between the buildings and stepped up onto the wooden walkway that spanned the dunes. At the end of the bridge was a small bench, and as she deposited her shoes there, she was grateful to see hers was the only pair. The beachgoers were still in their rooms eating breakfast and slathering themselves with sunscreen. She still had some time before things got busy.

As always when her bare feet finally met the sand, she paused and dug in, savoring the cool cushion that crept between her toes. People talked about the healing properties of salt water—she remembered her mother once telling her to take a mouthful of Gulf water and gargle it to soothe a sore throat—but in Violet's mind, the real healing was in the sand.

When she reached the firm, damp sand close to the water, she paused and took her clipboard from her backpack. She lifted the waterproof cover page and wrote the date and her name, then jotted down initial notes on the conditions. A quick look around with her binoculars, and she noted a group of birds to her left. *Royal terns, 3, juvenile.*

Violet had been volunteering with the local Audubon chapter for years. She attended lectures about bird migrations and endangered species and volunteered occasionally at the local nature center, mostly keeping kids from sticking their fingers through the bars of the injured-bird habitats. She'd taken an early retirement from teaching a little over ten years ago when Sugar Bend Academy merged with a larger school in the next town, which freed her up to accompany more seasoned volunteers on their regular bird surveys. After a while she was given an official clipboard and her own route.

Her job was to walk a one-mile stretch of beach, observing, counting, and identifying all birds whether on land, water, or in the air. During each survey season, volunteers were charged with recording and logging official data once a week, and Violet fulfilled her duty in rain or shine, heat or chill, and filled out the data sheets in her still-perfect teacher's penmanship.

Today she kept her binoculars at the ready as she made her way down the beach. She moved cautiously, careful not to disturb the birds as they went about the business of their daily lives. For each bird she saw, she made a hatch mark on the bottom of her data sheet, noting the bird's color, age, and sex. It was a morning for the laughing gulls, with several colonies dotting the beach and floating in the shallow water just beyond the gentle waves. The gulls always added a particular zip to the day, with their cackling laughter and slashes of black and white against the azure sky.

When a string of runners passed her, the birds took flight at once, their laughter carrying over the sound of the waves and the stiff breeze. Violet did a quick count, mentally untangling the wings into individual bodies, and noted their particulars—all juveniles, mostly females.

She continued on her route, making notes and occasionally pausing to dip her toes into the water. The time passed quickly as it always did when she was enjoying herself. When she reached the yellow chair-rental stand that signaled the turnaround point of her route, she adjusted the brim of her visor to block the sun, then headed back the way she came, continuing her observations until she reached her starting point. She made a few last notes on her sheet, including two birds she couldn't easily identify, which was rare for her, and finally tucked her clipboard into her backpack.

Back at the foot of the walkway where she'd left her shoes, she took the water hose looped over the handrail and rinsed the sand from her feet and legs. As chilly water ran down her calves and cooled the skin of her feet, something rustled behind her.

She turned just in time to see a large brown pelican stretch out its wings and take flight from the back of the bench. The magnificence of seeing the bird's huge, prehistoric wingspan up close blotted out all else, and she stood still, watching the bird as it soared away from her.

It swooped low over the beach, then glided even lower over the rolling waves, its wings flapping only once or twice as the ground effect kept it aloft. Finally it came to rest on the water, pulling its wings into its sides and bobbing on the surface. Violet's skin thrummed when the pelican cocked its head and glanced over its shoulder to where she stood, hose dangling in her fingertips and her toes turning cold from the flow of water. She reached behind her and turned off the faucet, keeping her eyes on the pelican.

A burst of conversation came from her right. She dragged her gaze away from the bird and took a step back as a family bustled by juggling four folding chairs, two inflatable rafts, a large cooler, and a string bag holding all manner of sandcastle-building gear. Two children, a boy and a girl, trailed the parents, their faces shiny with sunscreen and glee.

When the boisterous parade finally passed, Violet closed her eyes and inhaled the salty air. It invigorated, energized. It whispered and sang. *It's not just the sand that's healing*, she thought. *It's the air too.*

When she opened her eyes, her gaze snagged on something lying on the handrail at the top of the bench, right where the pelican had perched moments before. Fish bones. Though much smaller than those sitting on her top step this morning, the skeleton was unmistakable. Her eyes darted to the water, but the pelican was gone.

When Violet arrived at Two Sisters a couple hours later, her skin and hair fresh from a shower and dressed in her usual drawstring khaki skirt and cool, loose-fitting linen top, Trudy was already hard at work, bent over the long table in the back, her green banker's lamp illuminating her work space. Violet recognized some of the items spread out on the table—the long piece of driftwood from a few days ago, clumps of dried seaweed, and the ever-present tangle of fishing line—but there were some new additions Trudy must have found on that morning's scavenge: a bouquet of sea oat pods, a bundle of reedy grass, and a handful of clam shells.

"Starting a new project today?"

Trudy's answer was a nod, her eyes not lifting from the fishing line she threaded through a string of shells. Sometimes Violet didn't understand why her sister didn't just buy a fresh spool of fishing line. It'd be so much easier to attach the shells and baubles together if she didn't have to untangle the line first, but Trudy was adamant about using cast-off materials—items others had discarded along with left-behind shells and bits of broken wood. Forgotten, abandoned things. Trudy calmed them down and put them together and made them beautiful again.

Violet made her way through the shop, bringing it to life. She powered up the computer, filled the electric teakettle and flipped it on, then set the music to low and twisted the rod to open the window blinds. Mismatched chairs set up at round tables under the large bay window waited for the day's customers. As the water in the kettle began to bubble, Violet propped open the front door to catch the last of the morning's breeze before it turned too hot, Ella Fitzgerald crooned "East of the Sun," and the shop was ready for the day.

Sugar Bend wasn't exactly a tourist town—there were no outlet malls, high-end boutiques, or five-star restaurants—but it was known for its quaintness, its beauty, its winding roads draped with cool shade and Spanish moss, and its annual art festival held at the end of every summer. Vacationers from nearby Orange Beach, Gulf Shores, and Pensacola often made their way up the highway—usually well into their weeklong vacations when their skin needed a break from the sun—in search of the hidden turns and overlooked signs that took them to Sugar Bend, population 1,923. It wasn't by accident that the roads were hard to find and the signs occasionally went missing.

Still, some made it in, and when they did, they faced two types of locals. One type bemoaned the out-of-towners who came for a dose of small-town charm to take back to their regular lives. They barked at the cars that went the wrong way down one-way streets, rolled their eyes at college spring breakers who had the nerve to order a half-caff, sugar-free, "could you add a double shot of espresso" mochaccinos at Joe's Coffee on Cedar Street, and pretended to be cash-only when people pulled out their debit cards. Then there were those who welcomed strangers in with open arms, who were willing to share Sugar Bend's beauty and magic with outsiders, who gave directions and let them pay however they liked.

For the most part Trudy and Violet fell into the second camp—after all, if someone wanted to take a piece of Sugar Bend with them when they left, why shouldn't that be a hand-painted oyster shell with gold-leaf edges or a whimsical sculpture made from driftwood, sea glass, and coquina shells? Violet would wave good-bye as the visitors walked out of Two Sisters, content in the knowledge that while they might be taking home a small piece of Sugar Bend, the true secrets of the town—and of the river that flowed through it—were known only to the real locals. Those, like Trudy and Violet, who'd loved and lost in this place, who'd wept here, who'd been broken and fastened back together all along these shores and roads and under these shade trees.

By early afternoon Trudy was finished with her work—*My materials are not cooperating,* she'd scrawled on a note—and Violet had sold a dozen of their bestselling pinch pots. The little containers—perfect for holding small odds and ends on a dresser or by the kitchen sink—were made from river clay Trudy had shaped and fired. When they cooled, Violet glazed them to resemble birds' eggs: brown-and-cream speckled for nuthatches, bright blue-green for robins, a mottled gray-brown for sparrows, pale blue with scattered dark spots for house finches.

As Violet wrapped up a sale, Trudy appeared at Violet's elbow holding a note. *I'm heading home. I'll get things ready for dinner.*

Violet nodded at her sister. "I won't be too long. I'll probably close around four." Most shops in town had fluctuating hours, and no one but outsiders minded.

With her messenger bag tight across her chest and her tackle box of supplies in hand, Trudy slipped quietly out the door and headed west on Water Street toward home. Violet took off her glasses and cleaned the lenses with the hem of her shirt. As she put them back on, a young woman paused outside the front window. Long dark hair fell in waves down her back, one side tucked behind a delicate ear. Proud nose, full lips, and wide, long-lashed eyes scampered this way and that, as if she was searching for someone. She seemed too young for the worried crease between her brows.

After a moment of hesitation, the girl opened the door and walked in. The bell jangled a happy tune.

"Welcome to Two Sisters." Violet smiled warmly. "Are you shopping for anything particular?" The girl shook her head and ran her fingers across a set of dish towels splashed with bright yellow flowers on a table by the door. "Well, I'm here if you need me."

Violet puttered around, dusting shelves and neatening up displays. She kept an eye on the new customer as she moved through the shop, her face still etched with concern. What was roiling inside her, itching to be freed?

The girl lifted the lid of a shell-encrusted box barely larger than a deck of cards. The inside was lined with pale pink velvet.

"My sister Trudy made that." Violet's words startled the girl, who dropped the lid closed. Violet tried to set her at ease. "She collects little things everywhere she goes—shells, pieces of wood, bits of twine and feathers—and she uses it all in her artwork. Many of the sculptures and art pieces here are hers."

"I like them." Her voice was deeper than Violet had expected. Mature. Violet had guessed her age to be fifteen or sixteen, but now she wasn't sure.

"I'll tell her you said that. Where are you from?" Violet was sure she'd never seen the girl, and at this point in her life, she knew most everyone in Sugar Bend, if not by name, at least by face.

The girl didn't answer.

"Are you here on vacation?" Violet prodded.

"Not really." She fingered the lid of the box again.

"Trudy usually sits at that table back there to work. Those are her supplies." Violet gestured to the shelves that held everything Trudy needed to make her sculptures: clear jars for salvaged sea glass, shells, small pieces of driftwood, and bundles of dried sea grasses; a few rolling pins she wrapped with fishing line once she untangled the snarls; and large plastic bins that held the bigger pieces of driftwood. Next to them were her tools: a spool of wire, scissors, wire cutters, a scattering of beads, and the ever-present knot of fishing line.

"Are you an artist?" The way the girl's eyes lit up when she saw Trudy's things made Violet wonder.

But the girl just shook her head and went back to browsing. A few minutes later, the bell at the door jingled. Violet lifted her head from where she was wiping the counter under the teakettle and saw the girl walking out, one hand stuffed in her pocket. Violet called out a good-bye, and the girl glanced back over her shoulder but kept her feet moving purposefully in the other direction.

Later, as Violet did one last walk-through of the shop before she switched off the lights and locked up, she noticed the little shell box was gone.

After dinner Violet organized her backpack while Trudy sat at the dining table, hard at work. Trudy kept the bulk of her materials at the shop, but she used a tackle box to transport home the ones she wanted to continue working on at night. That night she'd toted home the most uncooperative materials from the morning—the dried seaweed and clunky clam shells—and she'd spread them out on the table, along with part of an old green fishing net and a length of chicken wire she'd pulled from the sand under their dock. It was a strange combination, even for Trudy, but she had a way with raw materials like that. She'd ponder and squint and move pieces around until they spoke to her and told her what they wanted to be.

At least that was how Trudy had explained it when that perky writer from *Bay* magazine interviewed her last year. The woman acted like there was some kind of magic to it, the taking of random, broken bits and swirling them around until they became something altogether different.

Trudy had scoffed and flipped to a new page in her notepad. *I'm an old woman and I like to make things with my hands. It's a hobby, not magic.*

But it was much more than just a hobby for Trudy. Violet knew that. It was why Violet never complained when she sat in a dining chair and felt the *crunch* of a forgotten seashell underneath her. Or when Trudy lugged home a driftwood log, leaving behind a scrum of fine sand all over the heart-pine floors or the cool tile floors of the shop. Trudy and Violet both navigated life the best way they knew how—for Trudy it was working with her materials and setting the pieces just right, while for Violet it was through the birds, savoring their ease of flight, identifying their needs, helping them on their way.

Violet had just set her binoculars carefully into their protective case when she heard someone coming up the wooden steps to the front door. A knock sounded, then Emmajean popped her head through the doorway. "Anyone home? I come bearing champagne. It was left over from a wedding shower at the library today."

"Someone had a wedding shower at the library?" Violet set her backpack down and met Emmajean at the door.

"One of our patrons met her fiancé in the fiction section, and they wanted to have the shower where they fell in love. Lucky for us, they overestimated how much champagne to buy."

Violet led her friend to the kitchen. "Surely your doctor didn't say anything about champagne being good for the heart. I know mine didn't."

Emmajean made a *pshhh* motion with her hand and plunked the bottle down on the table. "A glass of bubbly now and then won't hurt." After making quick work of opening the bottle, Emmajean poured three glasses—Violet placed one next to Trudy's elbow—and the two friends made their way out to the porch overlooking the river.

Violet relaxed into her rocker, and Emmajean took a seat at the small wooden table. They raised their glasses—"To the beauty of another day," Emmajean said—and sipped. Violet closed her eyes and savored the crisp citrus zing on her tongue. The bubbles made her feel like she was floating, and she suppressed the urge to giggle. She opened her eyes in surprise.

"It makes you feel young again, doesn't it?"

Violet nodded. "Champagne wasn't exactly a part of my younger years though. Our upbringing was a bit more humble."

"I hear you." Emmajean leaned back against her seat and

propped her feet up on the chair across from her. Ten years older than Violet, Emmajean was a beautiful woman. Her hair was a deep, cozy gray and still had the waves from her younger years, though it was much shorter now than when Violet first met her at Sugar Bend Academy more than forty years ago. Emmajean had been the school secretary, Violet the science teacher, and the two women became fast friends in those heady days of music, sun, and water.

Like Violet, Emmajean had taken an early retirement after the school merger, but unable to relax quietly into her golden years, she grew antsy and took a part-time job at the public library.

"How are things going at work?" Violet asked. "Other than drinking champagne at parties."

Emmajean laughed. "Oh yes, it's very exciting. Books coming and going, kids stopping up the sink in the children's department, teenagers kissing in the back of the computer lab. Again."

"What is it about libraries that makes people feel so affectionate?"

"Who knows—the cool air, maybe? The quiet? All I know is they should have made me a security guard instead of an assistant, for as often as I have to bust up the lovebirds."

A pontoon boat idled by on the river, music pumping from an on-board speaker. It was standing room only, with a gaggle of young women dancing to the beat and waving their slim, tanned arms up in the air. Violet watched as the boat passed, its wake winking like stars in the moonlight. "Does it mean I'm

getting old if I see those girls and all I can think is how danger-
ous it is to be dancing on a moving boat like that?"

Emmajean chuckled. "These days every woman is trying to
look younger and prettier than the gal next to her. You and I
may be getting older, but at least we're aging with dignity."

"Is that what this is?" Violet glanced sideways at her friend.

The two women sat in comfortable silence. A dove flew to
the feeder hanging from the eaves, picked at a seed, then flew
off again. Down by the water, the dock lights clicked on in the
falling dark, throwing out wavy beams in every direction.

"I bet that river holds a lot of secrets," Emmajean said.

Violet's pulse throbbed in her fingertips and inside her
elbows. "What makes you say that?"

Emmajean pushed her hair back off her forehead. "When I
was growing up, people always talked about how pirates used
to roam around here. Out in the Gulf, through the pass, and
all up and down this river. Sometimes I think about what all
might be at the bottom of that water. Old ships, treasure chests.
Maybe jewels."

While Emmajean stared at the river, envisioning gold coins
and rubies, Violet heard the high-pitched whine of a boat motor
as if it were happening right now. Saw the boat taking shape
through the misty fog. Felt those fingers, rough and hard,
against her neck. She absently rubbed her thumb across the
scar on her wrist.

"Violet?"

Emmajean's voice cut through the memories, and Violet
fought her way back to the present. "Hmm?"

Emmajean's eyes were soft, concerned. "I asked if you think there's any treasure in the river."

Violet drained the remaining champagne in her glass, her lips puckering at the now-flat effervescence. "I think anything buried in that water deserves to stay right where it is."

⁓

That night, Violet had the dream again. She was on the dock, waiting. Anger simmered inside her like a soup pot left on a hot eye. She was no stranger to anger, but this was something altogether different. This sensation had shape, taste, heat. And her guilt was a bitter root through it all.

At least she's safe. The bruises might have been shining even in the dim lamplight, the edges already beginning to darken, but inside the house, all was safe. Violet would make sure of that.

With shaking fingers she caressed the simple gold bracelet around her wrist, the delicate lines engraved on it. She lifted her chin to face the dark sky, hidden behind thick fog, and thought of the man who'd given it to her. He was so kind, so good. He had no idea the volume of hatred that lived inside her right this minute.

She ran her fingers around the edge of the bracelet over and over like a prayer, until the tinny drone of an outboard Evinrude made its way up the river toward the dock where she stood. Her heartbeat thudded again in her ears, and she clasped her hands together to stop the nervous tremors.

Then with a *whoosh* of air in her face, like a great flap of wings, Violet awoke in a tangle of damp bedsheets. She flung them back and nearly gasped with relief when the breeze from the ceiling fan hit her legs. She lay there a moment, then rose and opened the window an inch and returned to bed.

Nighttime noises had always been a comfort to her—light winds rattling the palm fronds, tree frogs serenading each other, the soft pulse of crickets—but tonight the sounds didn't soothe her as they usually did. Something bubbled deep inside her that had nothing to do with the champagne she'd sipped with Emmajean and everything to do with her friend's casual mention of the river's secrets.

With her eyes clamped shut in an attempt to entice slumber to visit, and hopefully more peaceful sleep this time, the whine of the boat motor started up again, the memory as real as life. It was as if he were still there on the river, still making his way toward her. Toward both of them. And she knew then she was still fighting him. Maybe she always would be.

***

The Sugar Bend Observer, Sugar Bend's Community News Source
Letter from the Editor, Liza Bullock
May 2022 | Volume 11, Issue 5

This week I had the privilege of attending a birthday gathering at the Home Under the Oaks for Sugar Bend's oldest resident. Mrs. Myrna Blaylock turned 102 on Monday, though to look at her, you wouldn't think she's a day over

80. With a glow in her cheeks and perfectly coiffed hair (styled at Cuts and Coffee every Wednesday at noon, thank you very much), she was the best-looking gal under the oaks by far.

I wrote this week's neighbor profile on Mrs. Blaylock, and you can find the feature on 2B. Prior to writing the feature, I corresponded with her grandson to get some background information on his grandmother. In an email he wrote that his grandmother has always loved animals and the wild life. Upon first reading it I assumed he meant "wildlife." However, after seeing the way Mrs. Blaylock hopped out of her chair and danced a foxtrot with one of the men at the party, I'm having second thoughts!

Summer is here and the possibilities are endless. Rest assured, if anything "wild" happens in Sugar Bend, we'll make sure to include it here in your monthly *Observer.*

Enjoy the issue!
Liza

t w o

Violet walked through the dewy grass, dampness curling over the sides of her rubber-soled slippers and tickling her toes. The bag of birdseed she carried was getting low. She'd have to remember to run by the feedstore to grab a new bag. Either that or ask Tyler to run her some by next time he was out this way.

As she walked she tipped the bag over each of the fourteen bird feeders scattered around their half-acre spread by the river. She'd learned long ago if she filled the feeders in the evening, the blasted raccoons would sneak in and empty them. So now, as soon as the first hints of pink streaked across the sky, she was out in the middle of it. The early rising birds thanked her for their breakfast with sweet serenades.

Usually this was the best, most peaceful part of Violet's day, but her dream last night had unsettled her. Instead of disappearing with the dark, it remained with her, its edges still sharp and painful, even on this fresh, clean-slate morning.

As she rounded the corner of the house, she saw the river

gleaming like liquid silver. A brown pelican floated out in the center, so still it made no ripple on the surface. As she stared at the slice of water that had made up so much of Trudy's and her life, her mind traveled back to the day she realized their lives were inextricably linked. More than just being sisters, more than sharing a home and parents and a fondness for chocolate pudding. It was a single request from their fragile, damaged mother that had bound them with something thicker than blood.

1973

Violet was running. It reminded her of the times her dad used to take her out on his boat in the dark early mornings. They'd skim across the river so fast, the wind would push her cheeks into a grin whether she was smiling or not. Occasionally she was, but not always. Her dad was unpredictable at best. At worst, he was terrifying.

But today her feet met solid ground as she ran home from school, and her smile was wide, genuine, uncontrollable. Her legs pumped, her heart raced, and the wind coaxed her hair out of the twin braids that thumped against her back. She was seventeen years old, but she might as well have been a kid again. She was giddy, and giddiness wasn't common for her.

"With grades like these you can go places," Ms. Cox had told her after the bell rang. As kids spilled out of the classroom, freedom etching each face, Ms. Cox took a step closer to Violet.

"Students like you don't come along all that often, Violet. What you have is special. I hope you can see that, and I hope you'll let this feeling—the one you have right now—carry you far." She gave Violet's shoulder a gentle squeeze.

It was like Ms. Cox had heard the desire that had coursed through Violet for as long as she could remember. The desire to leave Sugar Bend, the sun-baked elbow in the river where she'd been born. The desire to see new places, to do new things, to push herself. To be someone new.

She stood there a moment longer, basking in the glow from the bright red A+ written on top of her biology test, before she shoved it in her bag, thanked Ms. Cox, and started running.

Their home was half a mile from the school, and Violet sprinted most of the way. With a pang she thought of Trudy's face when she told her sister she'd see her at home. Violet and Trudy walked home together every day. Well, not together exactly. Trudy walked with her three best girlfriends, all of them giggling as boy after boy called to Trudy, flirting, joking, trying to be the one to make her smile and laugh.

Violet always walked a block behind, invisible to everyone but Trudy, who often turned around to see if Violet was still there. As if life as she knew it couldn't continue if Violet wasn't around to make sure things were okay. With a father who was often out on the road in his eighteen-wheeler, and a mother who spent most of her energy dodging blows from her husband, both verbal and physical, Violet had accepted her role as Trudy's caretaker long ago.

When she reached their street, Violet stopped and bent over, hands on knees, chest burning, legs rubbery. Her breathing slowed and she resumed her trek home, though slower now. She imagined what her mom might say when she saw the grade on her biology test.

"I knew you could do it."

"I'm so proud of you."

"Beauty is one thing, but what you have is better."

Her heart stuttered a little over that one. Her sister, Trudy, was beautiful, but it wasn't her fault. She'd been born with the best parts of both their parents, resulting in angelic blonde hair, light blue eyes, perky pink lips, and, even at fourteen, a voluptuous body.

Violet, on the other hand, had gotten the cast-off genes: mud-brown eyes, brown hair that was neither straight nor curly, and a frame that seemed to be more bones than anything else. She was gangly and awkward, while Trudy was a soft cloud, a velvet-petaled rose, a dream.

Violet had her grades, though, and that was the one thing that could catapult her out of this tiny town where nothing ever changed except the Friendly's Ice Cream girl-of-the-month. Her mom had told her that—quietly, when her father wasn't around—and now Ms. Cox had said it, too, so it must be true. Violet Figg was going places.

She flung open the front door, not worrying about making too much noise because her dad was eight hours into a long haul to Nebraska and wouldn't be home for four more days. "Mom?" The word pitched up at the end, coated in excitement. She dropped her bag by the door and ran to the den, then down the carpeted hallway that led to her parents' bedroom. "Mom! Where are you?"

The air in the house was thick and warm. Stale, as if no one had been there in days, which was crazy since the house had been buzzing with activity just that morning, as Violet spooned Cheerios into her mouth while reading through her biology notes, Trudy ironed her hair in the bathroom at the end of the hall, and her father stood in front of the pantry, complaining that her mom had "forgotten" to buy the six-pack of Michelob he liked to take with him in the truck.

When Violet saw that the back porch was just as empty as the rest of the house, her footsteps slowed. Her mom was always there when the girls got home from school. But today—Violet crossed the kitchen and opened the back door to confirm her suspicion—her mom's little red Datsun was gone.

She closed the door and pressed her back against it. Cleaning the kitchen was usually Violet's job. Her mom tried, but most days she ended up back in bed long before she cleaned up from breakfast. Violet didn't mind. Even as a child, she'd seen the toll it took on her mom to be chained to a hard man like her father. She usually tackled the cleaning after school, before she pulled out her homework or notes to study. Today, though, the kitchen was spotless—the sink empty, the counters wiped clean, the floor sparkling in the afternoon sun.

As her gaze fell on a piece of paper lying in the middle of the white kitchen table, dread slid through her like a faint pulse of electricity. The night before, after Violet had gotten out of the bath, her mom had called her onto the back porch. Her mother, Deena, sat on the love seat with her knees tucked in, her nightgown pulled down over them, and a wineglass at her elbow, a rare moment of relaxation that only happened when Violet's dad was out for the evening. Violet sat and her mom pulled her close.

"You're a good girl, Violet." Mom smoothed her hand down the back of Violet's head. "I know I can always depend on you."

"Of course you can."

"Good, good," her mom murmured, more to herself than to Violet. "If I asked you to take care of Trudy after I'm gone, could you promise me you'd do that?"

"After you're gone? Where are you going?"

"I just mean . . ." Her mom sighed and tucked her hair behind her ear. The sleeve of her nightgown slipped off her shoulder, exposing a stretch of pale skin. "I won't be around forever, Little Bird. When I'm gone, will you look after Trudy?"

Her mom hadn't called her Little Bird in years, and Violet would agree to practically anything when she heard her favorite nickname. "Sure. I'll take care of her."

"Look at me, Violet." Her mom's voice was suddenly firm, insistent, and she pulled Violet's face toward her. "You have to promise me you'll take care of her. You'll protect her."

"I don't understand why you're asking me this." Perspiration prickled behind Violet's knees and under her arms.

"Just promise me." The words came out as a whisper, but everything in her mom's face was shouting.

"Okay, I promise. I'll protect Trudy."

Her mom's shoulders sagged. "Thank you." She leaned down and kissed Violet's temple and pulled her closer against her side. Violet inhaled her mom's powdery scent and pressed her cheek against her shoulder.

Standing in the kitchen now, Violet reached for the note on the table, her heartbeat pounding in her ears. She already knew what it would say.

Girls, I'm sorry, but I have to leave. You two will be fine—you have each other. You always have and you always will. A cord of two strands is not easily broken.

It's three strands. Violet remembered it from an old Sunday school lesson. *A cord of* three *strands, not two.*

She turned the note over in her hand, searching for more words, an explanation, something. But that was it. *I have to leave.*

Leave where?

But she knew. Deena Figg was gone. Hadn't she just said it last night? *"I won't be around forever, Little Bird."* Honestly, Violet was surprised her mom had lasted as long as she had.

Violet walked back to her bedroom, and the electricity humming under her skin blinked out when she saw the second piece of paper. It sat on her favorite pillow, the one with the yellow ruffles at the edges. What now?

Violet, I need you to take care of your sister. You're the strong one, much stronger than I've ever been, and she's going to need you. I'm sorry to put this on your shoulders, but I trust you and I love you. Remember your promise.

Violet's fingers squeezed of their own accord, crumpling her mom's note in her hand. She could throw it away. Both of them. Maybe drop them in the river where they'd drift out into the Gulf, as if the words had never even been a thought, much less a request.

She was halfway down the hall toward the back door before she stopped. She couldn't do it. Couldn't throw the notes away, couldn't pretend like her mom hadn't asked such a monumental thing of her. For better or worse, Deena Figg had decided leaving was better than staying, and if she needed Violet to take care of Trudy, then that's what Violet would do.

She never knew there was a physical sensation when dreams died, but she felt it. All those hopes she had for herself—going places, doing things, becoming someone—peeled off her and dissipated in the stale air of the quiet house. She wasn't going anywhere, for she was Trudy's keeper now. She'd never be free.

Without realizing it Violet had moved across the grass toward the water, and her feet were now inches away from where the river whispered against the sandy shore. She curled her toes and was surprised to feel the cool sand of the riverbank rather than the worn shag carpet of her childhood home.

Sometimes Violet wondered how good a job she'd done in

taking care of Trudy. On her good days she was content in the knowledge that her sister was happy, fulfilled by her art and her daily scavenging trips, and perfectly fine in her cocoon of soft silence, *that night* safely buried in the past. She could tell herself she'd fulfilled her mother's request and taken care of her younger sister.

But on days like today, when the past bumped up against her, it reminded Violet it was never really gone. Could she have done more to protect Trudy, to shield her, to cushion her from the blows?

From behind her came the trill of a robin, and its cheerful song pulled her from her reverie. As she reached down to brush off a piece of grass that clung to her ankle, she saw it. The bones. The size of a matchbox and aglow as if touched by the morning sun, which hadn't yet risen above the tree line.

She swiveled her head, checking the shore and the lawn behind her, the shade under the trees and her back porch overlooking it all, but other than the birds, she was alone. Her heart beat fast and angry in her chest.

With trembling fingers she lifted the fish bones, and they sat cold in her palm, heavier than they should have been. With a swift stretch of her arm and a flick of her wrist, Violet flung them out into the river, so hard her muscles burned. Though the bones didn't come anywhere near the pelican sitting out in the middle, it took flight anyway, its wings a brown blur as the bones sank slowly under a ripe-peach sky.

Two Sisters already had a handful of customers by the time Violet arrived. Trudy was at the counter ringing up a lady purchasing a couple of hand-painted coffee mugs, while two more customers pondered the fish sculpture on a side table. This particular piece was a showstopper—three feet tall and just as wide. Trudy had made it from thin pieces of driftwood wired together in the form of a blowfish, complete with spiny fins and pursed lips made from pink sea glass.

The day carried on as it normally did, with regulars settled down for tea and conversation while customers—some familiar, some tourists—floated in and out on the breeze, most leaving with a little something tucked into a lemon-yellow Two Sisters bag. With Violet in place behind the register, Trudy returned to her work at the back table, determined to force the uncooperative fishing line into submission. Violet heard her now and then, sniffing in frustration or angrily swiping a hand through her hair. Trudy occasionally grew exasperated by her work—a shell not fitting where she thought it should go, or pieces of wood refusing to sit side by side—and Violet knew better than to make light of it.

"You know you can take a break if you need to," she offered as she waved hello to a pair of customers entering the shop. "Go for a walk or something. I'll be here."

Trudy reached for her notebook. *I have to keep at it. If I stop now, I'll never come back to it.*

"I understand. Can I help?"

Only if you can make these two pieces of wood stop arguing and sit nicely next to each other.

Violet laughed. "Like disobedient children."

A noise came from Trudy's throat that sounded suspiciously like the beginning of a laugh. Trudy's hands stilled on the table, as if the noise had surprised her as much as it had Violet.

"Trudy?" Violet stared at her sister. "Was that—?"

But the bell jangled over the door, disrupting the sacred moment like a finger popping a soap bubble. Trudy's gaze slid to the doorway, and Violet's eyes followed. There, standing just inside the front window, was the same young woman who visited the store yesterday. Violet glanced back at Trudy, still clinging to the startling sound she'd just heard coming from her sister, but Trudy gave her head a small but firm shake and motioned toward the door with her chin.

Violet forced her knees to unlock and her shoulders to lower as twin urges crashed in her chest. Remembering the delicate shell box, she wanted to ask—to demand—why the girl had taken something that hadn't belonged to her, but a ping in her chest cautioned her to go slowly. To take a step, not a leap.

"Can I help you with anything?" Violet's words were soft and tentative, the way she spoke to her birds so she wouldn't startle them and cause them to fly away.

The girl eased into the shop, her eyes scanning the space. Two men waited at a table under the front windows as their wives shopped, and a handful of other customers were scattered throughout the shop. The air was filled with a pleasant hum of sound. The door opened again, setting the bell to a jingle, and the girl flinched at the noise.

Her face was plain, without the heavy makeup and thick

brows Violet often saw on girls too young to be covering up all their skin. That fact alone—that the young woman braved the day bold and bare faced—softened the sting of knowing Trudy's box had slipped into her pocket yesterday. Unnoticed, the girl likely thought, but Violet saw everything.

A moment later, Violet had a line of customers at the register, and with one eye on the door to make sure the girl didn't leave again with something else she hadn't paid for, she rang up the customers, answered questions, and directed one hungry man to the Sugar Shack down the street for a plate of their famous fried-fish sandwich.

When the last customer had been taken care of, she was surprised to see the girl standing at Trudy's table behind the front counter. Judging by the irritation on her sister's face and the quick, forceful ways her hands were moving, her materials were still not cooperating. Finally Trudy exhaled and dropped the pieces of wood onto the table. Defeated, she swiped at her forehead with the back of her wrist and sat back in her chair.

When the girl reached out a hand, Violet opened her mouth to caution Trudy to—what? Guard her materials? As if the girl would steal right out from under Trudy. But then again, maybe she would.

But the girl didn't take anything. She lifted the pieces of wood Trudy had been struggling with and laid them next to each other on the table. Then she chose a small smooth stone from the top shelf of Trudy's tackle box and set it against the stones. A smile flickered on the girl's face as Trudy's eyes grew wide. She handed Trudy the wood and stone, and Trudy held it all up to the sculpture she'd been battling all day. The pieces fit perfectly.

Trudy tilted her head as she stared at the girl, then pulled out her notebook, scribbled a few words down, and handed it over. The girl read it and let out a small laugh. "I'm not an artist. I just sometimes know where things belong."

Trudy wrote something else, and the girl responded. If she wondered why Trudy wasn't speaking, she didn't let on. Their uneven conversation continued a few moments while Violet busied herself and tried to look like she wasn't paying attention. Trudy showed the girl her various materials and tools, and as the girl's hands moved over the bits and baubles, her shoulders dropped and the crease in her forehead smoothed out. By the time she checked her watch and said she had to go, the table was littered with small pieces of paper, the girl's spoken words mingled with them, and Trudy's sculpture now resembled a pair of wings, ethereal despite the rough materials.

Violet stopped her before she made it to the door. "I'm glad you came back." She cocked an eyebrow and the girl winced, likely fearing Violet's next words. It would serve her right, considering, and Violet was about to say just that, but at the last minute, even as she opened her mouth to speak, her words changed. "My sister had been working on that piece for most of the day, and it was giving her fits." Violet nudged her red-framed glasses up on her nose. "The two of you seemed to work well together."

The edges of the girl's mouth loosened, but she'd yet to look Violet full in the face.

"What's your name?"

"Maya."

"It's nice to meet you. I'm Violet."

Maya wore denim shorts and a green T-shirt with the Sugar Shack logo across the front, and she'd pulled her thick dark hair up into a bun at the back of her head. Long tendrils had escaped around her face, and Violet noticed the sparkle of a tiny nose ring as Maya glanced down to check her watch again.

"I've got to get back to work. I just had a short break between shifts." She hesitated, her gaze bouncing up to Violet's face and away again.

Violet thought she was going to say something else, but instead she gave one last wave back at Trudy, then slipped through the door and down the street in the direction of the diner.

Later, as they locked up for the day, Trudy handed Violet a piece of paper. *She said she's not an artist, but she has good hands. She knows how to use the materials.*

Violet gave a slow nod but didn't speak.

You don't like her?

"I didn't say that."

Trudy crossed her arms and eyed Violet, waiting for her explanation, but Violet grabbed her purse and walked to the door. "Come on. Let's go home."

At a stoplight on Chestnut Street, Trudy nudged Violet's shoulder and pointed across the street. Maya was climbing out of the driver's seat of a beat-up black car. She slung a bag over her shoulder and walked up the steps to the apartment above Fritz's Bait Shop.

Fritz Meyer rented out the room, often to drifters who came through town looking for work on one of the fishing boats that set out each day from the docks upriver. Fritz was a nice man, but the studio apartment couldn't be a very nice place to live. Did she live there alone? The bait shop was small, but the room above it seemed hardly big enough to house even one person.

Trudy's concern filled the nooks and crannies of the car. "I know," Violet muttered to her sister. "I feel it too." She rolled her window down a crack to have some breathing space.

The light changed to green, and just as Violet let off the brake, Maya unlocked the door and walked inside.

The bedsprings of the thin mattress dug into Maya's back between her shoulder blades, but the room wasn't all that bad. In fact, it was far better than many of the places she had slept: a cot in a concrete-floored garage, a middle bunk in a claustrophobic group home, a sweltering attic space she'd shared with two pigeons and a mouse. Some places had been okay—the cottage in the woods with the couple who raised goats, the big house in the suburbs with three other kids and two rowdy dogs, the couple in their fifties who made up for their disappointment at not being able to produce their own children with false cheer and promises for a bright future.

With each new placement, her social worker had told her she had to straighten up. Work harder. Be better. No more funny business. "This is better than the alternative," Debbie had often said, but Maya had always wondered about that. What if the alternative was actually better?

And now here she was, right in the middle of that alternative. On her own with no one behind her to make sure she didn't fall. That's how Debbie had explained it: "You're eighteen, Maya. You're an adult. I can't force you to stay in the system, but understand this: If you leave and end up on the street, no one will be there to help you. You'll be on your own."

Maya sniffed. *I'm not on the street, Debbie.* It might be a rented room that smelled like old shoes and dead shrimp, but it was hers. At least for now. She'd always taken her future in small bites, but at this point she was down to a day or two at a time.

Maya shifted and studied the photo in her hands. It had grown soft at the edges, its colors dulled by age and her own fingerprints. She'd slept with it under her pillow every night since her grandmother Maria had died, a childish attempt to keep the woman's memory close, etched in Maya's mind so it wouldn't leave her too. So far, it had worked. Though after eleven years the memories were more like flashes of color and sound, quick flutters of sensation: soft hands and softer words. A long blue-green skirt that whispered when she moved. The quick darts of her hands as she flipped her cards over one by one.

The photo—Maria with her head thrown back and eyes closed in laughter—was the only thing Maya had from her birth family, the people who had given her life and breath, her wide-set eyes and the freckles that scattered across her nose as soon as the weather grew warm. She had nothing tangible from her mother, who'd left long before Maya had made memories, but it was just as well. At least Maria hadn't chosen to leave Maya behind. She just died. No choice in the matter.

When Maya had finally convinced Debbie she wanted out, Debbie had taken pity on her. She'd bought Maya a car—nearly as old as Maya, with 197,000 miles on the gauge and a suspicious stain on the back seat—and given her an envelope with $500 inside. "It's the best I can do," she'd said. "What can I say, Maya? I really want you to make it."

Debbie didn't do that for everyone. Maya had known other girls assigned to Debbie, and when they'd had enough of the system that routinely chewed kids up and spit them out limp and ragged and angry, Debbie had sent them on their way with a farewell and a sigh of relief. But Debbie had grown to like Maya, despite her nimble hands that made quick work of taking things that didn't belong to her, the main reason she'd been booted from ten homes in eleven years.

Maya had made empty promises to call and let Debbie know how she was doing, then cranked the engine of the black Nissan Sentra. "Where are you headed?" Debbie had asked.

"I'm going home." She knew there was no home to head to, and worse, Debbie knew it too. But Maya wanted to say the words so badly. She wanted to say them and have them be true. Instead, she'd headed south on the interstate and waited for a sign.

Her grandmother had talked a lot about signs—watching for them, listening for them, waiting for them. She'd lived by signs given and received. Maya hoped a sign would jump up and reveal itself as she drove, but the farther she went, the darker the sky grew and the quicker her hopes slid out through the cracked windshield.

At a stop for gas, a flyer on the glass door advertised a River Days Art Festival taking place in August in a place called Sugar Bend. As her eyes focused on those two words, *Sugar Bend*, a cool rush of air caressed her overwarm skin and images flashed through her mind, as quick as her grandmother's hands: a handful of seashells and tumbled glass. A flutter of birds' wings in treetops and on porch steps. A boy standing next to her, golden hair gleaming in the setting sun. Comfort, security, and the indelible sense of belonging wrapped around her like a blanket. She was exactly where she was meant to be.

Maya was frozen, one hand on the door of the gas station, as the pictures in her mind snapped and fizzed.

"Ma'am? Are you okay?"

She blinked and it all disappeared. The only thing in her vision was the dingy gas station and the smudged door with the flyer taped to it.

Behind her the man had cleared his throat. "You okay there? You look like you done seen a ghost."

"I'm fine."

Inside the man took his place behind the cash register, and Maya paid for her gas. At the door she paused. "How far is it to Sugar Bend?"

"About ten minutes"—the man pointed down the road—"thataway. A sign will show you where to turn."

"Thanks." Back in her car, she sat and drummed her fingers

on the steering wheel. Finally she pulled out of the station and turned in the direction the man had pointed.

That was a month ago. Sitting here in her room above the bait shop now, she smoothed her fingers across her grandmother's face in the photo again. *Well, I'm here, Nana. I saw the sign. What now?*

A few minutes later, she tucked the photo beneath her pillow and reached under the bed for the shoebox. It was full of items she'd lifted from each place she'd lived, each one a reminder of days spent in a life that didn't belong to her. With each item she'd tucked away in the box, she prayed for a life that *was* hers, one where she could make her own choices, including when to stay and when to leave. A life no one could take from her.

She ran her hands across each item: the baby shoe that had belonged to the little boy she rocked to sleep every night for six months while his mom entertained a parade of boyfriends downstairs. The silver fork from the home where she never had enough to eat. A lint brush from the house that kept eight long-haired dogs, including one that had bitten her, leaving a wound on her calf so deep it required twelve stitches to close it.

And the newest addition—the small shell-covered box. It was the nicest thing she'd ever stolen. It was also the first time she'd ever felt a measure of guilt for her theft. Usually she stole from people who deserved it—people who had no idea how to care for a life placed in their hands and in their home—but the two women in the shop didn't deserve what she'd done.

The first one she'd met, the one behind the counter, had been so nice. She talked to Maya—talked *to* her, not just *about* her—and the relief Maya felt had been immense. Maya had always been able to sense where things and people belonged, and while this woman, Violet, belonged in her shop, there was something about her that didn't belong. Something she was carrying that was too heavy for her, a burden that wasn't hers to shoulder.

Trudy, her artist sister, was quiet, and that quiet spoke of something forceful and unmanageable, though Maya couldn't tell yet what that was. Regardless, she was drawn to the woman's silence. So much in Maya's life had been loud: babies and dogs, yelling and laughter, school counselors' harsh words, and the yearnings for belonging that trailed from strangers' fingertips and shoulder blades and the backs of their necks. Maya felt it all. Trudy's silence felt like a respite, even though Maya suspected it might not feel that way for Trudy.

But she couldn't keep the shell-covered box. As soon as she'd walked out the door with that familiar comfort in her pocket—the soothing weight of something that wasn't hers— she knew she'd have to figure out a way to return it. And to do it in a way that wouldn't spell her quick dismissal.

Because the truth was, she hadn't stopped thinking about the strange pictures that had rushed through her mind when she saw that flyer on the gas station door. The images were jumbled and confusing and out of place, but they felt strangely like a key slipping into a lock or a hand fitting perfectly alongside another.

Tyler Holt knew what that look meant. Cassie stood in the middle of aisle three, half hidden behind a spinning rack of seeds so Tyler's dad couldn't see her, and slowly hooked the tool belt around her hips. Her shirt was cropped and the taut, tanned skin of her stomach gleamed above that leather belt. She gave Tyler her best *you know you want this* glance.

But instead of getting up off his stool and walking toward her, like she'd expected and clearly wanted, he swiveled and opened up the ancient Dell laptop sitting on the counter. He leaned in and ran his finger down the screen as if he was studying something more important than the background photo of his family's store, Holt Feed and Seed.

"Tyler," Cassie called. "What are you doing over there?"

Tyler glanced up. His dad was already peering at him over the top of his wire-rimmed glasses, his thick eyebrows pushed together in consternation. Dixon Holt cleared his throat and tipped his head toward Cassie.

Tyler rolled his eyes and slapped the laptop shut. He walked around the end of the counter to where Cassie was waiting, the tool belt now dangling from her pink-manicured fingertip. "I'm working, Cassie. Like I do every day." He took the tool belt from her and hung it back on its hook on the wall.

"Can't you take a break? A bunch of us are heading down to the beach today. We already have a cooler packed." She took a step closer and pressed her ample chest against his. "I got a new bikini. It's real cute."

He reached up and nudged her off him. "I'm sure it is, but I can't go. You know that."

Cassie exhaled. "It's our last summer, Tyler. Can't we have some fun?"

"It's your last summer. Not mine. I've already started the rest of my life. I don't get a summer anymore."

Not that he'd had a real summer in years. While other kids spent the long summer afternoons sleeping off the party from the night before or swinging from a rope swing at Soldiers Creek, Tyler had spent most every summer day since he'd turned thirteen—and every day after school when he wasn't on one ball field or another—helping out at the store. He loaded bales of pine straw, pallets of horse feed, and bags of every kind of soil and fertilizer under the sun; chatted with customers and rang them up; and generally prepared himself for the day when he'd take over as the next owner of Holt Feed and Seed. It had been his future since he was a kid, and he hadn't spent much time considering any other outcome. He'd never had time to. It was only now, when all the other kids his age were looking forward to college and a future of their own making, that he was seeing the consequences of accepting what was right in front of him.

Cassie pulled her phone out of the pocket of her cutoffs and checked the time. "You get off at six, right? We'll still be there. We're bringing food and staying for the sunset." She grabbed the pen from the front pocket of his shirt and wrote *West Beach— come find me* on the inside of his wrist. She slid the pen back in his pocket, then with her eyes locked on his, called out, "Mr. Holt, I think you work Tyler too hard."

His dad grunted in response. Cassie lifted onto her toes and kissed Tyler full on the mouth, surprising him and causing him to take a step back. She laughed and sauntered out the door, where her friends were waiting in an idling truck.

Unable to face his dad, Tyler grabbed a rake and headed for the back parking lot to clean up the excess pine straw from that morning's delivery. A few minutes later, Tyler lifted his head to see his dad watching him, his shoulder propped against the door frame, arms crossed.

"Mr. Olsen called earlier and ordered five bags of horse feed," Tyler called out. "As soon as I'm done here, I'll load it up and take it out to him."

"That sounds good." His dad had a toothpick stuck in the side of his mouth, and he sucked on it. "Son, that girl . . ."

Tyler swiped his thick blond hair off his sweaty forehead with the heel of his hand. "I know, Dad."

"Not sure she's up to much good."

Tyler leaned on the handle of the rake. "You're probably right. But she thinks she is, which is all that matters to her."

His dad chuckled.

Tyler took up the rake again, his muscles burning as he pulled the straw into piles.

"You've always been a big help to me, son." Not one for public displays of affection or praise, his dad was staring down at his boots. "I appreciate your hard work. I want you to know that."

"I know, Dad. I'm happy to help."

His dad looked like he had more to say, but after a brief hesitation, he rapped the screen door with his knuckles and headed back inside. As his dad's footsteps retreated, Tyler stared up at the business that could no doubt provide him with a steady and solid future. It was right there for the taking. He chewed the edge of his lip, then tapped his rake against the pine straw–covered ground and pulled.

three

1979

Violet knew all about Friendly's Ice Cream. Everyone in Sugar Bend did. What had started as a single shop, barely bigger than a large closet, had grown into a chain of six stores across the county, each with twenty-five flavors and its own "Friendly's Girl." The owner of Friendly's Ice Cream, Jay Malone, told people he'd lived in Sugar Bend his whole life, though no one remembered seeing him before the day he drove up and unlocked the door to the coolest new shop in town. He had plenty of employees to work each store, but he often dropped by out of the blue to serve a few customers himself. That would get everyone excited, because Jay was known as the friendliest guy around.

Folks in town traded stories of the man until he became almost larger than life, a small-town celebrity sitting contentedly on a chocolate-chip pedestal. He was known to show up just when a person needed help the most, offering an umbrella in a sudden thunderstorm, a can of gas when the boat motor ran dry, or a spare tire after running over a nail in the road. And the girls he hired to be the faces of his stores were equally as awe-inspiring. The Friendly's Girls wore red-and-white shift dresses with wide white collars and slits at the thigh, knee-high white boots, and crocheted hats with a red flower on the front. Being named one of Jay's girls meant instant local fame in the form of radio jingles and TV commercials and, they hoped, a step toward becoming someone who mattered. Every woman in town wanted to be chosen, but it was an honor only bestowed on a few.

No one was surprised when Jay chose nineteen-year-old Trudy Figg, the prettiest girl in Sugar Bend, as the latest Friendly's Girl. Not even Violet was surprised, though her guard was up and strong. She had seen guys like this shower their attention and affection on Trudy countless times before, and Trudy never seemed to understand that some men needed much more than a woman's soft hand and gentle smile. And if they didn't get what they wanted as an offering, they'd take it with force. Violet and Trudy had seen it up close with their parents, but that didn't stop Trudy from thinking every man who tripped over his words or feet on his way to talk to her had a heart as pure as her own.

Jay Malone didn't trip though. He didn't flirt shamelessly or act like a puppy in front of a bowl of food. Jay was different. Older than Trudy by seven years, Jay showed his maturity in a quiet demeanor, a number of well-cut suits, an immaculate red Chevy Monte Carlo, and his apparent awed fondness for the lovely Trudy Figg. From the moment Trudy first donned the trademark dress and tall white boots and smoothed the crochet cap over her long blonde hair, Jay was a goner. And as soon as he directed his deep, soulful eyes and dimpled grin her way, so was Trudy.

For the first time it appeared that maybe Trudy's string of bad boyfriends had broken. Jay sent flowers and bought her clothes, took her out to fancy dinners and for long drives along the river. He even once invited Violet to have dinner with Trudy and him, and when they arrived at his house, he pinned a camellia blossom to each of their blouses and led them to a picnic he'd set out on a blanket in his backyard overlooking the river. They spent the evening eating and laughing and watching the sun creep into the blue horizon.

Having been Trudy's stand-in parent for the last two years, after their father had finally drunk himself into a stupor and driven his car straight into a water oak, Violet couldn't help but breathe a sigh of relief that her sister's heart had been captured by someone as kind and true as Jay Malone.

It wasn't until one night a couple months later, at the grand opening of yet another Friendly's shop, that Violet saw Jay's illusion of perfection begin to slip. He was supposed to pick Trudy up for the event, but he never showed up. He didn't even call. So out of character was it for Jay that Violet drove Trudy there herself. He was there when they arrived, but he was agitated. It seemed a newspaper reporter was supposed to have met him for an interview before the ribbon cutting, but a last-minute scheduling conflict had caused the reporter to cancel the interview.

"It's okay." Trudy took his hand and pulled him close,

her feathered blonde curls haloing her face. "You don't need a newspaper article to bring people in. Look around. They're already here."

Despite Trudy's sweet encouragement, Jay held his body stiff, his shoulders high. Finally he relaxed and laughed a little. "You're right, sweetheart. It'll be fine. I just really want this to go well." He kissed her on the cheek. "I'm sorry I didn't pick you up this afternoon. It won't happen again."

Later when it was time to cut the ribbon, Jay gathered by the shop's front doors with his employees at his side. Trudy, dressed in her Friendly's Girl outfit, was supposed to be in the photo, but she'd run into her old friend Billy Olsen, who'd shown up for the grand opening. When Jay noticed the two of them chatting off to the side, a shadow—so slight it was likely no one noticed it but Violet—crossed his face and he strode away from the group. He pulled Trudy by the elbow and positioned her right behind the ribbon, then took his spot in the middle holding the oversize scissors.

After the camera flashed and the ribbon fell in two pieces, Jay put his arm around Trudy's shoulders as he leaned in close and said a few words to her. Violet couldn't tell what he'd said, but the wary look in Trudy's eyes and the way his fingertips pressed firmly against the skin of her bare shoulder made Violet's stomach curl into a ball.

Later that night when it was just the two of them at home, Violet asked Trudy about Jay's odd behavior.

"What are you talking about?" Trudy kept her back to Violet as she ran a dishcloth over the kitchen counter.

"He just seemed a little tense. Then getting mad at you for talking to Billy, yanking you back behind the ribbon."

"He didn't yank me, Violet. You're just seeing things." Trudy dropped the dishcloth and faced Violet. "Sure, Jay was upset that the reporter didn't come. Can you blame him? It was the grand opening and the guy couldn't even be bothered to show up. And the thing with Billy . . ." She tucked a lock of hair behind her ear. "Jay just wanted me to be next to him in the photo. It was sweet, really."

Trudy seemed so sure, so calm and confident, Violet forced herself to relax. *Jay's different. He's a good one.*

Then came the night a scant few weeks later when Trudy walked into the kitchen with pink cheeks, perfectly mussed hair, and puffy, just-kissed lips. Violet was at the table studying for a biology exam—she was taking college classes over in Mobile with her eye on a career in ornithology.

"He says he wants to marry me, Vi." Trudy sank into the chair next to Violet and plopped her chin on her hand. "He doesn't have a ring yet, but he's working on it. He's letting all the other Friendly's Girls go and just keeping me. He wants me to be his one and only." Trudy smiled and closed her eyes, no doubt savoring the memory of Jay's whispered sweet nothings.

Violet bit her lip. It was so soon. She trusted that Jay was good for Trudy—it was easy to see that they were over the moon for each other—but why was he in such a rush?

And she couldn't deny that faint voice telling her not to ignore the small things. "What do *you* think?"

"About what?"

"About Jay. About marrying him. Trudy, you're barely twenty years old."

"So? Just because you've never fallen in love doesn't mean I can't."

Violet took shallow breaths to keep from feeling the full sting of Trudy's words. It was true, she'd never been in love, but oh, how she'd yearned for it—to have someone she could relax with, to lay down her responsibilities and duties and let herself be taken care of for once. To meet someone she could trust with her deepest heart and truest self.

When Trudy noticed the impact of her words, tears sprang into her eyes. "I'm sorry." She reached for Violet's hand and squeezed it. "I didn't mean that."

"It's okay." Violet swallowed hard. "But you're young, Trudy. We both are. Don't you think it's a little early to be talking about marriage? Besides," she said with a chuckle, "what would Billy think?"

It was no secret that Billy Olsen—the lanky and vaguely annoying kid down the street who'd grown into a quiet, thoughtful, and much less annoying young man—had stars in his eyes over Trudy Figg. Violet had once held a secret hope that Billy would somehow be able to sweep Trudy off her feet, but it had become clear it was Jay who'd succeeded in doing that.

Trudy picked at a thread on the tablecloth. "Jay doesn't like Billy. He says Billy's possessive."

"Billy's about as possessive as a washcloth, you know that."

Trudy shrugged. "But Billy's not talking about marrying me. Jay is. He loves me. Can't you be happy for me?"

Violet studied her sister, her companion, her partner. "I do want you to be happy."

Trudy grinned. "Good. When the time comes, I want you to be my maid of honor. I'll pick out the prettiest dress for you." She reached over the table and hugged Violet's neck, then headed toward the back hallway and her bedroom. It wasn't until she passed the lamp by the couch that Violet saw the faint finger-shaped bruises on the back of Trudy's left arm.

After Violet's morning bird survey, she stopped by the Audubon office to log her data into the online survey portal. Internet service in Sugar Bend tended to be spotty, and the cover of trees around Violet's house made it even worse. Naomi, the director of the Coastal Alabama Audubon Society, told Violet when she first started volunteering that she could always come use the computer in the office when she needed to, and she gave Violet a key in case she needed to use it when the office was closed.

As Violet entered the morning's data, her mind swirled around a comment from a customer the other day. "Have you ever considered teaching a class?" the woman had asked as she watched Trudy work on a sculpture. "I know a lot of people who'd be interested in learning how to do what you do."

Trudy paused, then cut her eyes at Violet. Trudy had mentioned it to Violet before, how she wanted to teach people how to hunt for materials on their own and follow their creativity to make their own artwork. Maybe even have a class for kids. But how was she supposed to teach a class when she couldn't speak to her students?

Violet entered her last bit of data—*reddish egret, female, with possible injury to right wing*—and zipped her backpack closed when the phone on Naomi's desk rang. Violet paused, unsure if she should answer it. The last time she'd tried to answer the phone for Naomi, it had taken her so long to find the darn thing, hidden as it was under mountains of papers, birdcages, and Audubon Society pamphlets, that she'd missed the call.

At the last minute she decided to let the ancient answering machine catch the call. She fumbled in her bag for the key to lock the door, and as the machine switched on, her fingers finally found the key in the bottom of her bag. Locking the door behind her, she could just barely make out a man's voice. "Yes, hello. I hope I've called the right place."

The voice was deep, warm, a little scratchy. It wasn't that she recognized the voice exactly, but hearing it flushed the skin of her chest and cheeks, and as she walked to her car, the warm air whispered memories in her ears. She fought them the whole way home—half-remembered words, the soft brush of fingertips, a hoped-for future she'd long ago stopped thinking of—and by the time she pulled up the driveway, sweat beaded above her lip and the hair against her forehead was damp.

Silly me. She grabbed her backpack from the passenger seat and got out of the car. *Getting all worked up over a few old memories. I'm an old woman, I have a lot of those.*

As she approached the steps that led up to the front door, scents from every blooming thing enveloped her—the heady

61

sweetness of the magnolia in its full glory at the side of the driveway, the Carolina jasmine twining between the porch rails, and a bed of rosemary growing in a sunny patch by the birdbath. She breathed in deeper, giving the scents permission to wash away the memories and start her over fresh.

When she opened her eyes, a brown pelican was perched on the bottom porch step. It was a familiar sight—the long gray-and-white wings tucked neatly in, orange-brown beak proud and straight, tufts of bright white feathers on top of its head—but she'd never seen one quite this close to the house. Instead of enjoying its massive beauty, she felt it stirring up a hot anger inside her.

When she started toward it, the pelican swiveled its head and trained its small eyes on her. She raised her arms and flapped them, making herself as large and threatening as possible, a difficult task for someone who stood only five feet one on a good day.

For a moment the pelican just stared, unaffected, but finally it stretched out its wings and took flight. Violet followed its trajectory with her eyes, afraid to check the step where it had been standing. When the bird disappeared behind the canopy of trees, she lowered her gaze.

Yet another set of fish bones.

It was similar to the ones before, with an eye hole, gently curved spine, and slender tail bones. The pelican had left them behind. Threat, hint, or warning, it didn't matter. As Violet charged up the steps, her anger mixed with a side of fear, and she sent the bones careening into the azalea bushes.

All day at the shop, Violet was fidgety and clumsy. She dropped a set of hand-painted wineglasses a customer was in the process of purchasing, dripped a blob of cocktail sauce down the front of her shirt as she ate a quick lunch behind the counter, and accidentally knocked a rack of note cards off the counter with her elbow while she was dusting.

At that last fumble Trudy approached and helped her gather the scattered cards. As Violet stood and set the rack back on the counter with a little too much force, Trudy crossed her arms and raised her eyebrows.

"I'm fine." Violet brushed her hair back off her forehead and adjusted her glasses on her nose. "Just a little out of sorts today."

The door jingled and Emmajean ambled in with her bag full of books over her shoulder. "Afternoon, ladies," she chirped.

Every day after her shift at the library ended, Emmajean headed down Water Street to Two Sisters and settled herself in one of the chairs in front of the windows. If a customer came in while Trudy and Violet were busy, Emmajean would take it upon herself to educate the customer about the pieces for sale and help the customer fill up her shopping bag, the fuller the better.

Emmajean set her bag next to her usual seat in the curve of the bay window and headed for the wooden table at the back of the shop that held the teakettle and a pitcher of ice water. A few moments later, she dropped down into her seat with a sigh. She dunked her tea bag up and down in her mug, sending scents of lemon and spice swirling above her.

"Any more lovebirds at the library?" Violet asked as a gentleman opened the door to leave, his purchase in a bag on his elbow. The bell jingled his good-bye.

"Not today, thank the Lord. Just a fella trying to steal half a dozen books."

Another regular customer browsing through a selection of books by the door took a few steps toward Emmajean. "What do you mean, 'steal'?" the woman asked. "They're free, aren't they?"

"They're free as long as you check them out before you leave with them. But this guy chose to bypass the checkout desk, and let me tell you those circulation managers love it when the alarm goes off when someone tries to leave with a pilfered book. Usually the patron will stop and go back to the desk, but this guy decided to make a run for it."

"What on earth for?" The customer sat next to Emmajean, fully invested in the outcome of the story.

It was one of the many reasons Violet loved the shop. Aside from it being a source of income and a space for Trudy to work and sell her art, it provided a place for people to be and to belong. To connect with friends and make new ones. And to get an earful, often compliments of Emmajean.

As Emmajean continued the story of the runaway reader, Violet took the broom to the back corner to sweep where two kids had munched on cookies while their mom browsed the aisles. The bell jangled over the sound of the women's laughter, and when Violet paused to stretch her back, Maya was standing at Trudy's worktable. Her hair was swirled into a long braid down the center of her back, and she wore another Sugar Shack shirt and a pair of shorts. Violet's gaze dropped to a square-shaped bulge in Maya's back pocket.

Violet swept while Trudy and Maya conversed, Maya's quiet voice and Trudy's quick notes swaying gently back and forth. Maya trailed her fingers through the jar of blue sea glass and pulled out a single piece, long and cylindrical. She handed it to Trudy, who set it against a slim black-and-white gull feather threaded through a snarl of driftwood. Trudy tilted the piece back and forth, and the light caught the sea glass like a winking eye.

It was uncanny. Her sister rarely let anyone be that close to her while she worked, usually preferring a healthy bubble of space between her and any curious customers, and sometimes even Violet. But this was the second time she'd let this stranger not just stand close but participate in the process with her.

As Violet watched from behind the shelf of straw beach bags, Maya's fingers worked swiftly, twining thin pieces of driftwood with a handful of sea oats. Trudy was still as she watched, then she took a lump of speckled sea glass and set it against the base of the wood. She scribbled a note and handed it to Maya, whose face lit up with a smile.

A few minutes later, Emmajean and her new friend gathered their things and rose from the chairs up front. "I need to be getting home," Emmajean said. "I asked Hap to take care of dinner tonight, but the poor man gets spooked when he has to do any little thing in the kitchen. You'd think I asked him to prepare beef bourguignon, but it's just a frozen lasagna!"

With a wiggle of her fingers, Emmajean walked out, the bag of books bumping against her hip. A moment later, Maya checked her watch and spoke quietly to Trudy before moving toward the counter, where Violet now stood. Maya's shoulders lifted in a deep inhale, then dropped, and she slipped her hand into her pocket and withdrew the small shell box. She set it on the counter between them, and they both stared at it. Violet bit her lip to keep from speaking first.

"I took this," Maya finally said.

Violet propped a hip against the counter. "I know."

Maya lifted her face and met Violet's eyes. "It won't happen again."

Violet took off her glasses and rubbed the lenses with the hem of her shirt. "I hope not. Trudy seems to like you."

A shy smile emerged on the girl's lips. "I like her too. And I'm sorry about the box."

"You should be. I heard you tell Trudy you know where things belong. If that's true, the opposite should be true as well. And something you didn't pay for does not belong in your pocket."

"I know. It won't happen again," she repeated, a whisper of obstinance in her tone.

"Okay then."

Later, as the sisters locked up for the day, Trudy handed Violet a piece of paper. *I think we could use an extra set of hands around here.*

"Do you?"

Trudy nodded and tipped her head in a way that let Violet know exactly who she was referring to. Violet wrinkled her nose in derision. The girl was a thief. Violet wanted to be mad at her. She deserved to be angry. But something in Maya's face had tempered Violet's anger, and all she felt was a stubborn softness.

Trudy's pen scratched across another sheet. *She only works part time at the Shack. Three mornings and a couple afternoon shifts a week. And she told you herself it wouldn't happen again.*

Violet stared at Trudy. "You know about the box?"

She told me she likes it here. And that sometimes she does things she doesn't mean to.

"She said all that to you?"

A lot can be said without words.

Tension leaked out of Violet's neck and shoulders. "Yes, I'm quite familiar with that."

1979

In the end Violet didn't get a chance to stand at the altar next to her sister as maid of honor. No one did. During a late-spring weekend trip to New Orleans, Jay officially proposed to Trudy on Friday, married her on Saturday, and drove her home Sunday with a new ring set on her finger and a pink flush on her cheeks.

On Sunday evening Violet expected Trudy to walk in their

house with nothing more than a suitcase full of clothes to wash and stories to tell of streetcars, jazz bands, and fruity drinks. Instead Trudy called Violet from Jay's house up the river.

"We got married, Vi."

"You did what?" Violet was at the kitchen table working on applications for master's programs in biology and conservation at schools from Tuscaloosa to Tallahassee. She dropped her pen on the table and rested her forehead in her hand. She hadn't mentioned anything to Trudy about having seen the bruises on the back of her arm.

"Jay proposed and I said yes. Then we passed the sweetest little church on the way home from lunch Saturday and the pastor was right there, so we went ahead and got married."

"Just the two of you."

"Well, and the pastor."

"What about a marriage license?"

"He'd already gotten one. Seems he expected me to say yes." Trudy laughed, but it was tense. "Can you believe it? I can't wait for you to see the ring. It's perfect."

Violet opened her mouth to respond, but no words followed.

"You like Jay. You told me so yourself. I thought you'd be happy for me."

Violet heard the hurt in her sister's voice, but she couldn't muster the happiness Trudy so desired. "This is . . . it's too soon. And Trudy, he . . ." She lowered her voice to a whisper, though there was no one around to overhear. "He hurts you."

"What are you talking about? He doesn't hurt me." Her words were so incredulous, Violet faltered. Maybe her hunch had been wrong. Maybe the bruises she'd seen were just a trick of the light.

"He doesn't mean to, anyway." Trudy let out a bright peal of laughter. "He loves me."

"Oh, Trudy. We talked about this. Don't you remember?"

"I don't know what you're talking about."

"Yes, you do. It was after Mom and Dad had that really big fight. The loud one. We sat on my bed and talked about how we'd never let ourselves fall in love with a man who hurt us. I know you remember." The image was still clear in Violet's mind, though she'd been all of thirteen years old, fourteen tops, and Trudy a tender ten or eleven. They'd been wearing nightgowns, and Trudy's hair was wrapped in pink sponge rollers.

"It's not the same thing at all. Jay married me, for goodness' sake. You don't marry someone unless you love them, right?"

"Don't you think Mom thought that too?"

Trudy was quiet for a moment, and Violet thought she'd hit her mark. She bit her lip as she waited for Trudy to speak.

"Jay is a wonderful man and he loves me. I know you haven't gotten to know him well, but you will."

Violet closed her eyes, unable to comprehend her sister's blindness, but Trudy had made her choice.

"So are you living there now? At his house?"

"Of course, he's my husband. Where else would I live?"

Violet gazed around the home she'd shared with Trudy their whole lives. It had gone from a home of four, to three, then down to two. And now it was just Violet.

"We'll come by this week to get my things. And I want to

show you the pictures. Jay was so handsome." As Trudy went on about what they wore—a gray suit, white lapels, and a new pair of sterling silver cuff links for Jay, and a high-collared, coral silk dress with flowing sleeves for Trudy—Violet slowly gathered her applications into a pile and folded them in half, then folded them again.

She wouldn't be going anywhere.

Moving away, following her dreams, meant leaving Trudy behind—entrusting her to Jay's keeping—and that was something she couldn't do. Trudy was Violet's responsibility, the one person she had left.

With a sensation like a sinking rock in her stomach, she dropped the applications in the kitchen trash can, shoving them under the morning's coffee grounds so she wouldn't be tempted to pull them back out again.

Two months later Violet finally moved out of their childhood home, though she didn't go far. She'd once imagined herself moving to an exotic location, studying her birds, and making a life for herself. A life of her own choosing. In reality she only moved a couple miles downriver and took a job teaching science to giggling, restless sixth graders at Sugar Bend Academy.

It wasn't quite what she'd envisioned—that onetime desire to see new places, do new things, push herself, become someone new—but she had a job and she had a new place to live. And Trudy was still close. That was what mattered.

four

Tyler jangled his keys, then opened the door to his truck and waited for the coming onslaught. It arrived a second later in the form of pounding paws, orange fur, and an oversized pink tongue. His golden retriever didn't wait for permission before bounding into the truck and up onto the passenger seat, head out the window, tongue lolling.

"Good girl, Ruby." Tyler ruffled the top of her head, then, with his truck bed full of pine straw, pulled out of Holt's parking lot and onto the highway in the direction of his morning delivery. When he came to the turnoff for Soldiers Creek, he kept his truck between the yellow lines, but he still felt a part of himself floating down that skinny road through the trees and ending up at the creek. Everyone there would be high on life and the future, squeezing every last drop out of hazy afternoons and wild nights before walking into the rest of their lives come fall. He wanted to be there with them, but he also didn't. The part of him that wanted more was glad he had a reason to skip the creek.

Tyler had learned long ago it wasn't cool to be too smart. The kids who loved to read, the ones who got the good grades without having to study, the ones the teachers smiled down on— those were the kids who got bullied, who found crude notes in their lockers, who were laughed at in the cafeteria. Tyler never wanted to be one of those kids, so he downplayed his grades, hid his stash of novels in a box in the garage, and learned to leave the classroom quickly after the bell so no teacher could stop him and talk about his latest A.

But the real truth was, Tyler loved learning. He loved to read. He could write a killer essay in the time it took most people to find their way to the library. He even enjoyed solving a good, hard algebra problem. He knew it was grounds for quick dismissal from the crowd he usually spent his Friday and Saturday nights with during the school year, but he couldn't help himself. He hated to say it, but most of those guys were *dumb.* They had his back on the football field and would defend him to the death, but ask them about Einstein's theory of relativity or, heck, even the laws of gravity, and they'd mumble something incoherent, then run off to their trucks and their girls and their coolers of beer in the back. Nothing wrong with that, but Tyler was tired of it all.

He was also tired of the store, but he couldn't do anything about that. His dad had no one else to take over Holt Feed and Seed when he retired. The entire family business and the hope and drive and dreams that came with it all sat squarely on Tyler's broad shoulders. It was a burden he felt every minute of every day.

And don't even get him started on Cassie Wellington. As Tyler waited at a stoplight, hushing Ruby when she barked at a dog in another truck, he rubbed the side of his neck where Cassie had left her mark. He and Cassie had dated back in tenth grade, then again in part of eleventh, but she'd broken up with him for good last fall when Sugar Bend Academy lost to Spanish Fort, their biggest rival, by a single touchdown after Tyler fumbled the ball at the one-yard line. He hadn't been particularly sad to see her cozied up to the quarterback of Spanish Fort the next weekend, but it wasn't long before they broke up and she came back for Tyler, hips swinging and hair bouncing. He kept telling her he didn't want to date again, but she wasn't one to take no for an answer easily.

Tyler turned onto Grove Street and looked for the wisteria-covered trellis that marked the long driveway to the Figg sisters' house. Violet Figg had been a customer of the Feed and Seed for as long as Tyler could remember, and probably longer than that. The woman loved birds, and she came in from time to time to ask about certain kinds of seed—safflower for cardinals or white millet for doves. She also occasionally asked for help in her yard—cleaning up after heavy storms, raking the impressive amount of leaves that fell from their trees in the fall, or trimming tree limbs that grew too close to the house—and Tyler was always quick to help. Today he was delivering five bales of pine straw for their front flower beds.

When he reached the end of the driveway, Tyler turned off his truck and the old thing ticked and exhaled. He opened his door and Ruby bounded out after him, nose to the ground and tail wagging. As Tyler lowered the tailgate and pulled out the first bale of pine straw, he spied Ms. Trudy around the side of the house, down by the edge of the river, in a similar position as Ruby, though without the tail. Ms. Trudy was bent over staring at the ground, her eyes trained for the little gems she pulled out of the sand and grass and then used in her art sculptures.

He thought her sculptures were kind of weird, but people loved them. His mom even had one, a sunburst on the wall of their kitchen made from twisted pieces of driftwood and little white shells.

A few minutes later he was hard at work, clipping the twine from the bales and spreading the pine straw under bushes and around the bases of small trees. Ms. Violet always said he could just leave the bales at intervals near the beds so she didn't have to lift them, but he liked to go the extra mile for them. The sisters were a little strange, with Ms. Violet's bird obsession and Ms. Trudy's little pad of paper, but Tyler liked them. Every time he pulled into their driveway and parked under the huge magnolia tree, it was like walking into another world—some fairy-tale place where the rest of the world slid away and he could relax.

When he was in places like this, separated from the rush and responsibility of the rest of his life, he dreamed about his future. Not his actual future—that was already laid out for him in the form of the two-story warehouse on County Road 23 that had been an institution in the lives of area farmers for nearly sixty years. "Farmers don't take vacations, and neither do we" was the motto of the store, open seven to seven, seven days a week. One day Tyler would don the navy blue hat with the trademark barn-and-silo logo and take his dad's place behind the counter. That was his actual future.

The future he dreamed about was decidedly less utilitarian. Tyler had let it slip several years ago that he thought he kinda, sorta, maybe wanted to be a teacher. Dixon Holt had no problem with education, of course, but he made it clear early on that teaching was a job for people who didn't have anything else to do. Who didn't have a business to run. He didn't have to say he thought it was a job better suited for females—his mom told Tyler that much, though her worry was more along the lines of how much trouble he could get in if he so much as looked the wrong way at a female student.

But Tyler loved the feeling he got when something finally clicked into place in his mind, whether a math equation or a novel's theme. He wanted to encourage kids in the same way his teachers had encouraged him, and he couldn't do that while tossing bags of horse feed in the back of pickup trucks and debating with farmers about the benefits of Bahia grass over Bermuda.

As he threw the last handful of straw down, the breeze picked up. He paused and closed his eyes, savoring the cool fingers on his face as his sweat evaporated and his breathing slowed. When he opened his eyes, the tops of the trees were swaying back and forth. With all the leaves fluttering in tandem, it looked like a school of minnows above him, first darting this way, then that.

A moment later, Ruby came running from the side of the house and plopped down next to him, her eyes focused on the trees above. For a large dog she was nervous about most every-thing, especially wind.

"It's okay, girl." Tyler scratched behind her soft ears. It *was* a strange wind. More like fall than early summer. He glanced up to see Ms. Trudy approaching, a bulging plastic grocery sack hanging by her elbow. She pulled her pad and a pencil from her back pocket. *Thank you so much. Looks great. Violet went to open the shop but she says thank you too.*

"No problem. The old straw had gotten pretty flat. This should keep your weeds down, and it'll help when summer rains start up."

She waved good-bye and he started toward his truck, then stopped. "Wait, Ms. Trudy, I almost forgot." She paused on the bottom step and he reached over his seat and opened the glove box. He grabbed the Ziploc bag and walked it over to her. "I found these last week down in Orange Beach. Thought you might be able to use them in one of your sculptures."

The bag held five small, perfect sand dollars. Ms. Trudy's art might be wacky, but as soon as he'd seen the sand dollars, he tucked them away for her, knowing she'd put them to good use. Cassie had begged him for them, but he held his ground, teasing her by saying they were for another woman.

He took the long way back to the store, cutting through town and stopping in front of the Sugar Shack. Next to drop-ping twenty feet from the rope swing into the always-chilled Soldiers Creek, the Shack's lemonade rivaled everything else as the best way to beat the summer heat.

Inside, the air was nearly as warm as outside. The diner's

ceiling fans whirled so fast they wobbled, trying to tamp down the heat caused by the massive grill in the back, but they didn't do much good. He took his place in line behind another customer at the counter. As he waited he flapped the front of his shirt to catch some breeze, his mind on the rest of the day's duties at the store.

He barely noticed when the double doors from the kitchen swung open, but a second later, something weird flooded through him. It made him nervous. Jittery. A girl with long dark hair passed him holding a tray of food, on her way to a table in the corner full of loud teenagers. As she crossed the room, a faint trail of silver mist, cool and clean, followed in her wake.

She unloaded the tray quickly and tucked it under her arm. When she turned around, her gaze met his and she froze. Time slowed as they surveyed each other from across the room, and it wasn't until the cashier cleared his throat—twice—that Tyler finally blinked and woke up.

"Hey, kid, what'cha having?" the man behind the counter repeated.

"Uhh . . ." Tyler blinked again and gazed at the cashier. He couldn't remember what he'd come in for.

"If you need a minute, I'll move on to the next customer in line."

"Lemonade. I'll have a lemonade, please."

"You got it." The man punched a couple buttons on the register and the cash drawer slid out. Tyler paid quickly and grabbed his drink, then turned, searching for the girl and the silver mist, only to see the double doors swinging closed.

Maya woke with tears in her eyes the next morning. She couldn't remember what she'd been dreaming about, but it must have been something sad, some memory she'd closed up and put away. She rubbed her eyes with the base of her thumbs and rolled over onto her side. Strong sunlight filtered through the thin curtains at the window and made lacy patterns on the floor.

For Maya memories had always been strange, skittish things. Take her mother for example. Every once in a while, Maya would be hit out of the blue with a memory of her mom so tangible, she could reach out her hand and see a hazy outline of it sitting in her palm. But just as she focused on it, tried to bring back the shape and feel of her mother's body, her hands, or the sound of her voice, it would disappear into fog.

But since moving to this tiny waterside town, her memories were multiplying, and they weren't as hazy as before. They bumped into her at strange times—when she was stepping out of the shower or tying her shoes before work or filling yet another glass of lemonade behind the counter. Just the other night, she'd shot up out of bed with a flash of memory about her mother's hair—blonde and curly, as far from Maya's dark waves as possible. And her grandmother had had a bird. Maya laughed when she remembered. The bird was blue with a white head and it perched on Nana's shoulder. Maya remembered the feel of the tiny claws on her forefinger when *Cielo*—that was his name!—would land there.

However, the memory that hit her yesterday at the diner had nothing to do with her mother or grandmother. She didn't know what it was. She'd pushed open the kitchen doors and walked out, tray balanced on her shoulder, and approached the table in the back corner. A couple of the boys sitting there had already given her trouble, flirting in that familiar way that meant they cared nothing for her but everything about how they came off to their friends. She handed out the food and backed away as quickly as she could.

But when she saw the guy standing in line at the counter, she couldn't move her feet. Tendrils wrapped around her ankles and snaked up her legs, rooting her in place and nearly snuffing out the air in her lungs as images cartwheeled through her mind: sand between her toes and a sweetness in her mouth. A boy with golden hair grabbing hold of her hand, his face hidden in shadow. The sensation of flying, with nothing but sparkling water all around.

They held each other's gaze until Leroy behind the counter grew impatient and grabbed the guy's attention. When he turned to give his order, Maya bolted back into the kitchen. As the doors swung shut behind her, she caught one with her hand, keeping a sliver of space open to peek out.

He stood in the middle of the diner, lemonade in hand, scanning the room. He was searching for her, she knew it. She waited until he gave up and walked out, then she released the lungful of air she'd been holding tight.

1981

For the year and a half that Trudy had been married to Jay, Violet had done as well as she could to hold tight to her promise to her mother—to look after Trudy, to take care of her, to protect her. It hadn't been hard to do. She loved her sister; she'd do anything for her. And she'd come to hate Jay Malone.

Not long into their marriage, Jay took to disappearing for days at a time. Sometimes longer than that. He'd never tell Trudy where he was going. He'd just drive off, either by car or boat, and she wouldn't hear from him until he decided it was time to traipse home again. Trudy told Violet—secretly, never when there was a chance he could overhear her talking about him—that sometimes he'd return and go on about his business like nothing had happened. Other times, though, he'd kiss her and tell her how much he missed her. But he still wouldn't tell her where he'd been, who he'd been with, or when he might leave again.

Violet wasn't typically one to harbor hate in her heart—it made her chest heave and her hands sweat—but Trudy had diminished into a shell of herself. Where she once had a cheeky sense of humor, she now rarely gave herself over to laughter or any kind of fun. Where she'd once been meticulous about her appearance, brushing her hair until it shone and carefully applying eyeliner and mascara to accentuate her almond-shaped eyes, now she often came to the door with disheveled hair or only wearing one earring, as if she'd forgotten what she was doing halfway through getting ready for the day.

In total contrast to Trudy, Jay had remained as robust and as charming as he'd always been. In public, that is. In private, when Violet would go to their house to visit with Trudy, his smile was half a shade off, the barest tone in his voice hinting at a passionate anger ready to be released, like a tiger pawing at its cage. He never let it out in Violet's presence, of course, but she saw it on Trudy's skin—a blooming purple ring around her wrist, a green-hued mark on her thigh, a bite on her neck. And always the trembly, watery smile.

Violet had even tried talking to the police about it. She waited until Jay was gone, another mystery disappearance that had left Trudy fretful and desperate. Passing the Sugar Bend police station on her way home from the grocery store, she saw an officer climbing out of his cruiser in the parking lot, then walking toward the front doors of the building. The man looked like the kind of grandfather she'd always wished she'd had. Someone who'd sit next to a hearth and stoke a fire and listen to everything his grandchildren wanted to tell him. Her heart nearly burst with gratitude as she turned her car around and pulled into the parking lot.

Finally. Someone who can reach in and help me with this mess.

Though she was hoping to be able to speak to that very same officer, she didn't see him in the front lobby. Instead she told the first person she saw that she needed to speak with someone about an abusive situation, and she was led directly to a back office. Three officers in blue uniform shirts sat at desks, and a fourth man sat with his hip propped on the edge of a desk.

Violet exhaled in relief—it was the kindly man from the parking lot. The badge on his white shirt read *Hutchins*, and when he smiled, his cheek dimpled. "How can we help, ma'am?"

After explaining the situation as well as she could, she folded her arms together and dipped her head. "I should have seen it coming, but I was caught up in all his charm and charisma just like everyone else. Jay's the friendliest guy in town, right?" She chuckled but stopped short when she realized the officers were all exchanging glances.

"You're talking about Jay *Malone*?" Hutchins asked.

Violet nodded.

His gaze slid quickly to the officer to his right. When he glanced back at Violet, the gentleness in his face had been replaced with something less than compassionate. "You must be mistaken."

"Mistaken? About what?"

The man's smile was just this side of condescending. "Ma'am, Jay Malone is one of Sugar Bend's most upstanding citizens."

"I suppose that depends on your definition of upstanding."

"We all know Jay," he said. "He's a good man. He supports other businesses, he's a friend to everyone, he's a model example of what makes this town great. You're probably just misunderstanding the situation."

"I'm not misunderstanding anything." Violet fought to keep her voice under control. "It's hard to misunderstand the bruises."

"Look, I don't mean any offense, honey, but maybe your sister's just clumsy. And if he's abusing her, like you say, why isn't your sister in here talking to us about it? Even if it were true, we couldn't do anything about it unless the victim asks for help. But trust me, we've known Jay Malone a long time. He's a friend to this police department. He's not that kind of man."

"With all due respect, you may know what kind of man Jay is with his friends, but you have no idea what he's like when he's home with his wife."

"Miss Figg, you are crossing a line." Officer Hutchins's voice was cold now. Hard. "And you should think twice about coming in here and placing blame on an innocent person. If anything should ever happen to Mr. Malone—even just a smear on his name—we wouldn't take too kindly to that sort of thing."

A few minutes later Violet was ushered out the door with a frosty, "You have yourself a nice afternoon, ma'am." She had to sit in her car for ten minutes before she trusted herself to crank the engine and drive away. Her hands trembled and her breath came in short spurts. *It's up to me.* The realization dawned like a bracing north wind. *There really is no one else.*

Some days it was all Violet could do to get through her classes for the day, sending her students home with assignments to label cell diagrams or identify simple machines or explain seasonal weather patterns in Alabama, before she hopped into her car and raced to Jay's home on River Ash Road. She'd wait down the street from the house, a sweet two-story cottage with white trim, dormer windows, and a lattice arbor, under the dappled shade of an oak tree with limbs that brushed the ground. She'd wait until she saw him walk across the grass to their dock and step down into his boat, a little green thing with a bright blue horizontal stripe down the side. Violet had nearly memorized every detail, as often as she'd watched him motor away in it, as he headed down the river while she headed inside to try to save her sister.

One particular night, just after the new year, Violet had jogged up the driveway as soon as Jay left. She had a few hours before she was to meet Emmajean at the Sandbar, a popular hangout overlooking a bend in Little River. Emmajean had set Violet up on a blind date, though Violet had zero interest in being set up. Plus, if she was successful in convincing Trudy to leave, she'd be a no-show at the bar.

She knocked, then pushed the front door open. The television was on in the den, but Trudy was in the kitchen sweeping up shattered glass, a wad of paper towels wrapped around her left hand.

"Let me see." Violet's voice was quiet.

"It's okay." Trudy averted her eyes. "I just dropped a jar and cut my hand."

"Mm-hmm." She took the broom from Trudy's hands and propped it against the wall, then peeled the paper towels back. Blood seeped from the cut in tiny red dots. "It's not too deep," she murmured. "I'll get a bandage."

"It's okay, Vi. I'm fine." Trudy grabbed a clean paper towel and pressed it to her hand, then took up the broom again. "You should leave. I don't know when he'll be back."

"It'll probably be a while."

When he was in town, Jay often spent evenings at the Showboat, the notorious houseboat docked just outside the city limits of Sugar Bend that allowed gambling on the bottom floor and offered an assortment of ladies upstairs.

"But I'll leave now if you'll come with me," Violet added.

Trudy shook her head. Her hair was shorter now but still thick, blonde, and lovely. Even with Jay's marks on her and the faint purple hollows under her eyes, her beauty still shone. It was burnished, but it was there.

"You can come home with me."

"And what?" Trudy asked, incredulous. "Just stay there? He'll know I'm with you."

"We could leave a bus schedule on the table. Make him think you hopped on a Greyhound and left town alone."

It was a flimsy plan, and Violet knew it wouldn't work. Sugar Bend was a small town, and Jay knew everyone—and everyone knew him, or at least knew who he was. There was no way to hide from him, but all Violet cared about at the moment was getting Trudy away long enough to put a plan together. A plan that would protect Trudy for good.

Trudy swept the last of the glass and dumped it in the trash. In the den *Magnum, P.I.* started with its familiar guitar intro and helicopter swooping down over the water. Trudy and Jay's house was simple and homey—soft pillows on the couch, books on the shelves, a kitchen window overlooking their wide backyard that stretched down to the river. But the details hid an ugly truth.

Trudy was a prisoner with a very cruel guard.

Violet left alone that night, as she always did, and Trudy remained behind, waiting for her husband's return and praying he'd come home with a little extra money in his pocket. That, they both knew, would bring back his friendly smile and maybe even a softness in his touch, which was much better than the alternative.

She promised Trudy she'd be back soon, but as she drove away, Violet wondered how much longer she could do this. How long would she try to convince her sister to see reality, to make a change, before she had to accept that Trudy was a grown woman and could make her own choices? How long was she tied to the promise she'd made to her mother years ago?

However long it takes.

She rolled down her window, ushering in the chilly January air and dragging it into her lungs. She exhaled as much stress and worry as she could, wanting for just one night to forget everything—Trudy's bruises, Jay's anger, the sisters' fractured childhood, Violet's own aching loneliness.

The loneliness had wrapped around her like an intruding weed long ago, taking root and squeezing tight. She didn't envy Trudy her life with Jay, but she wished for something different. Something better. A place to land at the end of the day, a safe-keeping hand and heart. Someone who wouldn't leave.

Inside the Sandbar she sat on a stool and flagged the bartender. All around her bodies swayed to the music and faces gleamed with buzzy happiness and the pulsing hope that they might not go home alone.

This sure isn't the place to find something better.

The bartender stuck a lime on the lip of her plastic cup. It wasn't long before a tall man, sweaty and overconfident, leaned in next to her, plying her with sweet talk about music and dance moves. He was pathetic, really, and she was just about to tell him so, when the air in the room changed. Prickles of heat ran up her arms and down her back, and she braced her hand on the bar as if the room were quaking. She peered over her shoulder just as another man approached the empty stool on her other side.

"Is anyone sitting here?"

And just like that, the cloak of loneliness tumbled off her shoulders.

Violet's morning bird survey began like all the others. The sand under her feet was cool and firm, and water tumbled over her toes like loose diamonds. Every surface, liquid or solid, was shining in the brilliant sun that coated the wide blue Gulf of Mexico. Usually on a day like this, the horizon would be dotted with sailboats and fishing boats out for a day's work or adventure, but a stiff breeze had kept most of them in. It was an uncharacteristic wind, stronger than normal for such a bright, clear day. But it did tamp down the heat, which Violet appreciated.

She was only a few minutes into her survey and the top sheet on her clipboard was already covered with data. In her experience, birding was often best on cloudy or even drizzly days, but it seemed despite the wind, the birds were taking advantage of the morning's clear brilliance.

Off to her right, among the grassy dunes, other volunteers had posted a temporary fence around an area where least terns had built their nests. These birds were annual visitors to the Alabama shore, and all the birders in the area knew to pay close attention to the activity there. Violet crossed the sugary-white sand toward the wind-billowed orange fence to get a better look. As she watched, two females flew low over the dunes and landed next to a third, which was already incubating a nest on the sand. The two newcomers ruffled their feathers and chattered, their noise a chaotic jumble of squeaks. The mother on the nest gazed at them, then glanced away, all but rolling her eyes. Violet imagined the two intruders as more experienced nest sitters giving heaps of unwanted advice to the new mother.

On she walked, making hatch marks on the sheet with each new bird she saw. She tried to stay focused on the task at hand, but her mind kept turning over old memories, like seashells tumbling in a rolling surf. Jay Malone. Bruises marring Trudy's pale skin. Violet's own fear and anger. The rush of heat and longing that first night at the Sandbar.

The particular beauty of this day—the beach empty but for the birds, the sun bright and fresh, the air laced with salt and pine—stood in stark contrast to the tumult of memories flooding her mind. She felt unanchored, caught between the present and the past, like the increasingly strong breeze was trying to carry her away.

Up ahead was the old chair-rental stand where her one-mile route ended. She paused, her gaze fastened to the sheets of wood and peeling yellow paint. She could almost see him walking toward the stand, the tiny shell pressed in his palm. It was an angel wing, broken in such a way that it resembled a bird in flight. An incoming wave had deposited it right by his foot, and he'd snatched it up.

"I'm leaving it here so every time you pass this stand, you'll think of me, even if I'm not with you."

Violet laughed. "I don't need a shell to remember you. And anyway, what makes you think it'll stay there? Don't you think some little kid will see it and drop it in his bucket to take home?"

"Not here, he won't." Violet stood next to him. At the top of the stand, where two pieces of plywood came together, there was a small indentation, a shelter just big enough to protect the nearly weightless shell. "There." He tapped it with his finger. "No one will know it's here but me and you. It'll be our secret."

Violet lifted herself on her tiptoes and kissed him. "I like a good secret."

She couldn't have known then how another secret would wrench him from her. Or her from him. If she had a chance to do it all over again, would she do it the same? Would she take the same path, make the same split-second decision, choose the same future?

Maybe. Probably. She couldn't be sure, though she was sure about one thing—her arms had grown tired from carrying her load all these years, and at certain times, in certain slants of light, she wished she could lay it all down and finally be free. She and Trudy both.

Before turning around and heading back, she picked her

way through the shells and clumps of seaweed to the stand that had hidden the angel wing for so long. It had been many, many years since she'd checked to see if it remained. She just hadn't let herself. But today, as she closed in on it, blood thrummed in her veins, her hopes pinned to that shallow indentation that had once held a silly symbol of young love, of an almost-promised future.

She closed her eyes as the wind whipped her hair out from under the visor, then peeked up between the two plywood boards. The space was empty. Just as she'd known it would be. All that remained were a few grains of sand.

Late at night the wind whips into a frenzy. Palm fronds slap against darkened windows, hammocks whip inside out, birds huddle in their shivering nests. And down in the far depths of Little River, a little boat quivers. A current prods the boat with persistent fingers until it dislodges from its protective tangle of barnacle-covered rope and sunken crab traps. The boat lifts from its resting place at the bottom and rises through thirty feet of brackish water until it breaks the surface for the first time in forty years.

After bobbing on the surface, sending ripples across the river in all directions like a gong, the boat begins to drift slowly but surely toward the shore. Finally it comes to rest in a patch of needle rushes along the water's edge, one side pressed against a dock piling. For a moment all is still.

Then out of the inky dark sky comes the sound of pounding wings. A brown pelican lands on the end of the dock and tucks its wings into its sides. Small brown eyes scan the dock and with a quick shudder, the bird lowers its head and deposits clean fish bones onto the old wooden boards, still warm from the day's heat. The bird's gaze rests on the little boat as it sways on the surface of the water. It tilts its head, then in a quick flap of wings and water droplets, the bird takes flight. The bones remain, bleached white and sharp as pins, and the boat presses a little farther into the shore.

PART TWO

soar

five

Justin Roby sat at his desk staring at the computer screen, bleary eyed and in need of a shave. He'd been scanning various social media pages for hours now, searching for tips on a string of car burglaries that had been happening in town, but he'd yet to find anything of substance. Justin knew most of the guys responsible for three-quarters of the crime in Sugar Bend, and he also knew they had secret social media accounts where they traded information about who was out of town, who just bought a new computer, who tended to leave car doors unlocked at night.

Many of the older officers at the precinct rolled their eyes anytime Justin pulled up Instagram or Snapchat, but he didn't care. All he needed was one good crime he could solve and they'd all look at him differently. He'd no longer be the rookie fresh out of the academy but a full-fledged and, most of all, capable officer.

The coffee on his desk was cold enough to grow ice crystals on the inside, so he tossed the Styrofoam cup in his wastebasket and made the trek down the hall to the kitchen in the back. The precinct was quiet this time of the morning, with a couple more hours to go on the graveyard shift before the next shift arrived, ready to patrol the streets of Sugar Bend, this small town four miles north of the Gulf. By then Justin would be buried in his bed at home, his head under the pillow and blackout shades securely drawn.

A local Girl Scout troop had dropped off a bag of snacks earlier in the week, and while most of the good stuff had already been devoured, Justin found a half-squashed Kind bar at the bottom of the bag and carried it along with a fresh cup of coffee back to his desk. Steam curled from the coffee cup as he sat in front of his computer again and navigated over to the familiar neighborhood news page on Facebook. It was where people in town talked about anything and everything—house break-ins, the neighbor who left his Christmas lights up all year, the overgrown lot where high schoolers congregated to drink cheap beer and listen to loud music.

He scrolled down, skimming his gaze over the usual names and gripes, then something stopped him. Two photos side by side, one of which showed a metal boat, possibly green but the amount of rust and gunk made it difficult to tell. The second photo was a close-up of a blue stripe running horizontally across the side of the boat. There wasn't anything special about it, nothing familiar to him, and yet something tapped on the inside of his chest. *Look at me*, it seemed to say. *Pay attention.*

Below the photo was a name he didn't recognize and a short caption.

This boat showed up under my dock on Little River a few mornings ago, half stuck into the sand. Boat seems pretty old, and it's obviously been underwater for a while. It's green aluminum with a blue stripe on the side. If the boat belongs to you or you have any information about it, please call or send a private message.

Justin leaned back in his chair and crossed his arms, staring at the photos. He wasn't supposed to be looking for a boat. He was trying to solve the car burglaries. On each of the driver's side doors of the vandalized vehicles, there was the same scratch, a deep mark that appeared purposeful. The mystery had teeth and Justin wanted to be the one to figure it out. Checking out this boat would only get in his way.

There was something about the boat though. He tried scrolling past it, but his finger kept coming right back to the photos of the murky green, the algae softening the lines of the hull.

He should ignore the photos—and that strange tapping in his chest—and keep his focus squarely on the car burglaries. But there was another option: Uncle Frank. Frank could dig up info about the boat while Justin did his real job. If Frank uncovered anything of importance, Justin could step in. He ripped open the Kind bar's wrapper, took a bite, and chewed slowly before he reached for the phone.

"You're up and at 'em early." Frank's voice was always deep, but in the morning it was deeper than ever, as if the night still clung to his vocal cords, trying to lull them back to sleep. "Must have had a night shift."

"I did. I'll be off in a little while. Sleep's calling me. Loudly."

"Oh, I remember those days. I always liked the graveyard shifts when I was your age though. Made me feel like Superman or something. Like I was the only one awake in the middle of the night to solve all the crimes."

If Justin didn't get to the point of his phone call quickly, Frank would be off and running on memories of his time on the force. He'd been retired for years now, but once a police officer, always a police officer. That's the way it was with the men in their family. They might hand over their badges, but they never gave up their dedication to duty.

"I found something here that might interest you," Justin said.

"Is that so?"

The sound of chirping fluttered through the phone, and Justin knew his uncle was in his backyard watching the birds. Justin's dad, Frank's youngest brother, always made fun of Frank for his fondness for birds, saying it made him soft. Frank never defended himself, but a steam of anger, or maybe embarrassment, would rise from his head and shoulders.

"What'd you find?" Frank asked.

Justin sat forward in his chair and sipped his coffee. "It's a boat. Seems like it's been in the river awhile. I thought you might be able to figure out who it belongs to. Or at least take a look at it."

"I don't know, I've been pretty busy lately."

Justin didn't comment. His uncle wasn't busy doing much of anything these days. He worried about Frank sometimes. He didn't see him all that often, though now that Frank had moved back to Sugar Bend from Pensacola, they only lived a handful of miles apart. But when they did see each other, Frank seemed lonesome. Or homesick. He was always patting his pockets or the top of his head or checking behind him as if he was looking for something—or someone—he couldn't find.

Frank had been forced to retire earlier than he would've liked due to a leg injury sustained on the job. As far as Justin could tell, he spent most of his time tending to his backyard birds and taking long walks with his cane. Justin occasionally called Frank when he came across some curious piece of information, a mystery that he doubted would amount to anything but would make Frank feel useful. Still valuable.

He also knew Frank always said no first.

"I understand," Justin said. "You're busy. And you know what? It's probably nothing. Just an old boat someone forgot about years ago."

Justin chewed on the edge of his bottom lip as he waited for the moment when Frank changed his mind. He always did.

Frank rubbed his cheek, the sandpapery sound swishing through the phone line. "I don't know, I might have a little time to check it out. Where is this old boat?"

Maya left early before her two o'clock shift at the Sugar Shack so she'd have time to run by the art shop first. She wanted to come every day, but she didn't let herself. Didn't want to be a nuisance. Plus, she'd stolen from them. She hadn't meant to do it, but it happened anyway. If she were a shop owner and some stupid girl came in and stole from her, Maya would probably bar the door. Why should they be any different?

But Violet, the one behind the front counter, had told her she was glad Maya came back, and that was *before* Maya returned the box. And Trudy let Maya help her with her sculptures. Maya didn't understand their kindness. Usually people being too nice to her meant ulterior motives. Or blatantly inappropriate ones. But she didn't get anything close to those vibes from these two.

The day was warm, the air thick and sugar scented from the doughnut shop on the corner. She lifted her hair off the back of her neck and twisted it into a knot, poking the ends under so it wouldn't fall down. She paused at the door as a customer angled her large shopping bag through the doorway, then took a step inside. Violet was behind the counter as usual, ringing up a customer, and Trudy was at work at the table in the back. With a cautious glance through the shop, Maya approached Trudy's table.

She sat to one side, her tackle box open on the floor next to her and an assortment of green and brown glass pieces scattered on the table in front of her. At the other end of the table were a pair of wire cutters and a spool of thin wire, a few pieces of driftwood, and the jar of clear tumbled glass. A small wooden bowl held clumps of dried seaweed, and the rolling pin of untangled fishing line sat perpendicular to the edge of the table. The second chair at the table was empty.

As soon as Trudy made eye contact with Maya, Trudy tipped her head to the side, toward the empty chair.

Maya raised her eyebrows. "You want me to sit?" Trudy nodded but Maya hesitated. She glanced over to where Violet was helping an older gentleman pick through a rack of sterling silver necklaces, then turned back when she heard the scrape of the chair against the floor as Trudy nudged it back with her toe.

Maya obeyed and stroked her fingers over the materials on the table—the cool wire and knobby wood. The rough seaweed and still-sandy shells. Her fingers itched and she could almost hear the various pieces telling her how they wanted to fit together and where they belonged.

Trudy slid a note toward her. *Go ahead. Just play.*

So play she did. For an hour she arranged and rearranged the pieces, intertwining wood pieces and tacking on feathers, knots of wire, and loops of twine. Iridescent jingle shells, coquinas as small as a pinkie nail, and tiny striped oyster drills. Everything mixed and mingled under her fingers as she shaped and wired and tested and pressed. In the end her creation vaguely resembled a tree, but it also somehow reminded her of her grandmother, with outstretched arms and a sturdy middle.

A moment later, she turned to Trudy and the words fell from her mouth. "I'd really like to work here." She pressed her lips together. She hadn't even realized that's what she was going to say until she said it, but once it was out, she knew that was exactly what she wanted. What she needed.

Trudy didn't say anything at first, and Maya assumed she was trying to come up with a way to let Maya down easily. But she picked up her pencil and wrote, *I was hoping you'd say that.*

Maya searched Trudy's face. "What do you mean?"

My sister and I need some help around here, Trudy wrote. *Two old ladies can only do so much when the summer crowds get going and the shop fills up. I told Violet I thought you'd be a great fit.*

"You did? Why?"

Trudy grinned. *You're a natural. You're good with these materials, even when they're finicky. You're patient, you're easy to get along with, and I think you'll be a big help to customers. And to me.*

"But Violet . . ." Maya peeked over her shoulder to where Violet stood by the front door chatting with a customer. "I don't think she'll be so eager to have me work here."

I wouldn't be so sure about that. All I need to know is if you're serious about wanting to work. If not we'll put a "Help Wanted" sign in the window tomorrow.

Maya thought again of her grandmother, how her hands were so quick they almost disappeared, flipping card after card as she doled out futures. Maya had never believed in anything the cards showed, but then again, neither had her grandmother.

"I don't tell people their futures, Maya," she'd once said. "All I do is give them courage. Usually they already know what they need to do. Sometimes it's fear that holds them back. Sometimes it's sadness or pain or hope. I just give them the push they need to walk the path laid out for them."

Maya didn't know what her future held, but she felt the push like a gentle hand at the small of her back.

"I do," she said to Trudy. "I want to work here."

Trudy nodded. *Okay then. I'll take care of it.*

Then she reached into a drawer of her worktable and pulled out the driftwood and sea oats Maya had twined together the last time she was here.

Remember this?

Maya nodded.

I was thinking we could do something with it. Trudy motioned back and forth between the two of them with her finger.

"I'd like that." Maya ran her fingers over the rough wood and prickly sea oats. "It needs to be softer."

Let's get to work then.

Together they fiddled with various pieces and positions, trying glass and shells and twine until something felt right. After a while, Maya glanced at her watch. "My shift starts soon. Can we come back to this later?"

Trudy patted Maya's hand and nodded.

As she leaned down to grab her bag by her chair, the bell over the door jingled. She slung her bag across her shoulder and stood and came nearly face-to-face with the boy she'd seen in the diner, the one whose curious stare had raised the hair on her arms, caused a pulse low in her stomach, and sent those colorful and electrifying images through her mind.

Next to her Trudy cleared her throat until the boy looked at her. Trudy tipped her head toward Violet.

"Oh, right." The boy glanced at Maya. "I have birdseed. It's for—"

"Tyler, you're a lifesaver," Violet called from the opposite side of the shop. "You can just leave it behind the counter. You've saved me a trip out to the store and I appreciate it."

"No problem." With one last lingering look at Maya, he walked toward the register and set the bag on the floor behind the counter. "I'll just . . ." He glanced back at Maya just as she felt a poke on her arm. Trudy held out a note. *That's Tyler. He works at the feedstore and does odd jobs for us. A nice boy.*

Maya swallowed hard and willed her cheeks not to flame with heat. It was a telltale sign of any agitation or embarrassment— her cheeks flared so red they almost turned purple.

"I have to go," Maya said to the air around her. At the door she paused and looked back over her shoulder. Tyler was slim but tall, with shoulders that strained the seams of his T-shirt. His hair was thick and blond and fell carelessly over his forehead. Dark, straight eyebrows sat over dark blue eyes, and he was watching her with the same intent stare as the other day. Then he flashed a smile so brilliant, it was like a sharp ray of sun on her chest. When the door to the shop closed behind her, she pulled her lips in between her teeth, but she couldn't keep the edges from turning up.

That night, lying in bed with a sliver of pale moonlight peeking between the yellowed lace curtains, she pondered the memory that had filled her mind when she saw the sign for Sugar Bend at the gas station over a month ago. The pull in the center of her being. That magical, comforting sense of belonging. She hadn't felt anything close to that in years, no matter how many homes she'd been shuffled into and out of.

But today, walking into Two Sisters, seeing that empty chair at the table, then feeling the shells and wood and glass under her fingers, she'd felt that pull again. Like a big magnet was hidden somewhere in the room, maybe in the pale blue paint on the walls or the smooth tile floor under her feet, and it was coaxing her in. She didn't understand it but she felt it. It was everywhere in this small, strange town, like arms outstretched in welcome.

Before the age of sixty Frank Roby never once dealt with insomnia. He'd spent most of his life falling asleep in three minutes flat and sleeping soundly without waking for eight solid hours. But lately, at least a couple nights a week, he lay awake in the dark thinking about life and his history and the future and every other intangible thing running through his mind.

This night, though, he didn't mind so much because he had a mystery to busy himself with. It was 3:15 a.m. and he'd been staring at the photos of the recently recovered jon boat for the last little while. His nephew Justin had sent him the link to the photos on Facebook, and that's where he was now, sitting in front of his computer with a finger poised over the mouse as he scrolled from one photo to the next, his face aglow in the dim blue light. The man who found the boat had posted a few more just last night, and he'd added the address where the boat had been found: 61 River Ash Road.

The man had managed to get the boat out of the water and up onto the sandy shoreline. The motor and tiller were still intact, though a hole gaped in the bottom and the whole thing was covered in barnacles and grime. Frank propped his chin in his hand, his mental gears working cleanly despite the hour. It could have been twenty years ago, when he was much younger and sprier and when a late shift energized rather than exhausted him.

He used to love those shifts, when the precinct was quiet until something happened, then he'd burst from his office, hop into his squad car, and show up wherever he was needed. Back then he'd never shied away from anything.

His life was much simpler now. Slower. And if he ever missed the frenetic activity, the near-constant buzz of his earlier working years, he had his nephew calling him up now and again to ask his opinion on some minor police matter—a squabble over a traffic ticket or a judge's indictment that had ruffled feathers on the force. Or, in this case, an old green boat that had been asleep under the water for who knew how long.

Justin was trying to make Frank feel needed, like his hard-won skills and intelligence from a career on the force weren't going to waste, and Frank appreciated the gesture. He even enjoyed the work. But sometimes all the phone calls did was remind him of just how quiet and empty his days really were.

With a sigh Frank rolled his chair closer to the desk and focused on the screen in front of him. There wasn't much left of the boat except that painted stripe down the side. The more he scrolled back and forth though, his gaze sliding over the bow, the hull, the stern, the more it began to take on a hint of the familiar. Something about that blue stripe set against the green. Somehow that blue was still crisp and clear, as if it had just been painted on yesterday, though the deterioration of the rest of the boat showed that was impossible. Frank's skin tingled as a wave of memory tried to kick his legs out from under him.

He stood from the computer abruptly, causing his chair to clang behind him. He paused, steadying both the chair and his shaking hands, then walked to the kitchen. In the dark he pulled a glass from the cabinet and filled it with water. He drank it slowly, relishing the coolness in his parched throat. When he finished, he set the glass in the sink and returned to the computer.

He leaned toward the screen again, his eyes tracing the slice of blue, the scum of algae along the bottom, the curve of the hull. He could almost see a pair of hands caressing the side of it, feel a stiff warm breeze against his face.

1981

Frank walked up the pathway toward the front door of 61 River Ash Road with one hand resting protectively on the butt of his gun. Not that he expected he'd have to use it, but the neighbor who called 911 said she'd heard a scream coming from the house next door, and Frank couldn't be too careful. It could be nothing—the woman could have heard a screech owl or a pair of brawling cats or a too-loud television—or it could be something else entirely.

Thunder rolled in the distance as the breeze picked up. The weatherman had reported a storm would be coming through overnight, and Frank wanted to be back at the precinct before the bottom fell out. His heart was already beating faster than normal, and he took a few deep breaths to steady himself. The caller hadn't given a name—neither hers nor the neighbor's—so Frank had no idea what to expect.

He knocked on the door. No response. Another knock, this time louder.

"Hello?" a voice called to him from around the side of the house.

"I'm Officer Roby." Frank walked toward the voice. "Just checking things out. I got a call from a neighbor about some noise over here."

When he rounded the corner, a man stood in the porch light, wiping his hands on a bandana, a smudge of blue paint on his forehead. "Must be old Frieda. She keeps everyone on the road in line." The man's face was open and friendly, and it sparked recognition in Frank, though he couldn't pinpoint how he knew him. "Sorry you had to come out here so late at night. I was out back painting my boat, and I just hammered the paint can closed. That must have been what she heard."

"I don't think so." Frank propped his hands on his hips. "She said she heard a scream."

"Ah. Must be the foxes then. A family of them lives out in the woods there." He pointed toward the thick, dark woods off to their left.

"Have you heard them tonight?" Frank asked.

"No, I can't say that I have. My wife's inside. Usually when the foxes are loud, they wake her up, but she's upstairs sleeping like a baby."

"How would you know that if she's in there and you're out here?"

The man laughed and shoved the bandana in the back pocket of his blue jeans. "Good point."

Frank waited, but the guy didn't offer any more. "What'd you say your name was?"

"I didn't. It's Jay Malone."

Frank snapped his fingers. "That's it. You're the ice cream guy. Friendly's Ice Cream, right?"

"That's right. Friendliest ice cream shop in town." His words were chipper and his tone light.

Frank nudged his chin in the direction of the boat. "What kind of boat do you have?" It was something he'd learned in the short time he'd been on the force. Sometimes asking off-subject questions could lead a person to say something he hadn't planned.

"Oh, it's nothing special. Just a jon boat. But I love it." He glanced behind him. "Want to see it?"

"Sure." Frank didn't know much about boats, but he'd humor the guy.

The boat was sitting on a trailer in the grass between the house and the dock. It was green aluminum, and a fresh stripe of royal blue stretched from the bow to the stern on both sides.

"It's a good-looking boat."

Jay ran a hand down one side, avoiding the still-wet paint. He was quiet, almost reverent, in his appraisal of his boat. It was a week until Thanksgiving, and a cool wind blew over

Frank's face and rustled the reeds growing along the banks of the river. Clouds skirted the moon and leaves fluttered in front of the porch light, casting strange shadows on the lawn.

Frank hooked his thumb toward the house. "Mind if I see inside before I head out?"

A shadow of irritation crossed the man's face, but it was gone as soon as it had come. "No, not at all."

Jay led the way up the back steps to the door and opened it. Inside, the living room was tidy and cozy. A woman's touch was evident in the needlepoint pillows and a couple vases of dried flowers. Through the doorway to the kitchen, an under-cabinet light illuminated clean counters and a row of jars with their labels perfectly straight.

"Your wife's sleeping, you said? Why don't you check on her while I'm here."

Jay raised his eyebrows. "You sure that's necessary? I'd hate to wake her up."

"I'd just like to make sure she's okay." *Seems you would too*, Frank thought, *if someone said she heard a scream coming from your house.*

Frank followed Jay up another set of stairs, this time to the second floor and a doorway to the right. Jay pushed the door open and light from the hallway pushed through the darkness within.

A sleeping form lay under blankets on the bed, and the soft shoulder sticking up over the blanket showed it was clearly a woman. She moved, held a hand up to her eyes, and peered back over that shoulder. "Jay? What's wrong?"

"Nothing, love," Jay crooned in a gentle voice. "Go back to sleep."

"Who's with you?" Her voice held just the barest measure of panic, easy to miss under the guise of poise.

"No one, just a friend. He's leaving now. I'm going to clean up the paint and I'll be up here with you in a few minutes."

The way he talked to her was almost childlike, as if he needed to dumb down his words and voice for her to swallow them. It set Frank's teeth on edge.

Jay pulled the door closed and tossed a satisfied glance Frank's way. "No screaming there, as you can see."

Downstairs Frank heard the beginnings of the rainfall. His heart still beat hard, but he'd seen Jay's wife with his own eyes, and there was clearly no screaming match going on in this house. If there'd been one earlier, the storm had passed, and anyway, it wasn't a crime to fight with your spouse, as long as things stayed on this side of physicality.

Jay reached his hand out to shake Frank's. "I appreciate you checking anyway. You men in blue always have my full respect, keeping an eye on everything for us. And good for Frieda for being careful, though I think she's just imagining those crazy foxes."

Jay walked him as far as the front corner of the house, then waved. "Gotta go cover my boat before the rain takes the paint off. Stay safe out there."

"Yeah, you too." Frank held a hand up to shield his face from the shower as he walked back to his squad car parked on the street.

He didn't hear anything—no words, no tap on the glass—but something pulled his gaze back to the house, and there, in one of the dormer windows upstairs, was Jay's wife. She'd turned on a lamp and wrapped the blanket around herself. Her face was somber, deliberate, as if she was trying to communicate something to him with her eyes.

He paused, testing the quiver of alarm that rippled through him. Just as he was about to walk back to the house, a scream ripped through the night. His hand went to his gun as he jerked his head to the left, toward the stand of woods. The scream came again, then another one, the two of them overlapping each other.

The foxes. He exhaled hard, fear draining out of his legs and off his shoulders, making him weak.

When he glanced back up at the house, the window was empty, the light off.

It took a few minutes for the present to chase away the past. Frank blinked a couple times, and the image of the freshly painted boat slunk away, to be replaced by the one before him on the computer screen, this one awash with age and river detritus. He blinked again, then pulled a piece of paper and a pen from his desk drawer and jotted down the phone number listed beneath the photos.

six

While most of Violet's volunteers enjoyed their work with birds, many of them complained about the monotony of logging their post-survey data into the Audubon portal. Violet never saw much value in complaining, and anyway, she always felt there was something soothing to the process of entering data. It was only simple words and numbers, no emotions, memories, or regrets involved.

Violet was absorbed in her task, adding in her notes on bird species, counts, and concerns, when the director opened the door and rushed inside with her characteristic flurry. Naomi's long black hair still fluttered behind her even after she'd come to a stop, her hand on her chest.

"Violet, you scared me to death."

Violet smiled. She'd talked to Naomi just yesterday and told her she'd be in after her survey to use the computer. "I'm sorry, Naomi. Didn't mean to scare you. I just have a little bit more to go and I'll be out of your hair."

"My hair's fine and you're not in my way. I just forgot you

were coming in." As Violet focused her attention back on the screen in front of her, Naomi crossed the room to her desk in the corner, the surface of which was as cluttered as Violet imagined her friend's brain was. "I'm glad you're here though. I have a new volunteer for you."

"It's about time." Violet tapped out her remaining notes. *Species: Black-necked stilt. Count: 5. Notes: One feigning injury to protect nest.* "We're down a few volunteers, and we always need extra during breeding. That last volunteer couldn't walk thirty feet without complaining."

"This one should be better. Let me see if I can find where I wrote his name down."

Violet typed, her fingers slowly pecking across the keys, while Naomi fished around for the piece of paper in question. "I know I have it here somewhere."

"Mm-hmm." Violet had become Naomi's go-to surveyor to train new volunteers in the finer points of birding surveys. Maybe it was her lingering penchant for teaching, or maybe it was the fact that Violet grasped the basic tenets of bird-watching better than most. To be a bird-watcher—a good one at least—required stamina, knowledge, the right equipment, and a dedication that many lacked.

"Ah well. I'll have to go on memory." Naomi came from around her desk and leaned against the wall next to the desktop computer where Violet worked. "Let's see." She tapped her chin like it was an antenna she had to tune to retrieve the information in her mind. "He's older like you." *Older?* Wasn't she just twenty-five yesterday? "He's from this general area—oh! I remember!"

"His name?"

"No, not that." She waved her hand, as if the name of a new volunteer was a frivolous piece of information. "But he's a retired police officer. That was the part I found interesting. He said not many people expect an ex-cop to enjoy bird-watching."

Violet's fingers stilled over the keyboard, and her mind flashed to a warm night, a cool drink, and a shy smile. Naomi was still talking, but all Violet heard was a buzz in her ears.

A moment later, Naomi leaned down to meet Violet's gaze. "Violet? Did you hear me?"

Violet blinked once, twice, then focused her gaze on the screen in front of her. She clicked the green Submit button, then stood and dropped her clipboard into her backpack. "Surveys are once a week. Let me know when he's ready to join in."

Naomi rubbed her hands together. "He's ready now. He wanted to start on his own, but I told him he had to complete training before he can take a route by himself."

Violet slung her backpack over one shoulder and moved toward the door. "Tomorrow then."

"Excellent. Where should I tell him to meet you?"

Violet opened the door and paused. "On the beach in front of the resort. Seven fifteen sharp. I'll have on a green hat."

The next morning, having shaken off the previous day's agitation, Violet headed to the beach for her survey and tried not to fidget as she waited. She always arrived early when she was training a new volunteer. It was important to earn their respect from the start, and being late would make them think tardiness, sloppiness, or, worse, apathy was acceptable, as if the bird surveys were merely a hobby or a way to pass the time during retirement. She expected a lot from her volunteers, and being on time was just the beginning.

Except this volunteer hadn't arrived early and wasn't on time either. She could tell by the height at which the morning sun sat above the horizon it was past her usual 7:15 start time, but she checked her watch anyway: 7:22. She sat on one of the empty lounge chairs lined up a few yards from where the Gulf licked the shore and curled her toes in the still-cool sand.

She'd give the volunteer three more minutes—that'd make him a full ten minutes late—before setting off on her route. Propping her hands behind her, she leaned back and tilted her face up to the light until her thoughts scampered away. She fought a wave of nausea as she remembered fish bones glinting in harsh late-afternoon light and a rip in the side of a bright red dress. Then she heard her name called behind her.

"Violet? Is that you?"

Her heart clanged inside her. She whisked the cobwebs away, the wisps of memories that clung to her despite years of sweeping out the corners, then stood and turned. It was him. Just as she'd known it would be.

My stars. He's gotten so old.

Then again, so had she. The last time she'd seen Frank Roby, her face had been as unlined as a sheet of drawing paper, her hair still a shiny chestnut, and her body as slender as a sea oat.

He cleared his throat, a nervous tic she remembered well. "I'm sorry I'm late." His eyes were the same warm gray, like soft flannel or the belly feathers of a chipping sparrow. His voice—the same one she'd heard on the answering machine at the Audubon office, she now realized—was older, of course, with a little more gravel, but it still had the same tenor, still caused the same vibration in her chest. His face was looser and deeply lined, but pleasantly so, and his hair was steel gray instead of its former dark brown.

Embarrassment flushed the thin skin of her chest as she realized she was staring and he was still waiting for her to speak. He shifted his feet and it was only then that she noticed the cane in his left hand.

"It won't be a problem." He lifted the cane and gestured to the round disk attached to the bottom tip. "This keeps me steady when I'm walking on sand."

She reached up and adjusted the brim of her hat, then pulled out the extra clipboard from her backpack. "We can start with this." Ignoring the wobble in her voice, she handed him the clipboard and a pen and gestured to the top of the page. "You'll want to fill this out first, before you get started on the surveys."

He kept his gaze on her a beat, then propped his cane up against the chair and took the board and pen from her. She waited while he filled in his name, date, and location. "For wind, precipitation, and cloud cover, you don't have to be too specific. Light winds, no precipitation, clear skies."

He made the notes, then looked up at her, a question in his eyes. Most people would stop to catch up on the intervening years before getting to work, but she'd long ago built a wall between her and her memories of him. She tried to keep it strong, but it occasionally cracked and the memories seeped through. More so lately than ever before.

She took the clipboard from him and clicked the pen closed. "A basic knowledge of coastal birds is helpful for this sort of thing." She had to ask, though she already knew the answer. "Are you familiar with birds along the shore?"

He stilled and stared at her, and in that moment, she saw him as he once was—the crisp blue uniform, close-cropped hair, and smooth, sharp jaw.

"I am."

She held his gaze as long as she could, then pointed to the west. "We'll walk this way first and I'll explain the process."

He fell into step beside her, the cane indeed not proving to be a problem, though their gait was slow anyway. That was one of the most important parts of the survey and bird-watching in general: move slowly, pause frequently, keep your eyes open. She'd found it was a good way to go about life, period.

"We take surveys four times a year, in each season, and each volunteer has his or her own one-mile route. Of course, we walk out and back, so it's two miles total." She glanced down. His limp was barely perceptible, but it was there. "Is that a problem?"

"No, ma'am."

"Good. So you'll walk your route once a week for each survey season. As a new trainee you'll stick with your trainer the whole season before you take a route on your own. It's sort of like a trial run."

"So I'll be accompanying you on this route all summer?"

Violet gave one quick nod. "Those are the rules. Each day you walk the route, you record your findings on the paper. Are your binoculars good?"

He patted the strap around his neck. "They're good."

She nodded. "Count every bird you see, even if you can't identify it. We focus on sandpipers, pelicans, gulls, and terns, but everything's noteworthy. Flying, floating, walking, it doesn't matter. If you see a bird, count it and identify it as well as you can. If you can estimate the age, even better."

As they moved she noted with satisfaction that he made a hatch mark on the bottom of the paper for every bird he saw. He gazed up as a flock of laughing gulls cruised above them, his mouth moving ever so slightly as he counted. Eight more hatch marks.

A few minutes later, four birds—plovers by the look of them—darted along the shore fifty yards or so ahead. Violet lifted her binoculars to her eyes, and next to her he did the same.

"Wilson's plovers," he said after a moment.

"Not piping plovers?"

He kept the binoculars to his eyes. "Piping plovers are a little smaller. And these guys have longer beaks." He pulled the binoculars down and squinted into the distance, then pulled them back up again. "Fella in the front just got himself a snack. Probably a coquina."

She glanced up at him, surprised by his accuracy. He

chuckled, though he kept his gaze straight ahead. "I do know a little about birds, Vi. Did you forget?"

She sighed as she lowered her binoculars. The mix of salt and brine and sand and the very nearness of him swirled her thoughts right back to the night they'd first met. The gentle sway of shoulders moving to the music. Hazy smoke-filled air coating her skin. Their shared laughter over a red-billed tropic-bird. Oh, she hadn't forgotten. The details were still there, etched. Engraved.

He angled his shoulder toward her, his voice low as if to keep the birds from eavesdropping. "You didn't seem nearly as surprised to see me as I was when I found out you'd be the one training me on bird surveys."

"You knew it'd be me?"

"That's what the woman at the Audubon office told me. I asked if there was anyone else who could do the training with me, but according to her, you're the best teacher. She also told me you don't tolerate tardiness." He paused. "I got all the way to the parking lot, but I almost didn't get out of my car. That's why I was late meeting you."

Violet reached up and brushed away a strand of hair caught on her lip. "What made you get out of the car?"

He shifted and gazed up the beach a ways. "I don't know. Curiosity?"

Please don't ask me. Her silent plea rang in her ears. Too much curiosity, any attempt to peel back the years and all that was left unsaid, would only result in pain. Much better to stick to the basics—counting birds, logging data, then going their separate ways.

At the sound of approaching voices, they both turned. Two men walked along the water's edge, running shoes in hand. After a moment, they broke into a jog, sand spitting back behind them and scattering the plovers ahead.

"It's just a little farther to the end of the route. Then we can head back."

They fell into slow step, with Frank still counting and making notes on the page.

4 Wilson's plovers—juvenile

8 least terns—4 adult, 4 juvenile

6 brown pelicans—age indeterminate

"So you knew you were training me?" he asked once they'd turned around at the one-mile mark.

She gestured to the clipboard still in his hand. "You'll want to keep counting, noting any new birds you didn't see on your way out."

He nodded and held the board at chest level, his pencil poised over the paper.

"I didn't have your name," she finally said. "But Naomi told me the new volunteer was a former policeman who likes birds." She tugged the brim of her hat down to better shade her eyes. "It could have been anyone. I told myself it wouldn't be you."

"If you were surprised, you hid it well." He slowed to a stop as a flock of gulls darted up from the sand and caught the wind. He did a silent count and marked the page. "I'd say it's good to see you, Violet, but the truth is I don't know." He rubbed the side of his face, the sound rough and papery. "I don't know what I expected."

She stilled every muscle, willing herself to remain steady. It had been so long—so many years—since anyone or anything had made her nervous. She liked it that way. This . . . stirring . . . was unpleasant. But also not.

Finally she tipped her chin up. *Hold yourself together, Violet.* "Well, we're both here now, and it's always good to have new bird-watchers who actually know about birds. I had to train a volunteer in the spring who I think was actually scared of birds. And she claimed walking in sand aggravated her migraines."

"Why'd she sign up at all?"

"Come to find out, she thought it was a paid position. Once she realized it was purely volunteer, I never saw her again."

He lifted the binoculars to his eyes again. "Well, I'm not scared and I walk in sand just fine."

They walked in silence a few moments. Even though Naomi hadn't remembered his name, even though they hadn't seen each other in too many years to count, it was true that she hadn't been surprised. In fact, it was just the opposite. When she heard his voice behind her, when she felt the shimmer that pulsed through her, she knew exactly who it was. It was as if no time had passed, as if they'd parted only minutes ago, their fingertips still warm from each other's hands.

My, how it ached, being this close to him again. If anything, *that* was the surprise—that her sixty-six-year-old heart could beat in such a way that didn't require a trip to the doctor.

When they made it back to the beginning of the route, Frank tried to hand the clipboard back to her, but she didn't take it. "Keep that. You'll use it each time."

He tucked the board under his arm. "So we'll meet back here in a week?"

"That'd be fine." Her tone was clipped. Professional. This was only training, after all.

"I guess that's it then. Are you headed back up?" He gestured toward the walkway that led back to the resort and the parking lot across the street where guests parked.

"I'll be a few more minutes. You go ahead. I'll see you next week."

"Okay then." He planted his cane and pivoted, then headed back up toward the walkway. After a few steps he stopped and turned back to her. "I take it back, what I said earlier. It is good to see you, Violet." He held her gaze and after a moment, he smiled. It was still shy, still kind, even after everything.

She bit her lip, but before she could speak, he was on his way up the beach, his back to her. She watched him until he crossed the walkway over the dunes and disappeared between the two towers, then she sat down, right where she was in the damp sand, her legs as weak as a Kleenex full of Jell-O.

Frank drove home from the training session on autopilot, his mind swimming in the years. It was all he could do to get home and make it out onto his back porch before collapsing. His bad leg was always nervous and jumpy after extended use, and he'd long ago learned the trick to alleviating the pain. Sitting in his favorite chair, he stretched his leg out in front of him and massaged the top of his thigh. After a minute or so of constant kneading, the jittery tension began to peel away. He only wished he could do the same thing to his heart.

Five years ago, on her sixty-first birthday, Frank's wife, Alice, had woken up and told him she was moving to Texas.

"Am I moving too?" he asked, bleary and barely awake.

She shook her head. "I'm sorry, Frank. I love you, but I need something different."

He sat up on his elbows and stared at her, reading everything written in her face. "Okay."

Alice had indeed moved to Texas and started a new business as a professional home organizer. She also took up with a former rodeo cowboy. Two years later Frank got an invitation in the mail for their wedding, which took place in the center ring of a rodeo arena north of Abilene, where her new husband had won his tenth World Championship title.

He didn't attend the wedding, but it wasn't because he had hard feelings. He and Alice had had a perfectly fine marriage. They got along very well, made each other laugh, and respected each other's careers—just the police work for Frank, though Alice had started so many LLCs over the years, Frank long ago lost count. They had two great kids and energetic grandchildren, and he was grateful for all she'd taught him about how to relate to and please a woman. But theirs was not a passionate marriage. He did love her, but was he ever fully in love with her?

He didn't think so, and if pressed, he thought she'd probably say the same thing.

So while there was a sense of disappointment and sadness when Alice left him, his heart kept on beating, air continued to flow in and out of his lungs, and in general the world kept spinning.

It was only late at night, when his defenses were down and the memories pressed in close, that he wondered if the presence of Violet Figg in his mind—burned into his synapses long before he met Alice—was part of the reason he hadn't fallen apart when his marriage did.

Despite all that had happened since he'd last seen Violet—all the work he'd done to move on—his heart had betrayed him today. He might as well have been that twenty-seven-year-old tongue-tied kid who couldn't put one foot in front of the other to go talk to her, but he wasn't. He was much older now and he'd lived a full life without her, but one glimpse all these years later, and his heart went and filled right back up again.

With his leg calmer he pulled the small stool over and propped his foot on it. Keeping an eye on his shady backyard and the birds flittering around his feeders, he gave himself over to the memory.

1982

The night Frank met Violet, he'd been assigned to a duty none of the cops at the precinct wanted to take: security detail at the

Sandbar. As the lowest on the totem pole, having only recently been released into the world—or at least the world of Sugar Bend—as a full-fledged police officer, Frank was often chosen for the weekend gig. But the truth was he didn't mind it much. Many of the other guys didn't like it because they'd rather be at home with their families or girlfriends than keeping an eye on intoxicated troublemakers at the local dive bar. Others preferred to specialize in something flashier like narcotics or criminal intelligence, which would keep them from having to take crap assignments like this.

At twenty-seven Frank wasn't married and didn't have a girlfriend, and he hadn't yet decided which path he wanted to pursue within the police department. And to be honest, he liked to people-watch. Almost as much as he liked to bird-watch, though he didn't admit either of those things to anyone at work.

He didn't work the security gig every weekend—a couple other guys shared the burden—but he'd been there enough to become a familiar sight at the door to the Sandbar, and he recognized most of the regulars who came every Friday and Saturday night, and some of them likely more often than that.

So when he saw the petite woman with chestnut-brown hair dressed in white pants with a wide belt and a pale yellow sweater, he knew he was seeing her for the first time. Something in him began to hum, a low roar that made his ears itch and his legs restless. As she approached the door she pulled out her ID and handed it to the man on the stool.

Inside, music swelled from the band onstage. The woman

seemed to steel herself before lifting her chin and walking inside. The man on the stool glanced at Frank and shrugged.

Another group of young people approached the door, but Frank's mind stayed with the woman. He imagined her walking inside, finding the person she was meeting, and settling in for the evening, a man's arm snug around her shoulders.

After waiting as long as he could, he told the man checking IDs he was going inside for a quick drink of water. He made his way through the crowd just inside the door and toward the bar in the back. As his eyes adjusted to the dim light and the haze of cigarette smoke in the air, he saw her sitting at the long polished bar. Everything in him wanted to obey the force pushing him toward her, but he remained there in the middle of the room, rooted and transfixed.

The truth was, Frank had never been good at talking to women. When he was younger, he'd get so flustered he'd have to walk away from them just to be able to breathe. But as he got older, and especially once he started wearing his police uniform, he learned he was good at faking confidence. At pretending to be easygoing and self-assured. At putting his shyness in his pocket and playing the role people expected from him. It usually worked out okay, but those interactions, especially when they involved a pretty girl, left him exhausted.

As the crowd swarmed around him, he saw her only in snatches—her rich brown hair, the curve of her spine, her foot hooked behind the bottom rung of her stool. The longer he watched her, the more familiar she seemed, as if he knew her somehow, but of course, he didn't.

He stood there watching. *Go say hello, idiot.*

Another man sidled up next to her. There was an open stool right there, but instead of sitting, the man squeezed in the small space between her and the person sitting on the other side of her.

That must be him, Frank thought. *The owner of the arm that belongs around her shoulders.* But the way the man leaned down and spoke—not to her but at her—made Frank wonder if the woman knew this guy at all. He kept at it, leaning down and grinning, gesturing wildly and talking too loudly, even for this loud place.

The woman had pulled back as far as she could without falling off her stool, clearly not sharing the man's enthusiasm for close-talking.

Then the man slid his hand onto her back—right on the strip of bare skin between the top of her pants and the bottom hem of her sweater. With three quick steps Frank was at the bar. "Ice water, please," he said to the bartender, then to the woman, "Is anyone sitting here?"

She gave Frank a questioning glance, then turned her attention back to the lime on the lip of her drink. "No."

"Hey, pal." The man leaned around her to peer at Frank. "I was just about to sit there." He opened his eyes wider, Frank's police uniform registering on the man's face. He held his hands up in a silly surrender. "If you don't mind, that is."

Frank held a hand out to him. "What's your name?"

"I'm Lawrence. And this is Mary." He placed his hand low

on her back again, a possessive gesture meant to show Frank his place.

"Hello," Frank said to Mary. Then, "Don't worry, Lawrence, I won't be here long." Frank hoped they didn't notice his shaking hands as he accepted the plastic cup of water from the bartender. He took a long sip as, behind them, the band started into a new song. "Just needed to rest a bit before heading back out."

"You can stay there as long as you need to." Mary's words were quiet enough that when the man next to her spoke again, his loud words crawled all over hers.

"Mary and I were just talking about birds. She's got these groovy earrings, and I thought, 'Hey, we have something in common!'" Lawrence gestured to the tiny gold birds on Mary's ears. His words were just this side of slurred, as if another big gulp of his warm beer would push him over the edge. "I love birds, man. Like that one." He pointed to a framed photo of a black-and-white bird behind the bar. "Love those seagulls. They're so happy all the time."

"That's not a seagull," Mary said.

Lawrence looked down at her, then back at the photo. "Sure it is."

"Nope." She squeezed a little more lime in her drink and took a sip. "It's called a red-billed tropicbird. See those long tail feathers? And the red beak?"

Lawrence was silent a moment, then he jabbed her in the shoulder. "You're pulling my leg. I see these birds all the time."

"Actually you don't," Frank spoke up. "The closest they

come to us is down in the Caribbean." Frank glanced at Mary. "Sorry. I didn't mean to jump in."

A smile played at the corners of her mouth. "It's perfectly fine."

They remained like that a few seconds longer, their eyes locked onto each other, until Lawrence pushed away from the bar and walked off. His movement jostled them back to reality.

"I think I ran your date off." Frank fiddled with the edge of his cup.

"He wasn't my date."

"Trust me, he wanted to be."

"Nah. He just wants a girl and I fit the minimum requirement."

Behind her, Frank saw Lawrence sling his heavy arm around another young woman standing right in front of the stage. He whispered something to her, and she giggled and pulled him closer.

"I think you may be right. Glad I saved you from him."

"I was doing just fine on my own, thanks. Though if you were planning to come help, it would have been nice if you'd shown up before he put his sweaty hand on my back."

He let out a quiet chuckle. "Sorry about that. I was trying to work up the nerve to come sit next to you." Heat flamed under his skin as she settled her warm brown gaze on him.

"Work up the nerve?" Her eyebrows lifted. "Last time I checked, schoolteachers weren't all that scary."

"Ah, you're a teacher. So that's why you know so much about birds."

She tilted her head. "Not really. My interest in birds came long before I started teaching." She tucked a strand of hair behind her ear.

His eyes followed her fingertips as they skimmed across her cheek and down her neck. Her skin was pale, with pink cheeks; straight, dark eyebrows; a small chin; and a strong nose. Taken separately, the features didn't belong on the same face, but together, they gave her a captivating beauty.

He cleared his throat, which was all of a sudden raw and parched despite the water he was drinking. "Do you teach around here?" It was foolish to hope she'd say she taught somewhere close by, so there'd be even a remote chance he could see her again, but he couldn't help it. Hope was a balloon rising stubbornly in his chest.

"I do. I teach sixth grade at Sugar Bend Academy."

"Sugar Bend Academy," he murmured. "That's great."

"Yeah. It is."

The bartender leaned over the sticky bar and shouted over the music, "Can I get you two anything else?" Frank shook his head no and Mary did the same. When he walked away, Mary dipped her head. "My name's not actually Mary."

"It's not?"

"I don't give guys like Lawrence my real name."

"Probably a smart move. Are you going to tell me your real name?"

"Can I trust you?"

"You can."

"Good. Then it's Violet."

"Violet." He held his hand out to her. "I'm Frank." Her hand in his was sturdy, warm, and pleasantly rough. "It's good to meet you," was what he said, but what he meant was, "Where have you been all this time?"

While they'd been talking, they'd moved closer together to better hear each other over the music, and it was only now that Frank realized mere inches separated their faces. The balloon in his chest stretched so big, he was afraid she'd see it.

She pulled her hand away. "So you know about birds too?"

"I know a little."

"Right. Only a little. Yet you knew about a tropical bird that doesn't even live in our country."

He shrugged. "It's in one of my books. It caught my eye because the tail feathers remind me of a stingray. And that red bill is striking."

She didn't respond but just looked at him, pensive.

"What?"

"Nothing. I just don't meet too many guys my age who have an interest in birds. They're usually decades older than me."

"My grandfather was the one who got me interested in birds."

"Ah. See? My point."

"I know. Trust me, I get it. I don't usually tell the other guys at the precinct I'm an amateur bird-watcher."

"Do you do any bird-watching around here?"

He nodded. "Sometimes."

She opened her mouth to say more, but a woman came up behind her and gently squeezed Violet's shoulder. "Come on, you, the band's taking a break. I want to introduce you to Kevin." The woman eyed Frank. "Hello."

"This is my friend Emmajean," Violet said. "Emmajean, this is Frank."

"Hi, Frank." Emmajean cocked an eyebrow at Violet.

Violet laughed. "I'm supposed to be meeting a friend of Emmajean's tonight." She met Frank's gaze and rolled her eyes just slightly. "She tells me he's cute and single."

"And he's in the band." Emmajean bumped her arm to Violet's. "Don't forget that part." She looked at Frank. "She never dates. I'm trying to get her out of her shell."

"She's already out of her shell," he wanted to say. "I already see her." But instead he stood from his stool and dropped his balled-up cocktail napkin onto the bar. "I need to get back to my post anyway. It was really good to meet you," he said to Violet.

"You too." Violet bit the edge of her lip, and it was all Frank could do to take a step back as he saw a man approaching Violet and Emmajean. Frank recognized him as the bass player from the band. Emmajean made the introductions, and while Violet was polite, she kept shifting her gaze back toward Frank, a tiny gesture that filled his chest yet again.

Finally he waved, then started for the door. But just before he got there, he felt a warm hand on his arm. A gentle tug. There she was.

seven

Tyler was stretched out on a flat rock at the edge of the river. With closed eyes he let the voices and laughter ringing all around him recede into a sort of faraway hum. With the heat from the rock seeping into his back and the breeze that felt almost cool, he was nearly asleep when a gauzy piece of cloth landed on his face.

He yanked it off and saw Cassie standing over him, one hand on her hip, a flirty grin on her face. She was wearing her new bikini, about three square inches of bright pink fabric and strings.

"Want to swing with me?" she asked.

He shook his head. "Too tired." He'd opened the store early that morning, which wouldn't have been a problem if he'd gotten any sleep last night, which he hadn't. His dad had let him off early that afternoon, and Cassie and a few others convinced him to come out to Soldiers Creek for some fun, but now he wished he hadn't come at all. His mind was singularly focused on the girl from the diner—who he'd then seen at Two Sisters Art—and she was all he could think about.

"Well, I'm going to swing. You can watch." Cassie sauntered off toward the rope swing. The next guy in line grabbed the end and pulled it back for her. She jumped up and hooked her feet around the knot at the bottom of the rope, then he let go. With a shriek she soared over the shallow river's edge and dropped into the depths farther out toward the middle. She came up sputtering and laughing.

He'd been having the craziest dreams since he saw her—the girl from the diner. He dreamed of soft bronze skin and a freckle behind an ear. A baby's cry and a bright white sailboat sailing on calm blue water. Red-painted toenails and cups of sharpened pencils. He never saw the girl in any of his dreams, but he couldn't shake the feeling that they had to do with her. With them both.

An ache spread through his belly, a yearning so acute, he didn't know what to do with it. With a groan he ran his hands down his face, then sat up. He remained there a moment, his unfocused gaze directed toward the river, then he jumped down off the rock, pulled off his T-shirt, and grabbed the end of the rope swing, pulling it taut. "Hey, Cass," he called, tipping his head. "Come on."

She squealed and hopped out of the water, droplets clinging and dripping, catching the afternoon light as they fell. A quick moment later, she was wrapped around him, skin to wet skin. He hooked his feet around the bottom knot, she pressed hers on top of his, and together they flew.

Violet waved to their last customer of the day and flipped the sign in the window to show they were closed. Maya had come in so the three of them could discuss the possibility of her working there in the shop. Violet had been surprised when Trudy told her Maya was interested in a job. It was true they needed to hire another employee, and Trudy had grown to like Maya—especially her skills with the sculpture materials—but Violet had expected the person they hired to be someone local, someone they were familiar with, someone they knew they could trust. Maya fit none of these descriptions, but Trudy was pushing hard for her, and as their life had shown, Violet would do nearly anything for her sister.

Trudy and Maya were already seated at a table at the front of the shop, Trudy scribbling notes and Maya responding.

"Can I bring either of you some tea?" Violet walked to the back of the shop and flipped on the teakettle. As she waited for it to bubble, she unwrapped a peppermint tea bag and dropped it in a white mug.

The only answer she heard was the scratch of Trudy's pencil, then soft laughter from Maya. Trudy glanced at the note in Maya's hands, then tipped her head toward Violet.

"She wrote that there aren't many people who drink hot tea when it's hot as blue blazes outside," Maya said.

"My sister can make fun of me all she wants. I've been enjoying a mug of peppermint tea every afternoon for more years than I can count." She poured boiling water over her tea bag, savoring the minty scent that rose from the mug, then pulled another chair to the small round table where Maya and Trudy sat.

Violet blew across the top of her tea to cool it. "So, Maya, Trudy tells me you're interested in working here at the shop."

Maya glanced at Trudy. "I could use the extra work. The diner doesn't pay all that much and Mr. Meyer just raised my rent."

"On that tiny room above the bait shop?" Violet asked. "He can't be asking for much—it's the size of a pea." Trudy lifted an eyebrow in admonition. "I'm sorry," Violet said. "That was rude of me."

"It's okay. It is small, but it's not too bad, actually. And his rent is much lower than anywhere else around here. I've checked. I'm making it for now, but I'll need to take on some more work if I want to keep paying it."

"You live there alone?"

Maya picked at the end of her thumbnail. She nodded.

"What about your parents? Where are they?" Violet was pushing, but she couldn't help herself.

"I don't have parents." Maya tucked a lock of dark hair behind her ear. "I mean, I did, but they're gone. I never knew my dad, and my mom left when I was really young."

Violet's eyes widened. "Honey, how old are you?"

"Eighteen."

Trudy handed Maya a note. "What brought me to Sugar Bend? I don't know. I just drove. My last home was in Montgomery, and I got in the car and drove south until I saw a sign."

A sign for Sugar Bend?

Maya glanced at Trudy's note. "As it turns out, yes. I stopped for gas and saw a flyer about the art festival in Sugar Bend on the gas station door." She rubbed her thumb back and forth across the note. "My grandmother used to talk about signs, and how one was always around when you needed it. I doubt she meant anything that literal, but I decided to follow it." She shrugged. "And here I am. I could use the work. And I like this place." She glanced around the shop, glowing pink in the early evening sun.

Trudy handed Violet a note. *You and I have talked about classes. Maya can help me teach. It'll bring in more money and it'll give her something purposeful to do. And she and I have already started working on a piece together.*

Violet took the pencil from Trudy and wrote her own note back. Trudy took it with raised eyebrows. *She stole from us. You think hiring her is wise?*

Trudy's mouth went thin as she scratched out her answer. *She deserves a chance. I think this could be good for her.*

Violet met Trudy's gaze. Despite her silence and her penchant for dragging sandy wood and bits of broken shells through their house, Violet could trust her sister. Could trust her decisions. She hadn't always been able to, but now that trust was strong, born out of choices and regret and time.

She also had a hunch that hiring Maya might be good for more than just Maya.

"Okay. How about we start with a couple days a week? Then if we're all happy with how things are going, you can add on more shifts. How does that sound?"

Maya nibbled on the edge of her lip, as if considering the offer. Then she nodded. "I can start tomorrow if you want."

Violet rubbed her hands across the tops of her shorts. "We'll see you at ten."

They all three stood and in an uncharacteristic move, Trudy reached forward and enveloped Maya into a hug. Trudy was not a hugger. The closest she ever came to physical affection was an occasional stiff pat on the shoulder or knee, but she wrapped her arms around Maya like she was trying to pass on something crucial, something necessary, to the young woman.

At first Maya's arms remained at her sides, but it only took a second or two before she melted. Her chin dropped onto Trudy's strong shoulder and her eyes closed. Violet swallowed hard over the lump in her throat. Finally Trudy pulled back and, with her hands still on Maya's shoulders, gave her a nod of affirmation, or maybe approval. Whatever it was, tears sprang into Maya's eyes.

A moment later, Violet and Trudy stood shoulder to shoulder in the doorway and watched Maya walk down the sidewalk away from the shop. She held her head high, proud, despite her solitude.

"I think this'll be good." Violet said it as much to herself as to Trudy.

Trudy opened her mouth and a noise escaped—not a word, exactly, or even part of one, but a sound nonetheless. Her eyes widened and she clamped her mouth shut.

"Trudy?" Violet stared at her sister, her own eyes moistening as tears pooled at the corners of Trudy's eyes. "What is it? Can you try again?"

It had been happening lately, these small sounds and beginnings. Trudy hadn't said a full word, nothing complete or even approaching it, but for her to be making a sound at all was groundbreaking.

Over the years Violet had tried to convince Trudy to see someone—a doctor, a counselor, someone who could help draw the words out or at least remove the stopper keeping them in. But Trudy always shook her head no, and Violet stopped trying to convince her a long time ago. But lately, with every sound of laughter or dissent, Violet wondered what was coming.

Trudy's lips moved but no more sound emerged. Finally her shoulders dropped and her face slackened. Whatever it was had retreated once again.

Violet slipped her arm into the crook of Trudy's elbow. "Come on, then. Let's go home."

The man on the phone had tried to give Frank directions to the house where the boat had washed up, but Frank told him it was unnecessary. He hadn't been there in decades, but after studying the boat photos and remembering the night the neighbor called about a scream, he realized he knew exactly where to go.

When he pulled up in front of the house at 61 River Ash Road, he stood from the car, closed the door, and gazed up. The trees overhead—live oaks, river birches, black gums, and longleaf pines, just to name a few—were giants, their leaves creating a canopy that stretched as far as he could see. Long, ghostly curls of Spanish moss hung low from every limb and branch, trembling in the nonexistent breeze, and under the canopy, the thick shade was alive with birdsong.

Down the road a ways, a row of old trees—pecan, by the looks of them—was all that was left of the woods that used to be next to Jay's house. *Those foxes.* Frank shrugged off a chill that crept down his arms, then he started up the front walk of the house. Paint peeled off the wood siding in thick chunks and some of the windows were broken. As he stared, a scrawny cat jumped through an opening and darted through the scrubby grass and across the street, yowling in irritation as it passed Frank.

The house had once been charming. The porch on the side was still wide and gracious, though it now sported a ripped screen and spiderwebs he could see from the middle of the yard. The windows boasted wide trim, though it was dirty gray now instead of white, and a lattice arbor over the front door was crisscrossed with ancient vines, now long dead. And there on the roof was the dormer window where Frank had seen Jay's wife standing in the lamplight.

He never knew if the neighbor heard an actual scream or not, but Frank had thought about the woman, Jay's wife, for a long time. He couldn't believe he'd never even gotten her name. Rookie mistake. Jay had given a believable, entirely plausible story, but had Frank missed something? Was there more to the story? He wondered it a lot more after the man went missing, along with that boat he was so fond of.

Wonder where she is now? Frank thought. There was no telling.

He knocked on the door, though he sensed the house was long deserted, then knocked one more time for good measure. At a sound off to his left, he turned to see a young woman walking around the side of the house.

"There's no one in there." The woman pushed a lock of red hair out of her face. She carried a small notebook in her hand, a pen tucked behind her ear, and she was dressed smartly in a green blouse, slim black pants, and black heels. Altogether too dressy and businesslike for this far end of town.

"If you're looking for Carl, he's out back on his phone," she continued as she stepped her way through the tall grass out toward her car parked on the street. He hadn't noticed it when he'd arrived.

"Thank you."

"No problem," she called back.

Frank followed the dirt path around the side of the house. The grassy lawn where Jay had once painted his precious boat was now mostly dirt and weeds, all covered by drooping tree limbs and shaded by giant azalea bushes. The river swirled just on the other side of a line of reeds and oats. On the far side of the yard, a man—Carl, he assumed—stood in the shade holding a cell phone to his ear. He was deep in conversation, one arm gesturing wildly, his back to Frank.

Frank surveyed Little River before him. Hard to believe this was the same river that meandered through downtown Sugar Bend. Down there, it was often dotted with cheerful sailboats, ski boats pulling kids in tubes, and kayaks gliding through the early morning and late evening hours. But up here the river was eerily quiet. With the vivid blue sky and bright sunshine hidden behind the crown of trees, a fog seemed to hover over the water. Either there were no neighboring houses, no nearby docks, or they were lost in the green-gray gloom.

He walked down toward the river. According to the Facebook post, the boat had washed up under the dock, but Frank saw nothing there except dark water. He was almost at the river's edge when the boat materialized out of the shadows on the sandy bank. The chill shivered down his arms again, and his hand tightened on the head of his cane.

At the sound of footsteps through the weedy grass behind him, his hand automatically went to his waist where for thirty-five years he'd carried his gun, but of course now all he felt was his leather belt and his cell phone in his pocket.

"You the cop?" the man called as he crossed the yard.

Frank cleared his throat and gave his head a noncommittal nod, hoping the man wouldn't ask about his lack of uniform or badge. "I'm Frank Roby. I called about the boat."

"Right. I'm Carl Waters." The man walked down to the boat and nudged it with the toe of his boot. "It's seen better days, that's for sure."

"And it just showed up? No one's come to claim it?"

"No, not that I know of." The man scratched his head. "I don't really know the neighbors. I just bought the house a few weeks ago, but I haven't started work on it yet. Obviously."

"You're fixing the place up?" Frank eyed the house, which appeared even more menacing from this side.

"That's the plan. We're fixing up several old houses on

this street, but it's just one thing after another with this one. Problems we didn't foresee—foundation, roof, walls. Here I was trying to preserve it, but it's like the house would rather be torn down than rehabbed." He nudged the boat again. "Boat doesn't even matter all that much. It's probably just a distraction from all the pitfalls with the house. Something about it catch your eye?"

The blue stripe on the side all but glittered in the hazy sunlight. "I don't know. Maybe. I wanted to see it in person to be sure."

"Whatever you need. I'll give it a little while, see if anything comes of it, then I'll probably have one of my guys haul it off for me. I'll let you know before I do that."

"I'd appreciate it." Frank scanned the rest of the shore and yard for anything that stuck out to him. The dock was falling in on itself, with boards poking out at all angles, and stretched across a portion of the yard were the crumbled remains of some sort of wall. Crusty, sun-bleached bricks were tumbled together in small heaps, and curiously, a single brick sat in the bottom of the boat, next to the large, rusted-out hole. Instead of cracked with dry age, the brick was slimy with algae and barnacles.

The man's cell rang and he answered, waving at Frank with his other hand. Frank nodded back and continued his study of the boat. The barnacle-speckled outboard motor, the mossy-green hull, the still-vibrant blue stripe—it clearly was Jay's boat. Frank didn't need serial numbers to know that. The vision of Jay running his hand along the side of the boat, the smudge of blue paint on his forehead that matched the stripe, and the sharp memory of the woman in the upstairs window were enough for him.

What had happened to them all? To Jay, his wife, and this boat? Frank gazed out at the river. It moved slowly, almost nonchalantly, but Frank knew the river wasn't always so innocent. Water could hold secrets, mysteries, and lies as well as any person. Maybe better.

With a wave to Carl, Frank walked slowly back to his car, his cane making a soft *plunk* in the sandy soil with each step.

Late evening was always Liza Bullock's favorite part of the day, when everything glowed lilac and rose and the rising moon threw wavy lines of light onto the river. It almost made living here in this tiny backwater town worth it. Liza had been the editor of *The Sugar Bend Observer* for close to a year, and the most exciting thing she'd covered was the farmer who pitched a tent in the middle of the highway last month to protest speeding logging trucks that scared his cows. And that was only marginally more exciting than the conflict between two spray paint–wielding neighbors who'd defaced each other's backyard fences. What would be next? A standoff between the two shoe stores on Water Street? A food fight at the Christmas Jubilee?

She hadn't gotten a journalism degree to spend her days writing about peeved farmers and crotchety neighbors. She needed something, just one little story, that would catapult her out of this sleepy inlet. If she could find a story with enough meat on its bones, she could write a sizzling exposé and land herself at a copy desk in Birmingham or Atlanta. Maybe even New York or Los Angeles. Why not aim high?

Liza stretched her legs out straight in front of her on the lounge chair at the end of her dock and closed her eyes. She was exhausted and the half glass of white wine she'd poured herself was only increasing her fatigue. Her day had started with a city council breakfast meeting at eight, followed by a ribbon-cutting ceremony at Palmer's Tires, a dedication ceremony for the new hospital wing, a staff meeting back at the office, then a trip to check on the housing development Fox Cove. It was a ramshackle stretch of town, but the developer, Carl Waters, promised that once the neighborhood was renovated, house prices would rise, which would attract wealthier home buyers and funnel more money right back into Sugar Bend. At least that was how he'd explained it to the zoning board, which was why they gave him the variances he needed for the work.

Once she'd asked her questions and taken the necessary notes to write her feature on the development, she strolled down to the water's edge and spied the old boat on the sand. Carl told her it had washed up onshore and that he was waiting on someone to claim it. Without thinking much about it, she snapped a photo of it with her phone, then went on about her day.

Sitting on her dock in the waning daylight, the photo called to her, so she pulled her phone out and scrolled to it. The boat wasn't much of anything—just a rusty hunk of green-blue metal with barnacles and algae clinging to its side—but it nearly pulsed with life there on the screen.

She pressed the button to darken her screen and rested her head against the back of the lounge chair, relishing the lift of the hair around her face as a breeze passed. She closed her eyes and drifted.

Later, the whine of a boat motor coming up the river made its way into her brain. Suspended in that loose space between wakefulness and slumber, she wasn't sure if she really heard it or if it was part of a dream.

As the noise grew louder, images began shuffling through her mind, behind her closed eyes: closed fists and raised voices, tear-streaked cheeks and broken glass. She tried to open her eyes but they were weighted, impossible to budge.

Just as the boat reached the dock where she sat, she reached her hands up to her face and her eyes opened. She sat up so quickly the back of the chair slapped against her, but when she scanned the river, it was empty. No people, no boat, not even a ripple on the surface. Then, like a trickle of ice water down her back, she realized where she'd seen the boat.

eight

When Violet awoke the next morning, rain was plinking off the windowpanes and the metal roof of the back porch. Her stomach was pinched with both nerves and anticipation at the thought of seeing Frank again.

She dressed quietly for the morning survey—after all, a little rain didn't stop the birds from going about their business—and walked barefoot into the den. She'd expected the rain to keep Trudy asleep for a while, but there she was, already hard at work at the long dining table, her woodworking tools spread out on newspaper, and her tackle box open to reveal the myriad compartments of pastel-colored treasures.

"Getting an early start today?" Violet peered over Trudy's shoulder to see what she was working on. It was the driftwood lamp she'd started on earlier in the summer. Violet noticed Trudy had added a thin line of iridescent jingle shells down one side of the wood, like a row of tiny buttons on the back of a dress.

Violet touched a shell with the tip of her finger. "This is lovely, Tru. Really."

A smile ghosted across Trudy's face, then her brow furrowed and she reached out and touched the white scar on Violet's outstretched wrist.

Violet pulled her hand back. "Just an old scar," she murmured, rubbing it with her thumb as if wiping away a smear of dirt or stray ink. "It's nothing." The lie gave her mouth a metallic tang, and despite the rubbing, the white line persisted, a slash of memory embedded in her skin. She'd never told Trudy where the wound had come from, opting instead to keep a Band-Aid on the cut until it healed. She'd chosen to keep the worst details of that night from Trudy—she'd seen no need to burden her sister any more than she already was. Violet didn't remember Trudy ever asking about the scar.

But the way Trudy's gaze remained focused on Violet's wrist, her eyes brimming with unease, made Violet wonder if Trudy somehow knew how it had gotten there.

Trudy's mouth tightened and she reached for her pen and notepad. *You've been such a good sister to me.*

Violet stared at the uncharacteristically tender note, then squeezed Trudy's hand. "You've been good to me, too, Trudy. We're a good team."

Trudy shook her head firmly and started to write again, and with a calmness she certainly didn't feel, Violet placed her hand gently on Trudy's. "It's okay. I'm your sister and I love you. That's all that matters." She took the pad from Trudy and tore off the page. "Now, how about some toast?"

She knew Trudy was staring at her as she walked to the kitchen, but she couldn't help it. Once upon a time she'd craved a chance to talk about that night, about all that had happened, all they'd both done, but she'd long ago accepted that for Trudy to move on—for both of them to—they had to leave it all in the past. And now, just the smallest reminder of it had caused Violet's heart to race and dampness to prickle under her arms.

An image of fish bones—winking in the sunlight, lying brazenly on the back step—rippled through her mind, but she mentally brushed them away, out of sight.

When she reached the kitchen, she crumpled the note into a ball and dropped it in the trash can.

The rain trickled to a stop in time for their survey, and when Violet emerged from the shadow between the two condo towers, she saw Frank already waiting for her down on the sand. Dark clouds still clustered here and there, but a bright line of sunlight shimmered several miles offshore, promising a sun-flooded day to come.

"Hello," she called as she approached. She didn't want to catch him off guard. But instead of startling, he turned slowly, a shy half smile already on his face.

"Good morning." He planted his cane in the sand and took a few steps toward her. "Glad the rain tapered off."

She nodded. "I thought we might have to push until tomorrow, but the day seems to be cooperating."

He readied his clipboard and tipped his head down the beach. "Shall we?"

They fell into step beside each other, moving slowly, pausing often, each making their own notes on paper. Occasionally one would question or comment—"Northern tern, you think?" or "Tricolor heron, haven't seen one of those in a while"—but for the most part, they walked in comfortable silence, and she was glad. She needed the time and space to collect herself. To allow the rhythm of the waves and the ordinary calls and chirps of the shore birds to settle the disquiet inside her.

She breathed in deep, willing the salty-fresh air into every yawning cavity inside her, every space that longed to be filled, and she remembered how it used to be. After that first night at the bar with Frank, the two of them had begun bird-watching together. And it was in those quiet hours that Violet had dared to imagine a future with him. The image of it shimmered at the edges of her mind, like a mirage she feared would dry up the closer she got to it.

They cared about the birds, of course—they both loved the thrill of seeing a new breed or a nest of perfect black skimmer eggs or the first warbler of the season—but the birding was also a cover. A reason for them to spend so much time together other than just not wanting to be apart.

Walking along the beach with him all these years later, Violet knew there was no reason she should feel this zing of familiarity, these strains of muscle memory, as if it had only been a short time since they'd walked down the beach together, fingers tracing circles on each other's skin and streaks in the cerulean sky as they learned each other and followed birds on their flight paths. It had been forty years. They were strangers. And yet the past felt as sure and solid as the sand under her feet and the wind against her face.

1982

Violet ran up behind Frank, her long brown hair wind-whipped and her skin goose-bumped, and tapped him on the shoulder. When he turned one way, she darted the other, her footsteps muffled by the cold sand. The sun was brilliant on this mid-February Saturday. It was chilly so close to the water, but the brisk breeze revived her lagging spirit, and now that she was here with Frank, her heart was light.

He took three running steps with his long, muscular legs and caught her, his hand warm on her wrist. "Hey, you." He pulled her toward him and kissed her. She rested her cheek against his and slid her hand into his.

"Sorry I'm late," she said as he wrapped an arm around her back. "I had to run by my sister's house." Violet had woken up that morning with an ominous sense that a crossroads was coming. She'd driven too fast on the curving road to Jay and Trudy's house, only to be turned away at the door by Jay.

"Your sister," Frank said as they fell into step together and headed down the beach, eyes alert to wispy feathers, thin legs, sturdy beaks. "Trudy, right?"

Violet nodded and nibbled her thumbnail as the cold Gulf water flowed over her feet. She inhaled sharply at the shock, and Frank guided her up a bit onto softer sand, away from the edge of the waves.

"Last time you mentioned her, you said she was going through a hard time."

It was true, Violet had said that, but she almost laughed at the absurdity of the cliché. *A hard time.* As if being married to Jay Malone was just a virus Trudy had picked up and would get over soon. The problem was Violet worried Trudy would never get over him, no matter how hard the times got. No matter how hard Violet tried to keep her promise to her mother. *"I promise. I'll protect Trudy."*

"You know what? I don't want to talk about Trudy." She met his gaze. "Is that all right?"

He closed the space between them and kissed her temple. "Of course." His eyebrows knitted. "She's okay though?"

Violet sighed. The random scrapes and cuts on Trudy's skin had transformed into dark, angry bruises, green and brown and yellow at the edges. Trudy tried to hide them, but there was only so much one sister could hide from another. Every time Violet asked about Jay or ran her finger lightly over another purple bloom—on Trudy's jaw, at her hairline, on the back of a leg— she would smile her perfect smile and toss back her mane of blonde hair and the haunted, anxious expression with it. *"It's fine, Vi. Everything's just fine."*

Trudy had said that so often, Violet was ready to take her sister forcefully from the home she shared with her husband. Either that, or give up on Trudy completely, which she couldn't, wouldn't, do.

"Violet?" Frank slowed their pace. "If it's anything I can help with . . ."

He didn't finish, but he didn't have to. She'd known him less than two months, but already she could tell he'd go an extra mile—or ten—for anyone who needed it. It was his nature, both as a police officer and as the earnest, loyal, good man she was finding him to be. And the poor boy had love written all over his face when he looked at Violet. Could he see the same in hers?

"She'll be fine," Violet finally said.

"You'll let me know if I can help?"

"I will," she promised.

Satisfied, he kissed her, his lips cold and salty from the breeze coming off the water. She caught his bottom lip gently between her teeth, then let go and pulled back. Even in his casual clothes and a ball cap on his head, he still had a commanding presence—broad shoulders, sturdy chest, strong jaw. He was twenty-seven—a year older than she was—but he could've easily passed for thirty or more on bearing alone.

They'd met up as often as possible to bird-watch together, though they did less of that lately, as focused as they were on learning every little detail about each other that they could. And Violet let him in on everything.

Almost everything, anyway. It was easier to keep some things to herself.

"I have to tell you something," she said, after kissing him once more and resuming their walk, not an inch of space between them. "I'm thinking about applying for a field study program this summer."

"A field study? What does that mean?"

"It's basically a temporary job, mostly for teachers and biologists. I'd be paid a tiny bit to work with scientists studying birds in their natural habitats. It'd be three months."

"It sounds perfect for you. Where is it?"

"They have programs like this all over, but there's one particular program in the Florida Keys. That's the one I'd apply for."

"Oh. Wow." He rubbed his cheek. "That's a long way away."

"I know. I've been thinking about applying for a couple years now. Since I have summers off, I have the time, and I've always wanted to see the Keys. I never thought I'd actually have a chance to go there though." She paused. "I have to turn in the application this week. I had it all ready back in January, but now I'm . . . well, I'm unsure." She swallowed. "The program starts in late May."

He glanced down at her and squeezed her hand. Good. She didn't have to spell it out that he was the reason she was unsure. Trudy was part of it, too, of course, but Frank played an increasingly large part in her uncertainty. It was so foreign to her—to have a man factor into a decision about her life. It had never been that way for Violet. Trudy, sure. She was the beauty, the desired one. Not just by boys and men but by everyone—friends, teachers, anyone with a camera. Since she was thirteen, Trudy had been quantifying and estimating herself based on how she was perceived, mostly by the opposite sex. Violet had always had complete freedom in her decisions. At least as it pertained to men.

And now here she was with a chance to go somewhere she'd always wanted to go, while doing the thing she loved to do, and she was waffling.

She kicked the sand with her toe, causing a cloud of it to fly back against their shins in the breeze.

"I think you should go for it."

"You do?"

"I do. Turn it in Monday and see what happens. If you get in, you'll go and study and learn. Then you can come back and tell me all about it."

Relief etched itself across her face in the form of a wide smile. She stopped and threw her arms around his neck. "Who knows?" he murmured into her ear. "Maybe I'll get some time off and I can come visit while you're there."

"I'd like that very much."

He put a gentle finger on her chin. "And I like you very much, Violet Figg." Her heart pounded but she didn't speak. "Where did you come from? You just walked into my life and changed my whole world."

"Actually, I think you walked into mine."

He chuckled. "Regardless, I don't think I'll ever be the same."

Frank's cane stabbed the sand with each step he took, and Violet was momentarily flustered, having nearly forgotten that it was decades later, and the man next to her was no longer the young, sure-footed, rookie policeman he'd been back then. And she was no longer the fresh-faced, ambitious young woman she'd once been.

Next to her Frank made a mark on his clipboard, then lowered it to his side. "I have some questions, if you don't mind."

She paused to steady herself. To ground herself in the here and now. "I'm surprised. You seem to have caught on to everything quickly."

"I don't mean about the surveys. I mean about you."

"Oh." She tucked a strand of hair behind her ear. She'd left her visor at home, thinking it'd be cloudy all morning, and her hair, no longer rich brown but mousy gray, tickled her cheek.

"It's been so long. I'm curious about you. About your life."

Violet swallowed hard and adjusted her backpack on her shoulder. "What do you want to know?"

"Did you ever make it down to the Keys?"

That long-ago desire. Her studious little heart. "No. I never did."

"Really? You were so excited about it. It seemed so perfect for you."

It was.

"Something else came up." She shrugged. "And kept coming up."

"What about kids?" She waited for the next, and it finally came. "Husband?"

There had been other men, of course. Later. They came and went over the years, some just wanting company for a little while, some wanting more, but she could never make them a priority. Not with her real priority holed up in her home, creating beautiful artwork out of cast-off shells and bits of wood, writing her words on pieces of paper, hiding herself within a bubble of silence and solitude.

"Neither."

He stared at her.

She laughed, a quick burst. "What?"

"I'm just . . . I'm shocked, honestly. I figured that was—" His mouth had started to form the next word—*why*—but he cut himself off.

What else would he have thought, Violet? Her words to herself were exasperated. *You flat out told him there was someone else.*

Everything in her wanted to set him straight, to assure him it hadn't been another man who'd pulled her away from him. But explaining that to him now would only trigger more questions— questions she'd orchestrated her life around not answering.

"It just never happened," was all she said.

He was quiet, waiting for an explanation she couldn't give him. "I have to admit, I'm surprised. You were quite a woman, Violet." He stole a glance at her, the corner of his mouth lifting just a little. "And still are, I imagine."

She smiled. She couldn't help herself, and neither could her heart, apparently. With the present and the past bumping up together, her heart raced just as it used to when she was with him.

Sandpipers coasted over the water and landed inches from the lapping waves. They dug their long, thin beaks into the soft sand.

Six sandpipers, four female, two male.

"What about you?" The thought of him loving another had once been unbearable to her, but years changed things. She thought she could take it now. "Did you marry?"

"I did. I married a woman named Alice. We have two sons."

Violet's heart stuttered, then resumed its pace. "And you live here in Sugar Bend?"

"I just moved back a few months ago. I'd been in Pensacola since . . . well, for a long time. But I wanted to be back closer to the grandkids." He paused. "Alice lives in Abilene with her second husband."

"Oh. I'm sorry to hear that."

"Don't be. We divorced five years ago. It was very amicable."

"Well then, I'm glad."

"Me too."

They'd turned around at the end of their one-mile route and were now headed back the other direction, quiet, the sun against their faces. Violet held up a hand to block the rays.

"How's your sister?" he asked.

"My sister?"

Her response was too loud, too sharp, and he tilted his head. "I remember you telling me a little about her. You always seemed worried about her."

"Trudy's just fine." She spoke quickly, almost before he'd finished. "She lives with me."

"Ah. I see. I'm glad you have someone with you. So you're not—?" He stopped.

"So I'm not what? A lonely old woman?" She smiled to take the sting out of her words.

He lifted his cane and set it down again a couple feet ahead. "You're not an old woman, but yes, I'm glad you're not alone. Or lonely."

She shifted her backpack off her shoulder and dropped her pencil and clipboard inside. "Trudy's a good companion." Quiet but steady as a heartbeat.

Back at the lounge chair that marked the beginning and end of their route, Frank lifted his face toward the sun and closed his eyes. Violet watched him a moment—his broad shoulders just a little bit stooped, the line of his jaw softer, his thick eyebrows wiry with age, and those same full lips—then she turned her face up too. The sun's rays were still soft, a little hazy in the morning breeze. Above them, gulls cackled to a nearly empty stretch of sand. Just Violet and Frank standing still as the years pushed against them. Leaning toward the sunlight.

Liza waited until the rest of the *Observer* staff had gone home for the day before she paused in front of the gallery wall of old Sugar Bend photos and newspaper clippings. She focused on one photo snipped from a 1981 front-page spread. She'd perused the gallery wall in the office many times since beginning her job at the paper, and while she'd seen this particular photo, she never paid it any particular attention. Today, though, she couldn't pull her eyes away.

The yellowed clipping showed a man with a wide smile. He held a string of just-caught fish in one hand, and the other rested possessively on the steering wheel of a green boat with a blue stripe across the side. The man was charming—cute and a bit flirty, as if he were trying to get a smile out of whoever was holding the camera. His hair was pleasantly disheveled, and his taut chest muscles gleamed in the sunlight. She thought back to the strange dream she'd had after seeing the boat washed up onshore—the fists and tears, the sound of a boat motor and broken glass. None of that jived with the affable face grinning from the photo.

The caption beneath the photo read, "Owner of Friendly's Ice Cream, Jay Malone, with his catch of the day."

The Sugar Bend Observer, Sugar Bend's Community News Source
Letter from the Editor, Liza Bullock
June 2022 | Volume 11, Issue 6

As I'm sure you've noticed, several new housing developments are under way in Sugar Bend. Each development is spearheaded by architects and builders intent on preserving beauty and charm while also renovating and rebuilding sections of the area that have fallen into disrepair. One of those areas is a neighborhood just up the river from downtown Sugar Bend. Carl Waters, with Southtown Contractors, has begun work on a new subdivision called Fox Cove. I recently visited Fox Cove, and Mr. Waters's teams are already in place beginning renovation work. The development will be anchored by River Ash Road, and a majority of the homes face the upper sections of Little River. I hear the sunset views are second to none!

In a nod to the history of our area, I discovered one of the homes Mr. Waters will be renovating was once owned by Jay Malone, who also owned several Friendly's Ice Cream Shops back in the 1970s and early '80s.

Additionally, on the day I visited, Mr. Waters pointed out a boat that had recently washed up onshore in front of the house. According to a photo from a back issue of *The Observer*, Mr. Malone caught quite a few fish from his treasured boat. I'll be doing a little digging to see if the boat that washed up did in fact belong to Mr. Malone. In the meantime please enjoy our feature on Fox Cove on 1B.

Happy reading!
Liza

nine

D o you mind if I move the tote bags to the rack here under the window? We could tell customers they can grab a bag to hold the items they plan to purchase, then when they come to check out, they'll realize the bag is so cute, it'll be hard for them not to buy it along with their other things."

Two Sisters had just opened for the day, and Maya was standing in the center of the shop, gesturing to the window, her dark hair in a high ponytail, a dustcloth tucked into her back pocket.

Violet smiled. "That's a great idea. Go for it."

They'd originally planned for Maya to work only two shifts a week to start, but she was a quick learner and had already come up with ideas for how to bring in more customers and increase customer satisfaction. For one, she moved a tray of pinch pots to the counter by the register, which had resulted in many customers adding a small pot to their stash of items to purchase. She also suggested bringing in someone from the library to hold a story time for kids and maybe even adding a coffee cart to sell flavored coffees and treats. She'd met a server at the Sugar Shack who worked nights as a pastry chef and was looking for places to sell her own gourmet cookies, cupcakes, and macarons.

With Maya there learning the ropes and helping with customers, it seemed people were swarming in at a thicker pace than before, and with the increased traffic, Violet and Trudy had already bumped her schedule up from two days to anytime she was free. If she wanted to work, they'd pay her for the extra help.

A week ago, with encouragement from Maya, Trudy had put up a sign in the front window about a mixed-media art class. The class would be for all ages, and students would have two hours to create a piece of art using a variety of materials provided for them—found objects as well as paint, charcoal pencils, and filament wire. The materials would vary for each class, depending on what Trudy had on hand, and their plan was to add more classes if turnout for the first class was decent.

Trudy worried no one would sign up, but two days after putting the sign in the window, they'd hit their maximum limit of students—all locals except for three women on vacation from Mississippi. They'd even had to turn people away, prompting Trudy to quickly schedule two more classes. This morning was the first class, and as Maya moved the rack of tote bags, Trudy burst through the front door with a box in her hands.

"I can help you." Maya set the rack down carefully and took the box from Trudy's hands. "Are these shells?" She set the box down on Trudy's worktable and peeked inside. "Ooh, these are perfect." Maya pulled out a plastic bag of small sand dollars. "Are these for the class?"

Trudy shrugged, then stuck her fists to her hips. She surveyed the materials on the table, then pointed to the small room at the back they'd decided would be their classroom.

"You got it." Maya was already well versed in reading Trudy's silent communication. "I'll help you move everything."

For the next half hour Maya and Trudy bustled back and forth between Trudy's work space and the classroom, draping plastic tablecloths over card tables they'd set out yesterday, moving boxes of materials, and setting up tools and supplies. Violet took up Maya's discarded dustcloth and finished the job and chatted with customers as they floated in. Some were shopping for particular items, while others were just browsing, lured in by the bustle and energy in the shop. Violet made herself available for help if needed but hung back and allowed customers the comfort of shopping without distraction.

With a few minutes to go before class started, the shop was pulsing with life. Emmajean stopped in on her way to the library, but finding the tables at the front of the store already occupied, she gave a thumbs-up to Violet and mouthed, *Looking good in here!* As class attendees arrived, Violet showed them to the room at the back, and by eleven o'clock, every seat but one was occupied. When the last attendee arrived with a flurry of apology about her lateness, Violet walked her back, then paused by the door before walking out.

Trudy stood at the front of the room with Maya at her elbow. She and Maya had already rehearsed—via myriad pieces of paper written and erased and rewritten—what they'd say and how they'd teach. Trudy nodded at Maya to begin.

"Welcome to the very first mixed-media class taught by Sugar Bend's own resident artist, Trudy Figg." Trudy's cheeks pinked at Maya's words and her brow creased, but Maya only smiled. "Don't worry, I'll stick to the notes from here on out."

"Trudy will be teaching the class today, but it'll be a little different than you might expect. The first thing you need to do is take a minute to get acquainted with the materials on the table in front of you."

As Trudy's closest companion for so many years, Violet was used to speaking for her sister. But watching Trudy standing at the front of the classroom, all eyes on her even though no sound came from her mouth, Violet understood that a baton had been passed. Trudy's own words finally had a voice. That voice might belong to a young woman, but the words were Trudy's. The voice was hers.

Violet closed the door softly behind her as Maya continued the instructions. With the students tucked away in class, the shop was much quieter. The only sounds were Maya's muted words through the door, soft music on the speaker, and the rustle of a newspaper on the seat of one of the chairs under the window.

Violet walked through the shop, straightening and neatening and thinking of her next survey with Frank tomorrow morning, then headed to the chairs up front to clear away a discarded receipt and an empty tea mug. The newspaper still fluttered, its pages rustling from the ceiling fan above. It was open to an article about a new neighborhood development called Fox Cove. As Violet reached down to grab it, her eyes snagged on two words at the bottom of the page. Two words that made her legs wobble and her blood harden to ice.

Jay Malone.

⸺

Trudy invited Maya over for dinner that evening as she and Violet closed up the shop. Trudy raised her eyebrows at Violet in question, and Violet nodded despite the thin coat of anxiety that had slipped over her shoulders after reading Jay's name in the article in *The Observer.* It seemed a boat had been found on the premises of a new housing development at the edge of the river, having washed up from somewhere. The housing development was situated on River Ash Road.

"Of course she can come," Violet had said to her sister, who hadn't read the article. Violet threw it in the recycling bin as soon as she read it, burying it under a couple days' worth of loose papers and cardboard. "We have plenty of food."

And now the two women had notes and sketches spread out all over the dining table as Violet threw together a salad to go with their dinner.

"What if we do a class specifically for kids and we add in some fun materials like pipe cleaners and googly eyes?" Maya asked.

Violet chopped the last of the cucumber and dumped it in the salad bowl as Trudy shoved another note across the table to

Maya. She picked it up and read it, then laughed. "You know, googly eyes. Those little plastic eyes with the black dots that move when you shake them."

Trudy's brow wrinkled.

"I'll find some and show you. I just think having some silly things would be good for the kids. Plus, parents might not appreciate us giving their little ones wire and glass to work with."

They'd been talking for half an hour, the conversation moving from classes to the sculpture they'd been working on together, as Violet puttered in the kitchen, making iced tea, pulling apart cold cooked chicken, and chopping veggies for the salad. Both women came alive when talking about the shop and their art, and Violet was struck by how similar they were despite their differences in age, verbal abilities, and background.

Then again, they didn't know much at all about Maya's background. Something Violet hoped to remedy tonight.

A few minutes later, Violet set the salad and chicken on the table. Maya cleared away the slips of paper and seashells as Trudy brought in the iced tea glasses, their conversation about future classes and ideas for the shop still floating in the air between them.

Once they began to eat, Violet waited a minute before asking, "Maya, I'd love to know a little more about you. Where you're from, your family, what brought you to Sugar Bend . . ."

Trudy cleared her throat and caught Violet's eye. Violet raised her hands and mouthed, *What?*

Trudy took up her pencil and wrote a note for Maya. Maya read it, then folded it in half. "It's okay," she said softly. "I don't mind." Maya sipped her tea, then wiped her lips with her napkin. "The truth is, I don't have any family. Not anymore. My mom left when I was three, and as far as I know, my dad was never around."

"You mentioned a grandmother the other day," Violet said.

Maya's cheeks lifted. "I lived with her after my mom left, but she died a few years later. I was seven."

She was so matter-of-fact, Violet was taken aback. Much like Trudy and her, this girl was alone. Left behind by parents who should have taken the job more seriously.

Maya went on to explain that she'd been put in the foster system after the death of her grandmother, and she'd lived in ten different homes since then. She'd finally had enough and signed her own papers the day after her eighteenth birthday, allowing her to leave and make her own path in the world. And somehow that path had led her to Sugar Bend. More than that, it had led her to Violet and Trudy.

Violet had never had a strong mothering instinct. She hadn't played with baby dolls when she was a child, and she didn't see women with babies or young children and feel she'd missed out on something elemental. But still, focusing on Maya sitting on the other side of her kitchen table, she felt something kick into gear and churn to life. Glancing at her sister, she could tell Trudy was feeling the same thing. They were getting up in years, but here was this young person in their life, working in their shop and eating at their table. It was something neither of them had prepared for.

Later, as they watched Maya drive away in her clanking

black car, Trudy pulled a pencil and a square of paper from her pocket. *She's great, isn't she? I have a good feeling about her.*

Violet read the note and let her hand drop, her gaze trained on the spot where Maya's car had disappeared under the wisteria arbor at the end of the driveway. "She's had a hard life, that's for sure."

Some might say we have too.

Violet tilted her head as her gaze skimmed across the familiar planes and dips of her sister's face. "At least we had each other."

Trudy smiled. *We did. And I think a little Violet in her life is just what Maya needs.*

Trudy slid her hands in her pockets and sighed contentedly, but Violet's mind was again awash in old memories and the two words she'd seen in the newspaper today. *I can't tell her*, she thought. *There's no need for her to know. No need to burden her with the past.*

Violet exhaled a puff of air from her nose. "I think it's you, Tru. She could use some Trudy in her life." She patted Trudy's arm as she walked back into the house. "Do you mind putting the plates in the dishwasher? I'm going to head on to bed."

The next morning, Violet was late for her survey. She'd once read that birds were creatures of habit, and though they might not have noticed—or cared—whether she arrived on the beach at seven or eight, it mattered to her. She didn't want to disappoint them. But she'd slept poorly the night before, her mind teeming with images of sharp metal, crumbled bricks, dried blood on a soft cheek, and air bubbles releasing on the surface of the river. Her legs had moved all night, trying in vain to find a cool, soft place.

When she finally succumbed to exhaustion, she slept hard, unable to rouse herself, even when a dreamy, high-pitched boat motor mixed with the sound of Trudy's sweet voice, calm and clear. Just as the motor threatened to overtake Trudy's voice, Violet wrenched herself up, yanking open her eyelids and commanding them to remain open.

Despite her unsettled sleep and chaotic dreams, she still could have made it on time if it hadn't been for the bones. Backpack in hand and visor in place, she'd left the house only to find yet another set of fish bones on the bottom step, like a casual forgotten shoe or an innocent gardening glove. But it was not casual to her. Not innocent at all. Her legs gave out when she saw them, and it was a few long moments before she could stand again.

By the time she made it to the beach—legs still trembly, breathless from hurrying, and damp at her hairline—Frank had started without her. He was a little ways up the sand with his back to her, his binoculars focused on three terns darting back and forth where the waves crept up the sand. She called his name, but her voice tangled in the strong breeze and flew back against her, so she just watched him a moment, unseen. A quiet stillness rolled off his shoulders and wrapped around his legs, the sight of it calming something frantic inside her, just as it had when she was a much younger woman.

Frank let his binoculars hang from the strap around his neck and jotted something on the clipboard. He glanced up again and made another note. A moment later, he checked his watch and glanced behind him, startling when he saw her. He held his hand up in a wave, grabbed the head of his cane that was propped against his hip, and began to walk back. She started toward him, the sand squeaking underfoot, and met him in the middle.

"Hello there," he said when he reached her. "Glad you could make it. I stayed close by because I didn't want to miss you."

Warmth spread up from her cool toes to her fingertips. "I'm sorry for being late. I was . . ." Unable—or unwilling—to chalk her lateness up to something as seemingly harmless as fish bones, she trailed off.

"It's okay. That's the beauty of being retired. We have all the time in the world." He held his arms open wide, knocking his cane to the ground in the process.

She bent down and retrieved it for him, then tilted her head up the beach. "Shall we?"

A line of gulls soared overhead, some with wings beating, some coasting, all of them brilliant white against the pale blue morning sky. Cotton-ball clouds rested just above the horizon.

"How long have you had this?" Violet brushed the cane with her fingers.

"Oh, about five years or thereabouts." He plunked the tip of the cane down in the sand a little harder than necessary. "Every time I think I'm ready to ditch it, my knee starts to ache again. When that happens, this stick is a lot stronger than my bad leg is."

"Why do you have to use it?" When he didn't answer right away, she apologized. "It's not my business."

"No, it's fine. Really. It was just a judgment call on my part. The wrong one, in hindsight."

She waited, curious but not pushing, and he eventually spoke. He told her he'd gone back to the scene of a burglary because something wasn't sitting right with him, and he wanted to work through the details in the place the crime had happened. It had been a week and they still hadn't found the suspects, so on the way home from work, he headed to the house to drive by and see if anything spoke to him.

He said that's when he'd seen the object lying near the gutter at the end of the street, as if someone had tried to throw it in but missed. Frank slowed next to the gutter and saw the whole scene play out in his mind—the intended quick-grab burglary, the chaos that ensued when the homeowner roared down the stairs, the burner phone tossed from a moving car. Just as Frank opened his door and leaned down to reach for the mangled phone, shots fired. His leg cracked and burned, and all went dark.

"None of the guys understood why I did it—why I went back there alone just because something didn't feel right. But I knew there was more to the story and the family deserved to know the truth. It was vain, but I felt if I didn't do it, they'd never find out who broke in and why. Looking back now, I see the utter stupidity. But at the time I thought I was doing the right thing."

"Would you do it differently now?"

He hesitated. "Probably not. The family had closure, and that's what I wanted. It felt right, even though it left me with a bum leg and an extra appendage." He twirled the end of the cane.

A memory pushed to the surface, and Violet remembered sitting hip to hip with Frank at the Sandbar years ago as the band pounded through the Allman Brothers Band's "Whipping Post."

"I had to do it, Vi," Frank had said, his elbows propped against the damp wood of the bar, his forehead in his hands. Violet pressed her hand to his back.

"He'll never talk to me again. None of them will. But I couldn't just ignore it. It was wrong. I can't look the other way, even if it's my friend."

Violet had heard about the raid at the Showboat, that ramshackle houseboat anchored just offshore in Little River. The boat's illegal activities had been going on forever, and a cop or two going in after a shift to try to win a little money—or the affections of the ladies upstairs—wasn't uncommon. But word was someone on the inside had gotten wind of these particular cops enjoying the Showboat and reported them to the chief.

Frank reached for his bottle and took a long swig. "I had no idea Hutchins already knew. Everybody knew and they didn't care." He pounded his fist on the bar. "They raided the boat to save face, but he said next time, I'm supposed to pretend I don't see it. That I know nothing." He swiveled on his stool and faced Violet. "How are people supposed to trust us if we choose to turn our heads when it's our friends doing the dirty things? What happened to serving mankind, safeguarding lives, protecting the innocent?" He dug his hands into his hair, leaving tufts of it sticking up in front. "Do you think I did the right thing?"

"Do you think you did the right thing?"

The band changed songs and the group sitting on the other side of Frank began to sing along. He glanced back over his shoulder toward the band—his troubled face a stark contrast to the joy and energy in the room—and faced Violet again. "I know I didn't join the force to be a crooked cop, and I wouldn't have been able to live with myself if I'd kept quiet."

Walking along the beach with Frank now, Violet marveled at this man's internal sense of right and wrong that had been with him from the beginning, and was still with him now.

"You always wanted to do what was right. I remember that." The breeze was cool on Violet's arms, but the goose bumps on her skin weren't due to the weather.

Frank gazed ahead to an egret perched on top of the lifeguard shack, then made a hatch mark on his data sheet. "I guess I did. But that urge to tell the truth was in me long before I joined the force. Just ask my brothers." He chuckled. "They couldn't pull anything over on our mom. Little Frankie was always there to blow the whistle on them."

Violet still caved inside at the thought of Frank finding out what had happened that night on the dock. His need to tell the truth, to bring justice and protect the innocent, was still just as strong as it had been when he was a young policeman. And that was just as it should be. He was a good, honest man, and she was the woman who had to leave him because of a foggy night on the water forty years ago.

She'd thought that everything associated with that night was gone and buried, but the first sight of fish bones on her top porch step had ripped open the past and brought it crashing back with sickening clarity. And the newspaper article—those two simple words—only confirmed her suspicion that the past wasn't as gone as she'd thought.

***

Tyler was on his way home from delivering another load of hay to Mr. Olsen, Ruby's head out the window, ears flapping in the breeze, when he rounded a curve and saw a commotion at the side of the highway. At first he thought it might be the crazy old farmer who'd held up traffic for hours earlier in the summer with a barbecue grill and folding chairs in the middle of the road, but as Tyler got closer, he saw it was a car with a flat tire. The old black car looked to be on its last leg anyway, and the deflated tire only accentuated its general dilapidation.

Tyler was glad to see someone else had stopped to help the unlucky motorist. That sort of thing happened all the time around here, and he would have passed on by with a wave and a nod to the good Samaritan if he hadn't seen the girl. It was the same one from the diner, then the Figgs' shop. She was standing back from the edge of the highway, deep under the shade, and her face was streaked with anxiety. The man who'd stopped to help stood next to her, his mouth *this close* to her ear.

Tyler slowed and the man raised his head, a veil of irritation on his face. Tyler threw his truck in Park in front of the man's pickup and got out. Ruby ran ahead, sniffing the ground, then stopped a few feet from the man, her ears pulled back, her tail lowered.

The guy planted a hand on the girl's shoulder. "Hey, man, I've got this taken care of. No need to trouble yourself."

"It's no trouble." Tyler kept his eyes on the girl. She was chewing on the edge of her lip, worry still pinching her features. "Anyway, I know her, so I can take over. Looks like you didn't get far with changing the tire in any case." He noted the hard glint in the man's eyes, but he walked to the car regardless and leaned down to check the tire.

"I was gonna do it. I just wanted to introduce myself to her first." He turned back to the girl. "Her name is Maya. Isn't that pretty?"

Maya.

"Maya, why don't you grab the jack while I loosen the lug nuts. I'll fix this up and get you out of here."

"I told you, I've got it." The man left Maya and came to a stop next to Tyler. "I'm taking care of her." It was impossible to miss the meaning in his tone.

"I don't think so." Tyler stood to his full height, towering over the guy, with only a few inches of space between them. "I've got it."

The guy stared at Tyler, his jaw shifting, muscles clenched. Finally he grinned. "Hey, man, she's all yours. Have fun with that tire." He kicked the tire with the toe of his boot, then walked back to his truck. A few seconds later, all that was left was a cloud of roadside dust in the air. Ruby scampered after a bird that landed a few feet away from her.

"You okay?" Tyler called.

Maya nodded and walked to her car. "Thanks for stopping. He was . . . pushy."

"I could tell. Why'd you get out of the car? Why didn't you call someone?"

She shrugged. "I don't have a phone."

"You don't have a cell phone?"

"I don't usually have too many people to call."

Tyler thought of Cassie and her ever-present iPhone with the glittery case and the constant notifications and rings. If she wasn't talking on her phone, she was thumb-typing on it nearly all day. It was exhausting.

He didn't want to think about Cassie when he was finally talking to the girl who'd occupied his dreams for weeks. He'd suspected it but wasn't willing to admit it until now. This was the girl he'd been seeing in his mind's eye at night, the cause of the strange images—of delight, of warmth, of comfort—dancing just out of his line of sight.

"I'm Tyler." He reached out his hand and she slid hers into his. When he let go a quick moment later, he could still feel the warmth of her skin.

"I'm Maya."

They stood there, eyes locked onto each other for an eternity, before Ruby pushed between them and lifted her eyebrows hopefully. Tyler reached down and scratched the top of her head. "Okay." He rubbed his hands together. "Is your spare in the trunk?"

"I'm not sure. I hope so."

"Let's check and see."

She opened the trunk but there was nothing. He pressed on all sides of the trunk space and pried his fingertips into every crevice, but nothing opened to reveal a tire. "No spare. But there's a tire store up the highway a bit. I could run you up there so you can buy a new one."

She bit her lip again. "How much are tires?"

He shrugged. "Probably around eighty dollars or so."

She rubbed a hand across her forehead and glanced back at the car. The front bumper was barely hanging on and dents dotted the side.

"You know what? I think I may have just what you need back at the store."

"You have a tire store?"

"No. It's a feedstore. Holt Feed and Seed. Up on County Road 23?" She didn't seem to recognize it. "You're not from around here."

"No. But why would you have a tire at a feedstore?"

He laughed. "Don't ask. We have a little of everything." He walked to the passenger side door and opened it. But instead of Maya climbing in, it was Ruby. The dog perched in the seat, ready for her ride. "Not this time, girl." He patted the back of the truck, and Ruby jumped out of the cab and into the bed, front paws propped up on the side.

Tyler held the door open for Maya, but she hesitated.

"You need a ride, right?" he asked.

She pulled the edge of her bottom lip in and stared at him.

"Right. You don't know me." How did he explain that though she didn't know him, he knew her? Or at least felt like he did. More specifically, how did he explain it without sounding like a total weirdo? "You can trust me." He closed one eye. *Great, Tyler. That's probably what every bad guy ever said to a girl before kidnapping her.* "Oh, I do some work for the Figgs sometimes. You could call them and ask them about me. I have a phone." He hooked his thumb toward the driver's seat where he'd left his cell.

But she seemed to relax. Her shoulders dropped a little. "You brought birdseed to Violet." He nodded. "Okay then. If they trust you, I will too."

"Good." He patted the door and she climbed in. A moment later, they were headed up the highway toward the store. He fiddled with the radio a moment and found an old Otis Redding song. The windows were down, the warm air filling the cab and fluttering the edges of their clothes and hair. Tyler tried to keep his eyes on the road, but they kept scampering to the right.

Her eyes were dark as the river at night, and her skin was a gorgeous tawny hue, like a new penny. Her hair was pulled up into a knot at the top of her head, but a lot of it fell down around her face, framing her cheeks with a fringe he wanted to reach out and touch. Just behind her left ear was a small brown freckle.

"So . . ." Once he started, he didn't know what to say.

She waited but when he didn't say anything, she gave a quiet laugh. "Yes?"

"I have no idea. Where are you from?" There. Safe territory.

But she didn't answer right away. And when she did, it wasn't in the way he'd expected. "I'm from all over."

"All over what? Alabama?"

"Sort of. I moved around a lot. Foster care."

"Oh, wow. I'm sorry."

"It's okay." She shrugged. "I'm just glad to be out of it and on my own."

"You live by yourself? That must be nice."

Her only answer was a murmur, neither a yes nor a no.

Tyler thought of his family—stoic, hardworking Dixon; his sweet, polite mom, Caroline; and his wild, athletic younger sister, Missy. They really weren't all that bad, but with Maya sitting next to him, everything seemed bigger. His future had seemed like this small tunnel he had to walk through to get to the other side, but now it was wider, like a big field that held all kinds of life and space and time.

When he pulled into the parking lot of Holt Feed and Seed a few minutes later, his dad was standing at the door.

"I'm glad you're back," his dad said as Tyler exited the truck. "You've got . . ." He broke off when he saw Maya climb out of the passenger side. His gaze darted inside the store, then back to Maya. His fingers went to the brim of his navy blue hat with the Holt logo and he gave it a characteristic tug. "Young lady."

"Dad, this is Maya. She's friends with the Figg sisters. She had a flat tire out on the highway."

"You gonna get her fixed up?"

"Yes, sir."

As Tyler and Maya approached him, his dad raised his eyebrows and tilted his head toward the store.

"What is it?" Tyler followed his dad's gaze and caught the edge of something pink in aisle three. He said a word under his breath that made Dad clear his throat.

"Maya, have you ever seen a Silkie chicken?" his dad asked.

"A silky chicken? I don't think so."

"They're the silliest things you've ever seen, but they're pretty friendly. We have a few in the coop in the back. If you want, I can show you while Tyler gets your tire."

Tyler sighed as they walked around the side of the building, relieved his dad understood the situation. Surprised too.

Steeling himself for what was to come, he squared his shoulders and walked inside. The familiar scent he loved so much—a mix of dusty hay, fertilizer, grass, and rubber—filled his senses and he closed his eyes for the briefest moment. Then she called to him. He followed the voice and found Cassie standing by a rack of wildflower seeds, her blonde hair pulled up into a high ponytail, her lips gleaming with gloss. She wore a short pink dress that showed off her tanned shoulders and a sizable expanse of her upper thighs.

"Where's your truck? I didn't see it out front."

"I parked around the side." A flirty smile tugged at the corners of her mouth. "I wanted to surprise you."

"Well, you did that."

"What took you so long? I've been waiting forever."

He sighed and rubbed a hand over his eyes. "I've been out working. It's what I do, Cass, in case you've forgotten."

"I know that." She rolled her eyes and walked toward him, coming close enough for him to smell her sweet, vanilla-scented perfume. "I meant, why didn't you call me? I thought after that day at Soldiers Creek . . ."

Tyler shifted his jaw. He shouldn't have done it—he'd gone off the rope swing with her several times that day at the creek, letting himself forget his frustration and yearning, drowning it all in Cassie's laugh and the feel of her small hand in his. And yes, even her lips a time or two when she planted hers on his, but both times he'd stopped her. Cassie wasn't the one he dreamed about. Cassie wasn't the one who made him feel like his future wasn't as small as he'd always thought.

Tyler glanced back toward the door where any minute, his dad could walk in with Maya.

"I thought maybe we could try it again."

"What, the swing?" he asked, his eyes still directed toward the back door.

"No, us. Me and you. I don't even remember why we stopped dating." She reached out to take his hand, but he lifted his hand and resettled his cap on his head.

"Sure you do. His name is Vince and he wore a big number four on the back of his Spanish Fort jersey."

Cassie laughed. "Tyler, I don't—"

Her words were drowned out when the back door opened and his dad's voice rang out. "Tyler, you in here?"

"Yes, sir." Tyler took a step back from Cassie and crossed his arms.

A moment later, his dad and Maya appeared at the front of

the store. His dad had a tire under his arm. "I went ahead and grabbed this for you." He set the tire down and propped it up against a shelf. "I figured you might have your hands full." He cocked an eyebrow up. "I showed Maya here the chickens, and we grabbed the eggs that were out there. I've got a customer up front, so I'm gonna . . ." His dad hooked his thumb back toward the register, then walked away, his relief at escaping the delicate situation so apparent on his face, Tyler almost laughed. Then he caught the expression on Cassie's face.

Tyler cleared his throat. "Cassie, this is Maya."

"Maya." Cassie lifted an eyebrow. "Who's she?"

He bristled at her tone, but he kept his voice even. "She's a friend. We met in town. She works at Two Sisters and at the Shack."

"Oh, the Shack. They have the best lemonade." It was an innocent statement, but there was nothing innocent about the way Cassie said it, or the smirk on her lips. She held out her hand to shake Maya's. "Any friend of Tyler's is a friend of mine. What's the tire for?"

"I had a flat and Tyler stopped to help."

"Well, isn't that sweet?" Cassie stepped toward Tyler and kissed his cheek. He could feel the gooey print of her gloss on his skin. "Tyler Holt's always willing to step up and help a stranger."

Though the barb was directed at Maya, Tyler felt it as if it had hooked him in the chest. He stepped away from Cassie and grabbed the tire. "She's not a stranger. I told you—she's a friend." With his free hand he touched Maya's elbow and nodded toward the door.

As they walked out Tyler could feel the weight of Cassie's stare on his back, but he let the front door close firmly behind them.

The ride back to Maya's car was quiet, with only Ruby's panting to fill the silence. Tyler tried to think of a way to explain Cassie's presence in the store, but when he glanced over at Maya, she was so untroubled, he decided to say nothing. She'd leaned her head back against the seat and was idly rubbing Ruby's back, the breeze lifting the hair around her face in a wispy halo.

Back at her car, it only took him about twenty minutes to change the tire. After throwing the flat one in the bed of his truck, he found Ruby flopped on her back next to Maya, who was stroking the dog's chest. Ruby's eyes were closed in happiness.

"That'll do it," he said.

Maya stood and brushed her hands off. "I really appreciate the help. I don't know what I would have done if you hadn't shown up."

"Without a phone you might have been walking back to Sugar Bend." Either that, or the other guy who'd stopped would have helped himself. Though it made no sense, Tyler already felt protective about Maya and didn't want to think about the other guy in relation to her at all. He unclenched his fingers, which had tightened into fists at the thought of the man.

Maya opened her car door. "So I'll see you back in town, I guess. Maybe you should come to one of our classes at the shop."

Tyler chuckled. "I'm not very artistic."

"You don't have to be. When I first sat down with Trudy, she told me to play. And that's what I did." She shrugged. "It's pretty fun."

He didn't see how playing around with seashells and old driftwood could be fun, but then again, she'd be there. He had a feeling he'd do anything—learn to knit, play bunco, try yodeling—as long as he could do it with Maya. "Okay, maybe I'll do that."

She smiled up at him. A divot dimpled each cheek, and the sun dazzled from a small dot of silver to the right side of her nose. A tiny silver bird.

"Cassie's no one," he blurted.

"What?" Maya reached a hand up to shade her eyes from the late-afternoon rays.

"Cassie, the girl back at the store? She's just—well, she and I used to—"

"It's okay. You don't have to explain."

"Yes, I do. We used to date, but we broke up a long time ago. She just . . . well, she's persistent."

Maya blew a puff of air from her nose. "Yeah, I picked up on that."

"I just don't want you to think that there's . . . anything happening there." He exhaled. *Come on, Tyler.* This girl made him feel so flustered and nervous.

"Okay," she said simply. Then with a wave, she pulled back onto the road and drove away. Behind her trailed strands of silver mist, curling and twisting in the summer sunshine.

t e n

Liza had to invent a reason to go back to the Fox Cove development. She'd already asked the contractor, Carl, all the questions she needed answers to the first time she went, but she needed to see the boat again, and she didn't feel comfortable just showing up to poke around down by the water.

Before photos. People love a good before and after.

She'd already walked up and down the street, snapping photos of all the houses in their preconstruction state, and now she stood in the middle of the yard behind the most dilapidated house in the neighborhood: 61 River Ash Road. She stared down at the river and the hunk of metal washed up on its shore.

Her mind told her to put one foot in front of the other and walk toward it, but it was like trying to push together two magnets with the same poles. She kept seeing that old photo— Jay Malone standing in this boat, holding his fish, with that big, wide smile on his face. Nothing should have felt off, but it did.

She fluttered her silk blouse away from the hot skin of her chest and forced herself to walk down to the edge of the river. As she approached the boat, it somehow seemed more barnacle covered, more grimy, more slimy with algae and plant growth than before, which was impossible since it had been drying out in the sun for weeks now. She stared a moment, trying to imagine what could have happened to send the boat underwater. Why did she care so much? It was just an old boat. It shouldn't matter at all.

"Did you get the photos you needed?"

She startled. Carl was walking down the grassy slope toward her.

"I did. Thank you. I was just taking a breather before heading back to the office."

Carl stood next to her and nodded, toed the hull of the boat with his boot. "Want to take this thing with you?"

She coughed out a laugh. "No, thanks."

"I need it gone. No one cares about it. Whoever it belonged to, seems they wanted to sink it anyway."

"What makes you say that?"

"Drain plugs are gone." He leaned over and pointed. "See those two holes? One on either side of the stern. Those don't just fall out. If it were just one, maybe it was an accident, but both? Looks to me like someone wanted this boat to go under."

One of the workers called to Carl from the side of the house, and he waved and started that way. "Let me know if you need anything else."

"I will. Thanks."

Liza watched him cross the yard and pause by the worker who'd flagged him. When they disappeared around the front of the house, Liza stepped closer to the boat. *What is it? What am I looking for?* She couldn't shake it.

She walked a circle around the boat, seeing it from all angles, and that's when she noticed the small door built into the side of the hull. It was only about six inches square, like a small glove box, and she would have missed it if not for the black knob sticking out. She reached down and gave the knob a tentative pull, and the door opened cleanly despite the sludge covering it. Leaning over, the boat inches from her body, its aroma of wet sand and rotten plant growth filling her nose, she peered inside the small space.

What she saw sent a jolt down the length of her spine. *What are you doing here?*

In stark contrast to the rest of the boat, what rested inside the small protected space was grime free, as if someone had just set it there for safekeeping.

With a quick look back to the house to make sure no one was watching, she reached inside and slipped the item into her pocket.

The Sugar Bend Public Library was housed in an old white-steepled church at the edge of downtown. Liza parked in the oyster-shell lot out front and walked inside, where the air smelled of paper and ink and history.

"May I help you?" asked an attractive older woman with short, dark gray waves. She was setting books from a rolling cart onto a shelf next to the circulation desk. The tag on her blouse said her name was Emmajean.

Liza bit her lip. "Maybe. I'm with *The Sugar Bend Observer* and I need some information. To be honest, though, I'm not exactly sure what I'm looking for."

"The library is a good place to start if you don't know what you need. I bet we can help."

Ten minutes later, Liza stood before a strange machine with a large roll on one side and a green glow coming from underneath.

"This is our microfiche printer," Emmajean said. "It's where we keep a lot of old documents and research materials. If you need something from pre-internet days, chances are you'll find it here." She clicked through a few pages on the computer sitting next to the microfiche. "Now, you mentioned old newspaper articles, right?"

"That's right. I need information about a man named Jay Malone. I think he owned an ice cream shop around here."

The woman's hands stilled on the keyboard. Her gaze dropped and a small sigh escaped her. "I read your article in the paper. About the boat that washed up. You think it's his?"

Liza nodded. "I do. Of course, I can't be absolutely sure, because no one by that name has come forward claiming the boat. No one seems to know anything about it. Or care, really. But I saw an old photo of him standing in the boat." She shrugged. "I'm just assuming it's his."

The librarian pressed her lips together and turned back to the machine. "I'll show you how to use this, then I'll leave you to it." She walked Liza through how to load the slides into the machine and how to scan through them quickly. There was no way to search for a specific word or name, like a microfiche Google, but if she had a general idea of what she was hunting for, she could move through the pages quickly with an eye peeled for particular words and headlines.

When the librarian walked out, Liza got to work. She started on slides from the midseventies, scanning through pages of newspaper headlines, minutes from city council meetings, briefs on land usage and zoning requirements. She found a list of every type of tree growing in Sugar Bend, reports on damage from dozens of hurricanes, and hundreds of real estate listings.

As her eyes began to burn, she scanned past an old advertisement, then paused and wound the knob backward to see the ad again. *Jackpot.* Three women were lined up across the page, their arms around each other's shoulders. They wore red-and-white dresses, knee-high boots, and little hats with a red flower on the front. Above their heads was the phrase, "Enjoy Friendly's Ice Cream—the best in town!"

She stared at the ad a moment, then scanned the following pages more slowly. Among articles of farmer's markets, housing prices, and a rare manatee sighting in the river, she saw several more ice cream ads, more photos of the Friendly

Girls, and a photo of Jay with one of the girls, a Trudy Figg, whom he eventually married. There was a short write-up in *The Observer* about their marriage, and how at the reception that followed an out-of-town wedding, they served ice cream in wineglasses.

She kept scrolling, but after the article about their wedding, photos of Trudy as a Friendly's Girl disappeared. Jay himself didn't seem to be in any more articles either. It wasn't until she was about to stand and take the slides out of the machine that she spotted his name one last time. She sat back down and read the article.

June 11, 1982—Jay Malone, owner of Friendly's Ice Cream, was last seen around midnight on Friday, May 16, leaving the Showboat on Little River. Witnesses report he was not alone when he left, and the motor of his single-engine fishing boat could be heard heading north on the river. No one has heard from him, and his boat hasn't been spotted anywhere on or near the river. Malone's wife, Trudy, too grieved to speak, has retreated to the home of her sister, Violet Figg. No evidence of foul play has been found.

Liza scanned back to the photo she'd seen of Trudy standing next to Jay. Jay's arm around her shoulders was affectionate, but now Liza noticed the indentation his fingertips made on the skin of her upper arm.

She sat back in her chair and stretched her neck. *Too grieved to speak*. What a strange phrase to use. Had she actually been unable to form words? Could grief do that, or was it something else?

At first glance Trudy bore the same wide CoverGirl smile that the other Friendly's Girls had sported, but when Liza peered closer, she picked up on something else. Call it a reporter's hunch, a premonition, or what have you, but what Liza saw in that woman's eyes was not joy or love or even happiness, despite her marriage to the man, despite the dazzling smile. Liza saw fear. Trudy was a woman on high alert, a woman wary of upsetting the man next to her.

Liza stood and pushed away from the table. She quickly pulled the slides from the machine and set everything back in its place. When she walked back to the front lobby, Emmajean was at the desk.

"Did you get everything you needed?"

"I think so. Thanks for your help." Liza was about to open the double doors to the parking lot when she paused. "Have you lived here long?"

"In Sugar Bend? My whole life. I was born on the river."

"Do you know what happened to Jay Malone? Was he ever found?"

Emmajean stilled. Finally she shook her head. "No one ever saw him again. I remember for a while there was a question of whether or not they were going to drag the bottom of the river to see if he'd drowned, but they never did. I'm not sure why. Eventually people just stopped talking about it."

"What happened to his ice cream stores?"

Emmajean shrugged. "They closed and that was that. Once Baskin-Robbins came in, no one cared anymore."

Liza sat in her hot car with the door open to release the wavy heat and let her thoughts settle. Could this be the story she'd been waiting for? A story bigger than feuding farmers and nosy neighbors? Maybe this was it.

She had a staff meeting at the paper in twenty minutes, but on her way back she pulled into the Sugar Bend police station. The woman behind the desk was as thick as a tree trunk, with a generous, sturdy chest and short, tight curls. When Liza mentioned that she was with the paper and had a question or two for a police officer, the woman sniffed.

"I'm afraid you'll have to call and make an appointment for that. We're pretty busy today."

Liza glanced behind the woman to the silent room. Three desks lined the wall, and a hallway at the back led to a kitchen, where the smell of burned coffee curled out of the doorway. She could see a single jail cell through a doorway at the back of the hallway. The cell was empty.

Just then, a young officer walked out of the kitchen, a Styrofoam cup to his lips. He swallowed and winced. "How long has this coffee been sitting here?"

"Well, let's see, I made it when I got in this morning, so . . ." The woman glanced at her watch. "I'd say about five hours. I only make one pot a day. You want any more, you best make it yourself." She shot a glance at Liza. "Boy's old enough to know how to make his own coffee."

"I heard that and I know how to make coffee, Fay."

"Good. Now, this lady here is wanting to ask you some questions. I told her she needed to make an appointment."

He raised his head and seemed to notice Liza for the first time. He straightened. "What kind of questions?"

"I'm with *The Sugar Bend Observer* and—"

"Police don't make a habit of talking to reporters," Fay interrupted.

Behind her, the officer laughed. "It's okay." He pointed to a chair in front of his desk. "You can come on back."

She hung her bag on the back of the chair and sat. The placard on his desk read *Officer Justin Roby*.

"Don't worry about her," he said loud enough for Fay to hear. "Her bark is worse than her bite."

"My bite is bad enough," Fay said. "I'll be in the kitchen, *not* making another pot of coffee."

When she was gone, he stuck his hand out. "I'm Justin. Sorry about all that." He sat back in his chair. "How can I help you? You said you're with the paper?"

"That's right. I'm doing some research on a story, and I'm curious about something. What would you say if someone had information about a missing-person case?" His eyebrows lifted a bit. "From forty years ago."

He laced his fingers together and rested them on the desk. "It depends. What missing-person case are we talking about?"

She puffed out a laugh. "You don't read *The Observer*?"

"Not really."

"Oh. Well, I found something that could, maybe, have something to do with a man named Jay Malone who went missing in 1982."

He sat forward in his seat. "Right, I did hear about this. It's the boat that washed up, isn't it? I asked my . . . well, I've been doing a little digging of my own. Are you just talking about the boat itself, or did you find something else?"

"I did find something else, but I don't know if it's—" She stopped when the squawk of a radio reverberated through the quiet office.

"Come in, Banger One, this is unit 4–5–0. We have a shoplifter speeding down County Road 40 with a tailgate tent protruding from both back passenger windows."

Fay ran up from the kitchen and pressed a button on the radio. "This is Banger One, go ahead, 4–5–0. Did you say a tailgate tent?"

"That's right. He stole a tent from Riverside Market and left with it sticking out of his car. He just sideswiped a truck carrying boxes of okra. Okra's all over the road, and it's a heck of a mess."

As Fay radioed back that an officer was on the way, Justin rubbed his head and stood. "Sorry, but I gotta go take care of this." He pulled out a card from his desk drawer and handed it to Liza. "This has my direct line. I'll be here until six this evening, then again tomorrow. Give me a call, and we can go over any information you may have."

As Liza was getting into her car a moment later, she heard

Fay call to Officer Roby from the door of the station, "If any of that okra's not smashed, think you can grab me some?"

⌒

The Sugar Bend Observer, Sugar Bend's Community News Source
Letter from the Editor, Liza Bullock
July 2022 | Volume 11, Issue 7

Since the news last month of a boat found in front of the home that once belonged to Friendly's Ice Cream owner Jay Malone, we've received many emails and messages regarding Mr. Malone. It seems some of you have long memories and remember the man who was often called "the friendliest guy in town," along with his subsequent mysterious disappearance.

Mr. Malone was known to have a beloved boat with a blue stripe across the side, and locals often saw him in it, fishing and cruising up and down the river. The boat that washed up onshore had that same blue stripe, and we're fairly certain the boat did belong to Mr. Malone. Despite its mysterious past, we're heartened to see the reappearance of the boat, and we will continue to keep you updated on new developments as they arise.

See you around town!
Liza

⌐⌐

Frank woke with a start in the middle of the night. His heart raced, sweat beaded on his scratchy upper lip, and his hand twitched as if yearning to reach for his nonexistent gun. He reached up and rubbed a hand over his forehead, absently smoothing down his flyaway hair.

The bracelet. He saw it in his mind, as clear as if he'd slipped it on Violet's wrist just the day before. He'd taken her to his parents' house—ostensibly for dinner, but mainly to introduce his boisterous family to the woman he hoped to marry one day. She'd been so nervous.

1982

"I don't know why I agreed to this."

Frank pulled his hand away from the doorknob of his parents' house in Pensacola and faced Violet. She'd clamped the collar of her jacket closed as a chilly wind bustled around them. He stepped closer to her and nuzzled his cold nose to her cheek. "Why are you so worried? They'll love you. Just like I do."

She whipped her head around and stared at him.

He lifted his eyebrows in laughter. "Are you surprised?"

The corners of her mouth dimpled and she leaned into him. When she spoke, her voice was muddled. "You love me?"

He leaned down until he met her eyes. "I do. I love you, Violet Figg."

"I love you—" He pressed his lips to hers, cutting off her words. A new urgency flowed through him, a desire that was nearly overwhelming. When he finally pulled back, she kept her arms tight around him. "They're probably expecting someone prettier. Or at least taller."

Frank laughed and put his mouth close to her ear. "You're perfect. Perfect for me. And they'll see that."

Before he'd pulled away from her, the front door opened and a burst of noise tumbled out. "Frank!" Pete bellowed. "Get in here and bring your woman with you."

Frank winced and glanced down at Violet, whose eyes were frozen open. All the Roby men were tall, but Pete's size even caught Frank off guard sometimes. His police uniform was tight around his shoulders, as if he'd grown even broader, and his leg muscles nearly overpowered the seams of his navy blue pants.

"Violet, this is my brother Pete. Pete, don't scare her."

"She doesn't look like she scares easily." Pete reached his hand out and took Violet's in his. "Good Lord, these are the tiniest hands I've ever seen."

"*Pete.*" Frank put an edge of warning in his voice, but Pete just winked at Violet, who grinned.

"Boys, let the poor girl in." Around the side of Pete's massive shoulder came their mother, with her curly hair and checkered apron tied around her middle. She shook Violet's hand. "I'm Glenda, and I have the distinct pleasure of being the mother of these boys." She rolled her eyes, then ushered Violet and Frank in. She kissed Frank on the cheek, then turned to Violet. "So you're the Violet who's stolen our Frankie's heart."

"Frankie?" Violet nudged him with her shoulder. "I didn't know you had a nickname."

"I don't," Frank said through gritted teeth. He put his hand on Violet's back and led her through the entryway and into the kitchen, where his father stood at the stove stirring something in a pot. "She put you to work, Dad?"

"I volunteered."

His mom snorted and eyed Frank. "I threatened to with-hold his dessert if he didn't help me with dinner." She grabbed Violet's hand and pulled her farther into the kitchen. "Violet, how do you feel about salad?"

Violet glanced back at Frank. "Um, I like it?"

"Great. Chop those tomatoes, will you, then drop them in the salad? No seeds though. No one likes those."

"Yes, ma'am."

"And while you're at it, tell me all about yourself."

Throughout dinner prep and dinner itself, Frank's family asked Violet every question under the sun, and for the most part she answered them with humor and honesty. Anytime they asked something specific about her family, she redirected the conversation back to Frank and his brothers, their work on the force, or what recipe Glenda used for the chicken. She did it so gracefully, the rest of his family didn't notice, but Frank did.

After driving her home that night, he parked in her drive-way and pulled a small velvet box from the glove compartment. Violet's breath caught when she saw it. "Frank?" Her voice held mild panic.

"Just open it." He set the box in her hand.

She lifted the lid. "Ohh," was all she could manage.

In the overhead light the little gold bracelet gleamed. Birds were engraved all around it, along with leaves, branches, and tiny berries.

"It reminded me of you." He took it from her hands and clasped it around her left wrist.

"It's the most perfect thing you could have given me." Her voice was hushed, reverent.

"I'd like to one day give you something that means a little more, but I figure this will tide us over until then."

She rotated her wrist, seeing the bracelet from all sides, then looked up at him. "Thank you. I'll wear it all the time."

They'd only known each other a few months, but already he knew he didn't want anyone else. He'd marry her right now if he could. It was like she'd changed the arrangement of his cells or the pattern of his brain waves—she'd etched herself into his mind and heart so indelibly, he couldn't imagine spending his life in any other way except by her side. He didn't know everything there was to know about Violet. Parts of her were still a mystery, but he was okay with that. If there were things she felt she still needed to keep close to her chest, he wouldn't pry. He'd be patient, and when she was ready to tell him, he'd be ready to listen.

eleven

R iver Days Art Festival," read the sign stretched across Water
Street between two light poles. "Art, food, and music—
meet us at the river!" As Maya parked on the street in front of
Two Sisters, she remembered the flyer she'd seen on the gas station door three months ago, the flyer about the art festival that
had caused her to point her car in the direction of Sugar Bend.
Actually it wasn't the flyer so much as the dreams it had stirred
up. Dreams, sensations, memories, she still wasn't sure what to
call what she'd seen in her mind, but she'd been following that
scent of belonging ever since.

An older gentleman strolled down the sidewalk in front of
the shops with a small dog on a leash, and two ladies came
out of the bakery a few doors down with sugar-smudged paper
bags in their hands. Maya loved early mornings in Sugar Bend
before the stores opened, when the dew was still fresh and the
day's heat hadn't set in quite yet. Violet had told her yesterday
that a shipment of cookbooks from local chefs was scheduled

to be delivered before the shop opened, and Maya had offered to come in early so Violet wouldn't have to.

Maya wanted to be helpful, but she also secretly loved being the only person in the shop. She liked to pretend the shop was hers, that she'd handpicked all the items to sell, chosen the paint colors for the wall, and hung the driftwood chandelier over the cash register herself. The truth was she was an eighteen-year-old girl with no family, a tiny rented room that smelled like shrimp, and a likely future of living paycheck to paycheck, but she loved to pretend she was capable enough to own and run her own business. To show the world she could do something with herself, could be someone though no one had ever believed in her. Well, except for her grandmother. And these two sisters.

The UPS man showed up at eight thirty. Maya signed for the delivery, opened the boxes, and walked around searching for the perfect place to display the books. As she moved through the shop, she trailed her fingers over rolled tea towels, delicate silver and mother-of-pearl jewelry, the sisters' clay pinch pots, and Trudy's mixed-media sculptures. Finally she found the perfect spot for the cookbooks, right next to the oyster shell–handled cheese spreaders and hand-turned wooden spoons. After that, she grabbed a broom and dustcloth and got to work.

Violet arrived at ten, just as Maya was propping the Open sign in the window.

"It looks nice in here." Violet slid her purse under the counter and tucked her hair behind her ear. Today she wore a khaki skirt, Chaco sandals, and a lilac button-down shirt. "Did you move some things around?"

"Just a little." Maya eyed Violet, trying to determine if she was annoyed or pleased. "I can move it all back if you want." She'd rotated a shelf of pottery toward the side wall to make room for the table holding the new cookbooks and kitchen utensils. Though the sisters tended to keep things the same, it made sense to Maya to move things around occasionally. Not so much that it confused regular customers but just enough to keep things feeling fresh. Maya had so many ideas for the shop, but she wanted to tread lightly.

"No, I think it's nice." Violet slowly scanned the shop. "Change isn't always a bad thing, is it?"

Running the shop required a whole lot more physical work than Maya had realized, and she sometimes wondered how Violet and Trudy had managed it for so long, just the two of them. Trudy often seemed strong enough to do the work of two people, but the truth was, neither of the two sisters was young enough to continue going at the pace they'd been working at for years.

Maya had only been at the shop for a month, but she loved every minute of it. She loved working side by side with Trudy as they tried shell after shell, feather after feather, to see where each abandoned item belonged in a particular piece of art. She enjoyed hand-selling particular items she'd purchase if she had enough extra money to buy something other than food and necessities. She loved feeling like a part of this vibrant little community. She even loved the mundane responsibilities like sweeping the floors, breaking down boxes, cleaning the huge front windows, and shutting down the register after closing time. And it was only then, late in the evening when the waning sunlight was amber and the shadows were long, or here in the dewy early morning sunshine, that she dared to imagine herself at the helm.

Despite the ominous warnings from everyone she'd lived with since the death of her grandmother, Maya had hopes for herself that kept her up at night. She wanted her life to mean something. She wanted purpose, a reason to get out of bed every morning, people who would miss her if she were gone.

She wanted a place to belong.

And here at the shop, she'd come as close to finding it as she'd experienced since losing her grandmother. Here in this small town, with these quirky people and these kind sisters, she was slowly realizing that maybe she could belong again. That maybe this could be the place for her. The place where she could be someone who mattered.

All day, Violet had been fidgeting. She picked at a fingernail, then drummed her fingers on the counter. Later, when she wasn't busy with customers, Maya caught her staring off into space, her lips moving in tight, nervous words. She'd rolled up a section of the newspaper and stuck it down by her purse, and every little while, she'd come back and scan through it again.

After lunch, Maya made a cup of peppermint tea and brought it to Violet. "Is everything okay? You seem a little distracted today."

"Hmm?" When Violet saw the mug of tea in Maya's hands, her shoulders dropped a little. "Oh, I'm fine. Just fine." Violet blew on her tea, sending peppermint-scented swirls into the air, then took a sip. "Well, I suppose I am distracted. The older you get, the more you have to think about."

"I saw a banner today for the art festival." Maya made her voice cheery to try to pull Violet from whatever malaise had gripped her. "What's it like?"

"All the shops close their storefronts and operate out of booths set up down near the river." Violet pulled a paper towel from the roll under the counter and swiped at the side table where the teapot was set up. "Then when the booths close down for the evening, they bring in food trucks and bands and it becomes a big street party."

"It sounds fun."

"Oh, it is." Violet balled up the towel and threw it in the trash can, a little harder than necessary.

"Does the shop have a booth?"

"Yes, we will." She seemed to snap back to reality. "And you'll be able to work that day, I hope. I can talk to your boss at the Shack if necessary. We could really use an extra pair of hands on the festival day."

"I'll make sure I'm here."

Maya left the shop on a high that night, her mind filled with possibilities for the festival and what products they'd heft down to the edge of the river to sell at their booth. When she arrived at the bait shop, however, she found Mr. Meyer standing at the top of the stairs outside the door to her small apartment.

He was fiddling with his fingers, his face mottled and damp. He didn't have to say any words. She already knew it'd be bad news.

He walked down the stairs toward her. "I was just leaving this for you at your door. I didn't want to miss you when you came in."

She reached for the envelope in his hands. "What is it?"

He pulled on his fingers so hard, she heard one of his knuckles crack. "I'm sorry to have to do this to you. You've been real good at paying your rent on time, better than most of the people who've stayed here, but my brother is coming back to town."

"Your brother?"

"Yes, and technically, he owns half of the bait shop business with me. It was our father's, you see. And he wants to live here." He flipped his hand around halfheartedly to the room behind him. "You'll need to find a new place to live. I'd be happy to talk to anyone and tell them what a great renter you are." The thought seemed to cheer him, or at least take away the sting of kicking her out.

"But I can't afford anywhere else."

"I'm so sorry." He twisted his hands again. "He'll be here next Saturday."

"A week? I have a week to find a new place to live?"

"I'm sorry." He was still saying it as he opened the screened door to the bait shop and disappeared into its fragrant depths.

The next day Maya worked a shift at Two Sisters in the morning, then an afternoon shift at the Sugar Shack before she was back at the art shop for an art class with Trudy at six thirty. The frantic pace of the day had left her no time to even think about finding another place to live, but the extra money at the end of the month would be nice. Anywhere else she lived would no doubt cost more than the spare room above Fritz's Bait Shop.

As she and Trudy prepared for class, filling small jars of shells, wood fragments, sea grasses, beads, and other odds and ends for the attendees, Maya could feel Trudy's stare on the tips of her hair and the back of her neck. Finally, she felt a jab at her elbow. Trudy held out a note.

Out with it. What's going on?

Maya exhaled. The first class attendees were just beginning to trickle in. "I have to move out," she whispered. "Fritz just told me last night."

Where are you going to go?

"I have no idea. He acted like I can go out and just find a new place, but has he even seen the rent prices of most places around here? Have you? They're insane." Her voice rose, and a man settling down in a chair at the end of one of the tables glanced up at her. Heat flooded her cheeks and she gave him an apologetic smile.

More students came in, and they started the class promptly at six thirty. Maya gave verbal instructions to the class as Trudy went around and pointed out various materials to the assembled students. Once the class got started, everyone's hands and mouths busy in work and quiet conversation, Maya stepped to the side and crossed her arms. A moment later, she felt Trudy at her elbow. Trudy reached an arm around Maya and squeezed. Maya leaned into her and rested her head on her shoulder. When she moved back, Trudy handed her a piece of paper.

You'll come live with us.

Maya read the paper, then stared at Trudy. "What? You can't say that."

Trudy pulled the pencil from her pocket. *I just did. It's done. You need a place and we have the room. Pack your bags.*

Trudy patted Maya's cheek, her hand rough and calloused, then walked back to the front table and sat down. Trudy often worked on her own sculptures while the class was working on theirs.

Maya's eyes blurred as she focused on the words, waiting for them to change into something else, to prove that this was too good a thing to be true for her. But they remained, stark graphite against the white paper. *It's done. Pack your bags.*

As Trudy showed the class a new technique she'd been using to fasten the most delicate shells to her sculptures, the door opened and someone slid into the room late. Maya grabbed an extra set of jars for the student and set them down on the table. When she glanced up in greeting, Tyler smiled back at her.

"Surprise," he whispered.

"What are you doing here?"

"You said I should try one of the classes." He shrugged. "So here I am." He took in the materials on the table in front of him. "Now, what am I supposed to do?"

"I told you. Just play." She smiled and walked back up to

the front of the room next to Trudy, who was holding up a length of wire with a collection of shells threaded onto it. A few moments later, the class got to work with their own materials. A student at the back of the room raised her hand, and Maya walked over to answer her question. As she did, she kept one eye on Trudy, who had opened the door and motioned for Violet to come to her.

"I brought this conch shell in that I found a few days ago," the student said to Maya, "but I'm not quite sure what to do with it."

Maya leaned down and picked a few smaller shells out of the woman's stash and added a handful of beads from one of the jars. As she spoke quietly to the woman, she saw Trudy hand Violet a piece of paper. Violet whispered something to Trudy, then they both glanced back at Maya, who quickly looked down. A moment later, Trudy closed the door and walked back up front. She caught Maya's eye and winked.

A laugh bubbled up in Maya and would have tumbled from her mouth if she hadn't clamped her lips closed. The weight of her worry evaporated, leaving something like giddiness behind.

"Excuse me, Teacher?" The voice came from the other side of the room. Tyler had his hand up in the air. "I have a question." When she reached his table he frowned. "I don't know what I'm doing." He had a large cockleshell in front of him, along with a few scattered coquinas, some dried seaweed, and a knot of fishing line. "I just put it all together but . . ." He laughed. "It's really ugly."

"Let's see what we can do." Maya reached past the man

next to Tyler and grabbed a few feathers and a couple other odds and ends, then pulled up an empty chair and sat next to him. "What happens if you put these feathers to the back of this pink cockleshell?" She played around a moment, then showed him.

"Hmm. Kind of reminds me of a hay bale with a chicken on top."

"That makes sense, coming from a guy in the world of farming."

"That's me all right. The next owner of Holt Feed and Seed." Tyler spun a shell around like a top.

"You don't seem too happy about that."

He lifted a shoulder. "It's just the way it is. My dad took over the store from his dad, and one day it'll be my turn." He pressed a feather against the cockleshell, then pulled it away and replaced it with an auger shell, but he didn't like that either. She slid a slim, curved piece of driftwood to him. He took it and fit it against the curve of the cockle.

"Is there something else you want to do instead of the store?"

"I don't know." He rotated the sculpture in his hands. "Teach." His voice was quiet. "I want to teach English."

"What age?"

His head snapped up, a quizzical look on his face, as if he'd expected her to respond in another way. "Middle school, probably. Kids that age are old enough to have really smart ideas but not so old they've checked out. I want to share good books with them and teach writing and ideas and have conversations." He shrugged again. "That probably sounds dumb."

"It doesn't sound dumb at all. Do you love what you do at the store? Do you love helping customers and selling seeds and, I don't know, feed?"

"I mean, I don't hate it, but no, I don't love it."

"Do you love teaching? Or at least the idea of it?"

He smiled. "Yeah. I do."

"Then it's clear. That's where you should be. In a classroom with kids."

He scoffed. "Try telling my dad that."

"Have you tried telling him?"

"I once mentioned going to college and getting my teaching degree, and he actually thought I was making a joke."

Maya nudged his shoulder. "Maybe you should try again. Because it sounds like your dad chose farming. You haven't. You can choose the way your life goes."

"What about you?" Tyler lifted his chin and peered at her with his deep blue eyes. "What do you want to do?"

In all her eighteen years, Maya hadn't spent much time thinking about what she wanted out of her future. She'd always been focused on the here and now—who she was living with and where and what might be coming next. Even when she lived with her grandmother, she always had the sense that it was temporary. For the first time possibly ever, Maya felt a measure of safety. Of security. And it was possible what she wanted most was not to leave.

But she couldn't say all that to this boy. Not yet, anyway.

Maya looked down at his sculpture. He'd continued attaching random pieces to his hay bale and now it resembled something like an octopus with a shell on each tentacle. "Right now what I want to do is help you with this octopus."

He laughed. "I thought it was a hay bale and a chicken."

"It was, but . . ." She grabbed hold of a feather on each side. "I think it's more surf than turf now."

Someone else asked her a question and she stood and walked over, feeling Tyler's closeness in every hair and nerve ending on her body. It wasn't too long before Trudy began walking student to student, writing notes of instruction about gathering materials and cleaning up. As she did this Maya handed out info sheets about the art festival, letting them know what to do if they wanted to sell any items at the festival.

By the time she made it back to Tyler, he was all cleaned up, his creation sitting proudly in front of him. "I'm definitely not entering this into any art show, but I think I like it."

"You should. It looks great." She waved to a group of students as they walked out, and as Tyler stood to leave, he put a hand on her arm.

"Some friends of mine are going out to Soldiers Creek tomorrow. Will you come with me?"

"Soldiers Creek?"

"You've never been? Everyone goes there. All the young people anyway."

She shook her head no. It had been a long time since Maya had been young.

"Well, that settles it." He grinned. "You're coming with me." His smile slid from his face. "Only if you . . . I mean, I'd like you to come, if you want—"

She laughed. "Okay. I'll come."

When he walked out a moment later, he waved over his shoulder and flashed a smile that warmed her all the way to her toes.

Violet was standing in her yard, her mind tangled in long-gone memories, her fingers idly rubbing the skin around her wrist. The bracelet had been there for such a short time, but in certain moments—like this calm morning tinged with the scent of brackish water, freshly cut grass, and jasmine blossoms—she could still feel its weight, the cool brush of metal against her tender skin. As she gazed out at the river, her mind spooled backward to another morning just like this one.

1982

Violet walked carefully through the grass around the side of the little cottage, birdseed in hand. She'd been collecting unique bird feeders for years now, and she had seven posted at various spots around her half acre. Each one attracted specific kinds of birds—the umbrella-shaped feeder hanging from the thick pine tree held safflower seeds for the doves and cardinals, the round feeder covered in blue mosaic glass staked near the hydrangeas was for the robins and jays, and of course, the bright red glass feeder up near the porch was for the hummingbirds.

She was just tipping seed into a ceramic feeder in the shape of a magnolia blossom when she heard footsteps behind her and smelled the nutty, caramelized scent of fresh coffee.

"I thought I'd find you out here." Frank reached around her and handed her the coffee mug, then kissed her. A sleepy, good-morning kiss. "Greeting the day and the birds." The sky behind him, peeking through the tree canopy, was a wash of pink sherbet, and a light breeze stirred the air.

"They expect me every morning now." She shifted the bag in her hand so the seed wouldn't spill, and as she did, the clasp on her bracelet—she hadn't taken it off since he gave it to her—came undone and it fell to the ground.

He retrieved it and slid it back on her wrist, then clicked the clasp together. "We certainly can't let them down, can we?" His fingers trailed across her skin, making her shiver. "How many more do you have to fill?"

"Four more."

"Show me where and how. Just in case I'm out here doing it on my own one day."

Warmth spread through her body, from her cheeks down, as they walked through the grass to the feeder hanging from a low oak branch. He was going to ask her to marry him, she was sure of it. She'd sensed it for a while now, the question waiting behind every word that came out of his mouth. It tried to elbow its way in every time they were alone together and all the other words fell away, but he hadn't let it out yet. Part of her was glad, but the other part wondered, *What are you waiting for?*

Violet often imagined what it would be like if they did

marry. Waking up together every morning and filling the bird feeders. Scrambling eggs and frying bacon hip to hip at the stove. Waiting up at night, wondering if he'd make it home safely after a night shift. Welcoming him back home with grateful arms and lips.

"I was accepted into the program," she said as she opened the lid of the feeder hanging under the oak and poured seed in. She'd been waiting for the right time to tell him, and though she wasn't sure this was it, the words fell out anyway. "In the Keys. It starts in two weeks."

He didn't say anything for a moment as he reached up and closed the lid, then took the bag from her and set it down. He laced his fingers through hers and pulled her close.

"I'll be gone all summer." Could she do it? Could she be away from him for that long, this man she was considering handing her future to? She'd never known a good man before him, and here she was, saying yes to a program that would pull her hundreds of miles away for three long months.

He leaned down and kissed each temple, then the edges of her lips, then finally kissed her on the mouth. His lips were warm and full. "I'm proud of you. You go do what you need to do, and I'll be here when you get back."

"What about coming to visit me while I'm gone? I think you'd like it there."

He grinned. "You say the word and I'll figure out how to get the time off. I'll be on the next plane south."

She leaned forward and pressed her cheek to his chest. His strong, steady heart thumped under her ear. As she leaned into him, she couldn't help but think of Trudy, stuck in her scary house with her equally scary husband. Violet had done everything she could think of to try to get Trudy away from Jay. She'd offered her home as a refuge, she'd offered to buy her a plane ticket so she could go far away, she'd even tried to confront him. But Trudy always brushed off the help. She explained it in all kinds of ways—she was fine, it was just a bad day, he had his good moments. But Violet wasn't stupid. Jay Malone didn't have good moments. All the ones he showed to the world were just that—a show. Trudy saw the real thing at home.

And Violet was the only one who could save her sister, if she could just figure out how to do it.

⌒

Violet heard a sound behind her, and there was Maya climbing out of her old car. She opened the back door and pulled out a large duffel bag, then slammed the door behind her. *Poor girl*, Violet thought. *Everything she has to her name fits into a single bag.* Before Violet could make her way through the grass and up to the house, Trudy walked out the back door, her arms outstretched.

After Fritz took the bait shop room back for his brother, Violet and Trudy had decided to ask Maya to move in with them. It was Trudy's idea at first, but the more Violet thought about it, the more she realized it was the obvious choice. The right choice. Their home—three bedrooms, quiet, with space to move around and *be*—had been a refuge for the two of them for decades. It was a place to retreat, to gather courage, to feel safe. And looking at Maya, this young, beautiful, lonesome girl, Violet knew she needed a place to call home.

The two sisters were getting up in years, too old really to be caretakers of someone so young, with so much life left, but there they were, walking into the little cottage by the river, the place they'd all call home. Three motherless women braving whatever came next.

Violet and Trudy had spent the day before sweeping and dusting, rearranging and cleaning, and now the house was as spiffed up as it had ever been. Violet walked behind Trudy as she fluttered up the hall to show Maya to her room at the end.

The scent of lavender floated from the attached bathroom, where Violet had unwrapped a new bar of lavender soap and placed it in a dish. Trudy had picked an enormous blue mophead hydrangea and placed it in a milk glass vase on the nightstand. The bed was made up with a rag quilt in shades of blue and green, and the dresser by the wall was bare except for a mirror and a glass tray.

"We didn't know how young people like to decorate their bedrooms, so we figured we'd let you decide if you want to make any changes."

Maya set her bag on the floor at the foot of the bed and smoothed her hand across the quilt. "It's perfect. I don't want to change a thing."

Trudy smiled and gestured for Maya to follow her down to the kitchen. Violet stood in the doorway as her sister, so full of light and energy despite her silence, led this young woman through their home and into their world.

Later the three of them poured tall glasses of iced tea and cut slices of pound cake for an afternoon snack. Violet watched as Trudy and Maya walked out to the porch side by side, Trudy's hand on Maya's back a small brush of motherly affection. On the porch Maya sat on one end of the swing and Trudy settled onto the other. From behind, Trudy's short, gray, out-of-control curls next to Maya's smooth, dark waterfall made them look like two mismatched bookends that somehow fit together perfectly.

twelve

On the drive to Soldiers Creek, with Ruby perched over her legs and hanging her head out the passenger window, Maya asked Tyler repeatedly to give her details about the place they were going. What would they do? How many people would be there? Did she have to swim? All he'd told her was to wear a swimsuit and bring sunscreen. He had a cooler in the back of the truck full of she didn't know what, but it didn't matter. She wasn't hungry or thirsty; she was nervous.

Tyler was easy to be around. He smiled a lot, he always seemed happy to see her, and conversation came easy now. They talked about books they'd read and reread, about Ruby, about his sister, Missy, and about Maya's vibrant grandmother and the bird that would sit on her shoulder. Tyler was a known factor, which made him increasingly safe. But he'd said a bunch of his friends would be there, and she didn't know them. Didn't know if they'd like her, if they'd accept her.

As the wind whipped her hair against her cheeks, she smoothed her shorts over her thighs. She didn't own a swimsuit cover-up, so she'd just worn shorts and a shirt over her swimsuit. And as for the swimsuit, she had no idea if it was in style or anything like what everyone else would be wearing. It was the only one she had—black and modest and purchased for a family lake trip a couple summers ago with a family that wasn't hers.

"They're going to like you," Tyler said, as if reading her mind. He did that a lot. "Don't worry. They probably won't even notice you."

"Ha. How can they like me if they don't notice me?"

"I don't mean that, I'm sorry. I just meant you'll be just another new person coming to the creek. It won't be a big deal."

But he chewed on the edge of his bottom lip, and his fingers beat a nervous staccato on the steering wheel. She had a suspicion her presence at the creek would be a big deal to someone.

Finally they pulled off the road onto a path through scrubby twisted oak trees and tall pines. It was shaded by climbing ivy that stretched from tree trunk to tree trunk, and a mixture of scents flooded the car—sweet honeysuckle, heady gardenia, and musky wisteria, though she saw none of those growing along the path. Every third trunk or so had a red piece of tape fastened around it, presumably leading them to where they'd end up.

After another minute of creeping through the trees, the path opened to a wide but shallow beach along the river. It was sort of like a cove—the shoreline was in the bright sun, but back from it just a little bit, the shade darkened everything to a cool blue. Cars, mostly trucks like Tyler's, were shoved under the trees like shoes under a bed, and kids were everywhere— lying on huge rocks in the sun, swinging from a long rope and splashing down into the river, dancing to music coming from someone's speakers, and congregating in groups talking. Maya's stomach churned.

Tyler climbed out of the truck, Ruby close on his heels. He walked around the truck and reached for her door handle, but before he could open it, they both heard a loud, feminine squeal. "Tyler!"

"And so the fun begins," he muttered as a girl came flying out of the trees in a few yellow scraps of nylon and flung herself at him.

"I didn't think you were coming!" Cassie peeled herself off his chest and tiptoed up to kiss him—right on the mouth, right there in front of Maya and everyone else. Maya's cheeks heated and she suddenly wished she was sitting on Violet and Trudy's back porch.

Tyler gently pried Cassie's hands from his shoulders. "Um, Cassie, you remember Maya." He opened Maya's door and extended his hand to help her out. He'd never done that before—was she supposed to hold his hand? She grabbed her bag holding her towel and a bottle of sunscreen and climbed down on her own.

"You brought her?" Cassie's gaze scraped Maya's body, starting with her toes and going up. Then, like a flipped switch, Cassie grinned and flicked her hair off her shoulder. "Welcome to the creek. You wanna try the rope swing?"

"Um, maybe later."

"Great. Y'all grab a drink and come hang out." Cassie turned and revealed her toned rear end barely covered by her bikini bottom. She sauntered toward a group gathered on towels in the sun on the other side of the beach and put her arm around another girl in an equally small bikini. Cassie leaned her head toward her friend, then they both stared back at Tyler and Maya.

"Well, you're right." Ruby ran up to them and Maya reached down to scratch her ears. "She probably didn't notice me."

Tyler laughed and took a step closer to her. "Look, Cassie doesn't matter. I'm glad you're here. Come on." This time she let him take her hand as he walked her over to a couple other groups of people. As he introduced her to everyone, most of them smiled and a few said hello, but for the most part, they went right back to their conversations, talking too loudly about touchdowns and fumbles, late-night parties and drunken brawls.

When they walked away from a particularly loud tangle of boys, she tugged him down so she could whisper in his ear. "These are your friends?"

He exhaled a puff of air from his nose. "They're guys I play football with, but . . ." He shrugged. Then he tipped his head toward a small group gathered on a rock at the base of the tree where the rope swing hung. He pulled gently on her hand and led her to the group. "These are my real friends." As he introduced her to each one—five guys and a couple girls—they all smiled at her, and she knew right away they were different. The tightness drained out of her neck and shoulders.

"Maya, what kind of music do you like?" One of the guys, Thomas, picked up his phone and scrolled.

"Uh, do you have any Beatles?"

"What self-respecting music man wouldn't have any Beatles?" Thomas tapped the screen and the funky intro to "Come Together" poured from a tiny speaker sitting on a higher rock behind them.

Tyler chuckled. "Thomas thinks he's a rock star."

"I am a rock star, man." Thomas shoved his sunglasses up to the top of his head. His floppy hair and goofy grin took away from any rock star persona he hoped to achieve, but Maya liked him anyway. "You should come hear my band play sometime," he said to Maya.

"What's the name of your band?"

"Right now we're Black Light Mailbox, but that's—" He stopped when everyone else laughed. "What? It's a rad name. People will remember it." Someone threw a flip-flop at him, and he grabbed it and threw it back. "You're right. It's terrible. We've got to come up with something else."

Tyler spread out a beach towel and gestured for her to sit. She lowered herself down and he sat next to her. For the next hour the conversation flowed like calm river water, and she was relieved to know all his friends weren't like Cassie. The whole time they were sitting, Cassie alternated between squealing from the rope swing and soaring into the water, and sunbathing on the sandy beach, on her stomach, with the back of her bikini top unfastened.

Later, Tyler pulled chicken salad sandwiches from the cooler in the back of his truck.

"Dude, did your mom make them?" Thomas grabbed a wax paper–wrapped sandwich. "I could eat five of these."

"His mom makes the best chicken salad in Sugar Bend." The girl next to her, Melissa, handed Maya a sandwich and a napkin. "I like your bathing suit, by the way."

"Thanks." Maya smiled as she unwrapped her sandwich.

"How long have you all been friends?" Maya asked Tyler a little later.

He glanced around the group. "I've known Thomas since preschool. His mom was my teacher. Davis and I played peewee baseball together. Melissa started at Sugar Bend Academy in third grade." He shrugged. "I guess we've known each other most of our lives."

"I've never known anyone that long."

Everyone else had started a robust debate over what Thomas should rename his band, and Tyler scooted a little closer to where she sat, back a little bit from the group. "What do you mean?"

"There's no one in my life who I've known forever. Everyone has come and gone." She chuckled. "Quickly."

"The foster system," he said quietly.

"Yep. Some kids get lucky and their foster parents adopt them. Well, if they're good people. They're not always good people."

"Have you lived with bad people?"

She blew out a laugh. "You could say that."

He reached over to the dog-bite scar on the side of her calf. She was embarrassed by it—it was still red and bumpy though it happened over five years ago. He traced the puckered skin with his finger, and goose bumps trailed behind his touch. When he pulled his hand away, she could still feel his fingers on her skin.

"They haven't all been bad. I've lived with some nice people."

"But you never stayed with them?"

"It just never worked out." She couldn't tell him about the things she stole, and how the families reacted when they realized the kid they'd kindly brought into their homes had been so sneaky and disrespectful.

"What happened to your parents?"

"They left early on. My dad before I was even born, and my mom when I was three. My grandmother and I never heard from her again. For all I know she's dead." Maya propped her knees up and wrapped her arms around her legs. "Or maybe she made another family. Who knows?"

"Tell me more about your grandmother."

"I lived with her after my mom left. She was great. She read cards for people."

"You mean like tarot cards? She was a fortune-teller?"

"Not really. She just gave people courage to do what they needed to do."

"I don't get it. So what did the cards say?"

"I think the cards were a prop, honestly. She'd just get a sense about someone, about what they might be struggling with or hoping for. And she'd help them figure out a way through it."

"Did she ever help you like that? Give you a not-prediction?"

Maya shrugged, her cheeks warming again.

"What was it?" He bumped his shoulder to hers, and sparks cascaded down from where their skin touched.

Maya closed her eyes, remembering one of the last times she saw her grandmother, when she was in the hospital with all kinds of tubes and lines coming out of her arms and hands. Maria had cupped Maya's cheek. *"One day your family will welcome you with open arms, Maya Papaya."*

Maya sighed. "She just told me I'd have a family one day. See? Definitely not a fortune-teller."

"You're eighteen, Maya. Your life isn't over yet." Tyler popped his last bite of sandwich into his mouth, then stood. He reached his hand down for her to take.

"Where are we going?"

"You'll see."

Next thing she knew, she was clinging to the thick, scratchy rope swing, her feet perched on the huge knot at the bottom. Tyler was standing on the rock, holding on to the rope and counting. When he got to three, he jumped on the opposite side and together they soared over the sand, then the glittering green-blue water.

"Now! Let go!"

She released her tight grip and fell toward the river's surface. It was both terrifying and exhilarating. A second later she splashed down, the water catching her like a soft, cool hand. When she popped back up to the surface, Tyler was already there, grinning and shaking water from his hair. She treaded water, her arms and legs moving in tandem to keep her afloat, then she started swimming back toward shore.

"Maya?" he called behind her. "Are you okay?" He appeared next to her, his arms slicing through the water to keep up with her. "I'm sorry, I shouldn't have made you do it. I know it's really high up."

Finally she made it to the shore. She reached up and squeezed her hair, then grabbed his hand. "I want to do that again."

⁓

Later, as they packed Tyler's cooler into the back of his truck and peeled their damp beach towels from the rock, Maya heard Cassie's voice. Cassie had eyed them all afternoon as she'd lain in the sun, laughed with friends, and danced in truck beds. Maya had also seen her tipping more than a few beer bottles back, and the way she stepped through the sand with exaggerated care told Maya all she needed to know.

"Tyler, will you come talk to me a minute?" Tyler glanced at Maya, but Maya kept her eyes on the cooler where she was scooping out melted ice. "It'll be real quick," Cassie said.

Tyler sighed and followed Cassie to the tree line on the other side of the rope swing. Their voices were low at first, but as Cassie grew more frustrated, she spoke louder. Maya tried not to listen, but it was hard to miss what she was saying.

"She's not your type, Ty. She's not one of us. She doesn't know you like I do."

Cassie stopped talking and Maya took a chance and peeked over her shoulder at them. Cassie ran a finger down the side of his face.

"You don't know me that well," Tyler said.

"I do." Cassie pressed herself against him, still wearing nothing but her bikini.

"Cassie, stop."

Maya let the lid of the cooler fall shut and climbed in the passenger seat of the truck where Ruby was already waiting. Through the open window Maya heard their low voices again. She reached over and ran her hand down Ruby's soft back.

Despite their conversation and fun during the day, Maya and Tyler were mostly quiet on the way back to Violet and Trudy's house. The noise of the wind distracted her from the silence between them, but only for so long.

"Why are you with her?" she finally asked, her gaze focused out the window. She didn't say Cassie's name, but she didn't need to.

"I'm not with her. I'm with you."

Maya turned and raised her eyebrows at him.

"Or I'm . . . well, I—I'd like to be with you."

His stumbling was cute, but it didn't matter. "She thinks she belongs with you."

"Cassie thinks she belongs with everyone. That she can have anyone and anything she wants."

"That's probably because she usually gets it. Am I right?"

He lifted a shoulder. "Pretty much."

"What do *you* want?" she asked him when they stopped at a red light near downtown Sugar Bend.

The way he stared at her sent ripples of heat through her belly and out to her fingertips. She kept her gaze on him as long as she could, then faced out the window again.

"I don't belong with Cassie," he said as the light turned green. "That much I know." He paused. "Do I belong with you?"

Above them, a handful of brown pelicans flew in a V, each

one flapping its wings in tandem. The warm air was thick and salty and Maya drank it in.

"I don't know yet," she said.

———

Every week, Frank looked forward to driving down to the beach, walking between the two condo towers, and seeing the first glimpse. Not of the wide blue Gulf or the sugar-white sand, but of Violet in her green sun hat, freckled arms, and bare feet. It reminded him of long ago when just the thought of her sent sparks of hunger and longing through his body. Honestly he was surprised that after all this time, the sparks were still there. A little muted, maybe, by time and life and choices, but there nonetheless. And gaining in strength every time he saw her.

They'd started talking some, as they walked the two miles in the wet sand and counted the birds. They talked about their lives and the directions they'd gone—Violet from teaching to living with her sister to co-owning the art shop, and Frank from the Sugar Bend police department to the precinct in Pensacola to retirement. He'd met Alice at a bowling alley and, within a year, had married her and started a family. He found himself wanting to admit to Violet that he hadn't truly been in love with Alice, that he'd married her primarily because she was a nice, pretty woman and he'd wanted children and a family of his own so badly. But he didn't want to dishonor the woman he'd been married to for thirty-three years.

Today was a survey day, and Frank was just walking out

the door of his house when the phone rang in the kitchen. He paused, then opened the door again and grabbed the phone. Violet told him she couldn't make it to the survey this morning.

"Is everything okay?"

"It's fine." He waited through a heavy pause. "I'm just busy at the shop. The festival is coming up, you know, and there's a lot . . ." She trailed off.

"Violet?"

"Do you remember how to log in your data back at the office?"

She'd taken him to the Audubon office the other day to show him how to enter his findings into the data system. It was an easy enough process, one he could have figured out on his own, but he let her walk him through the whole thing, asking a question here and there, until she was comfortable with his proficiency.

"I remember."

"Good. Then I'll just plan to see you next week."

"Violet, are you . . . ?" The *sure* scrambled away before he could say it. Violet was a strong woman, always had been, and the years hadn't worn away the armor she wore to show everyone she could handle everything. He didn't want to sound like he didn't believe her . . . but he didn't believe her. "If I can do anything, you'll let me know?"

"Of course. Thanks."

So Frank walked the morning survey on his own. He made sure to do everything exactly as Violet did it—slipped his shoes off on the wooden walkway, paused at the lounge chair to pull out his clipboard and flip to a fresh page, made the initial notes about cloud cover, precipitation, beach conditions, and wind speed. Then he started walking.

The birds were out en masse this morning, despite a large group of early sunbathers setting up umbrellas and towels and tossing beach balls on the sand. A large gray heron stood among the dunes to his right, its thin neck a dark line against the waving, wheat-colored sea oats. Twelve tiny sandpipers dotted the shore, their thin beaks quickly darting into the wet sand to grab the clams that scurried under the surface after each wave receded. Three gulls, two males and a female, ran just ahead of him, daring him to get any closer to them. When he did, they cackled and took flight.

He and Violet always turned around at the chair-rental stand, but today he went a little farther. His leg felt strong and he wasn't ready to return to his quiet, empty house just yet. He was having dinner tonight with his son, but he had a lot of solitary hours to get through before meeting him at seven o'clock. He laughed to himself when he realized he considered the birds decent company. Violet had said the same thing just a few days ago.

When his data sheet was almost full, he turned around and headed back. Passing the rental stand again, he thought of that sliver of space where he'd once tucked the bird-shaped shell. The space was empty, of course. He'd come back to that spot soon after . . . well, after everything happened . . . and reclaimed the little shell. It had accompanied him to Pensacola when he moved, and he'd even kept it through the years he was married to Alice. He never looked at it, but he knew it was there, buried in the bottom of a shoebox full of random things he'd emptied from an old desk drawer. He'd brought the box back to Sugar Bend with him when he relocated, and it sat in his closet now, quiet as a promise.

When he left the beach, he drove to the office and logged in his data, then drove back home. A local news program came on every morning at ten—it caught him up on everything he needed to know in less than thirty minutes. That was about all the news he could handle these days.

He checked his watch: 9:55 a.m.

Two Sisters also opened at ten. He could skip his morning news and instead purchase one of those new cookbooks they had in the front window. He wasn't a half-bad cook, but maybe it was time he learned to cook something more adventurous than grilled chicken and a decent steak.

He chuckled and filled a glass of water at the sink. Here he was, sixty-seven years old and trying to come up with an excuse to go see a lady. He set the glass by the sink to use later, then sat at the table to stretch his leg. The most recent *Sugar Bend Observer* was there on the table, so he pulled it toward him. *The Observer* was okay—it wasn't the same as the paper he used to read, but then again, none of them were. He missed the days when he got a daily newspaper, chock full of everything he needed to know and then some. Now the papers came so infrequently, the news they reported was like days-old coffee, forgotten in the bottom of the pot.

He paged through the paper and skimmed the headlines:

"Things to Do in Sugar Bend This Weekend." "Public Meeting August 15 to Discuss New Community Park." "Raccoons Terrorizing Phoenix Bay Neighborhood." "The Mystery of the Old Boat Continues."

He sat up straighter in his chair and peered closer to read the small print under that last headline. "Jay Malone's boat that washed up in Little River continues to perplex Sugar Bend residents, who wonder how his boat got there and how it sunk in the first place. As if that wasn't mysterious enough, a new piece of the puzzle has been discovered sitting in a dry box in the side of the boat's hull—a delicate gold bracelet engraved with birds."

Frank's eyes blurred as he read the words. He saw the downtown jewelry store, saw himself standing by the display cases, his forehead damp with perspiration as he scanned the velvet cases for a gift for Violet. The gold bracelet, etched with birds in various states of flight, had seemed perfect for her. How in the world had it found its way into Jay Malone's boat?

Then, with sickening clarity, he knew. *It was him. This is who she left me for.*

It was a gut punch, realizing why she'd pulled away. And the worst part was, he'd met the man. That night at his house—the boat in the yard and the smudge of blue paint on his forehead. The woman standing at the window and the screams of the foxes in the woods.

Jay was a married man, with his wife in the upstairs window, worry painted on her face, and yet Violet had been with him? How could that be?

A paper napkin lay on the table in front of him. Frank took it and slowly, methodically, folded it in half, then in half again. Smaller and smaller he folded it until it was the size of a quarter, then he clenched his fist around it, his knuckles protesting against the crush. In the middle of his sunlit kitchen, he closed his eyes. He wanted to go straight to Violet and ask her. After all, maybe he was wrong.

But another, meaner part of him wanted to sit in his hurt and feel it. To stew in self-pity for a while, to lick his wounds and his battered male pride. It was childish, yes, possibly even cruel, but deep in his heart, he felt the betrayal like he was still a hopeful twentysomething, high on love and the future he wanted with Violet.

He didn't go to Two Sisters that morning, and he didn't switch on his news program. He sat in his chair at the table until the shadows grew long, mourning the loss of that long-lost future and the woman he'd once—and still—loved.

thirteen

With nerves jangling like live wires, Violet couldn't shake the feeling that things were coming loose. Everything had been fine until that first set of fish bones showed up on her top step earlier in the summer. She'd known they were an omen as soon as she saw them, but she tried to ignore that particular feeling in her gut. Then the boat had washed up, the reporter started talking, and now there was the bracelet. Coincidence or connection, she didn't know, but it sure felt like more than she could handle.

Yesterday she was supposed to have met Tyler at the house to show him where the eight-foot ladder was so he could clean out her gutters, but as she approached the house, she saw a van in her driveway with the words *Action 10 News* on the side. She drove right on past her wisteria arbor and didn't stop until her stomach grumbled, signaling she'd missed dinner.

She drove back home, thankful to see the driveway empty, only to find the tiniest set of fish bones yet—barely the length of her thumbnail—sitting on the base of a mason-jar bird feeder hanging from the magnolia in the driveway.

Today she was at the shop, pretending everything was fine, though the way she kept catching Trudy, and even Maya, glancing at her, then quickly averting their eyes, she knew she wasn't fooling anyone.

Just before lunch, the door to the shop opened and the bell hanging over the door tumbled to the ground in a noisy heap. Violet had startled so badly she cracked her elbow against the corner of the counter. When she turned, rubbing her screaming elbow, it was just Tyler. He scooped up the bell and rehung it, apologizing and smiling at Maya all at the same time.

As Tyler and Maya headed to the back, Trudy nudged Violet's arm and handed her a slip of paper with raised eyebrows. *What's going on with you?*

"I'm perfectly fine," Violet retorted. "That blasted bell just scared me."

You're jumpy.

"I am not jumpy. I am sixty-six years old. I don't jump."

A muffled snort of laughter came from Trudy. Violet stared at her sister, but before she could say anything, Tyler walked back to the front of the shop. "I'm going down to the Shack for a quick bite to eat. Can I bring y'all some lunch?"

"That'd be great," Maya said. "Let me grab my purse."

"It's okay. I got it. What about you two?" He tipped his chin toward Violet and Trudy. "Can I get y'all anything?"

Trudy nodded and reached for the pad of paper on the counter, but Violet stopped her. "You know what? Why don't you both go with Tyler and eat there. I'll keep an eye on things here."

"Better yet, why don't you come with us and we'll flip the Closed sign around for half an hour," Maya said. "People will understand."

"No, you all go on. I'll wait here. Just bring me some catfish and a lemonade."

With the three of them gone and the shop empty of customers, Violet exhaled in the stillness. Her hands were shaky, so she busied them by grabbing a duster and moving through the shop, dusting and refolding and adjusting. After a few minutes, her hands calmed and her breathing slowed, as it always did when she meandered between the racks and shelves in Two Sisters.

When the bell jangled a moment later, she smiled, ready to greet her next customer. But she felt certain the man who stood just inside the door wasn't a regular customer.

The police officer was young, with light blond hair, a strong jaw, and broad shoulders. His uniform was crisp, navy, and official.

Violet's heart stumbled. "Can I help you?"

"Hello. I'm looking for a Trudy Figg. Is she here?"

"I'm sorry, she's not." She didn't mention Trudy was just down the street. Violet prayed for a long lunch line.

"Are you her sister, by any chance?"

Violet straightened her shoulders. "I am. I'm Violet Figg."

"Violet, I'm Justin." He offered a small smile. "I just have a few questions. Would you mind if I run them by you?" He was already pulling a small notebook from his chest pocket.

He clicked the button on his pen and wrote something on the top page.

"What is this in regard to?"

"Earlier in the summer, I was trying to find information about some car burglaries in town when I ran across a photo of a boat that had washed up in the river. I'm sure you've heard about it by now. Seems like everyone has." He rubbed his forehead with the back of his wrist. "It shouldn't have been anything—things wash up in the river all the time—but after a little digging, and a very persistent newspaper reporter, I'm . . . well, I'm starting to wonder if this is more than just an old, forgotten boat."

"What do you mean?"

"It seems the boat belonged to a man who disappeared a long time ago. Around about forty years, actually. Man by the name of Jay Malone."

The way he watched Violet told her he expected the name to have a particular effect on her, but she kept her expression as placid as possible. "Oh?"

"Yes, ma'am. The case was closed not too long after he disappeared—seems there were some debt issues, and at the time there was no suspicion of foul play. The boat was never found and he was never heard from again. Now correct me if I'm wrong, but I believe your sister, Trudy, was married to Mr. Malone. Is that correct?"

With her throat suddenly as parched as dry pavement, Violet swallowed hard, a minute movement that did not go unnoticed by this young man. She dipped her head in assent.

"I looked back in our records from the years when

Mr. Malone and your sister were married, and they showed that an officer was called to the Malones' house one night, obviously before Mr. Malone disappeared. A neighbor claimed she heard a woman in distress."

A woman in distress. Violet's hands began to shake, and she clasped them together behind her back. "Did the officer find anything?"

Justin's gaze flicked down to his notepad. "Not exactly. The officer's report stated that the neighbor had heard a couple of foxes in the woods. He didn't find anything else amiss." He clicked his pen—once, twice. "Is there anything you think he should have found there?"

But Violet barely heard him. She was remembering the single time she had tried to involve anyone else in her attempts to help Trudy. The police, sworn to protect and serve, to give aid to those who need it. But what she found was condescension, arrogance, and thinly veiled ridicule. A veritable boys' club. *"Jay Malone is one of Sugar Bend's most upstanding citizens . . . You should think twice about coming in here and placing blame on an innocent person."*

"Ms. Figg?" Justin's voice roused her from the past, bringing her squarely back to the middle of her shop, standing before an officer from that very same police department where she'd been swiftly disregarded and shown the door. "Is it possible that officer missed something?"

"I don't know what you're talking about." Violet picked up her duster where she'd set it down on a table and continued her dusting.

Justin shuffled his feet. "It was my uncle, actually, who visited the house. He's the officer who made the report. Frank Roby."

Violet froze. Frank? "Your uncle is Frank Roby?"

Justin nodded.

"When did you say he visited the house?"

He gazed at her a moment before he flipped a page in his notebook. "It was 1981. Mid-November."

She'd gone to the police close to Christmas, and she met Frank at the Sandbar for the first time just after the new year.

"Do you know anything about your sister being mistreated?" His voice was professional, curt even, but there was a kindness in his eyes that nearly brought tears to hers. He had his uncle's eyes.

"I—I don't . . ." Her mind spun and her fingers went to her throat. The clammy hand squeezing, the bruises, the blood.

And no one willing to believe her.

Justin—*Justin Roby*, she now read on his silver name tag—scribbled something on his pad. "Do you think she could have tried to take matters into her own hands?"

"Wh—what are you talking about?"

He held his hand up. "I'm just trying to get to the bottom of what might have happened."

"Is it even possible . . . ? I mean, after all these years, is there anything that can be done? Even if you did find out new information? It was forty years ago. You said so yourself."

"Well, it depends on what we find. New evidence could open the case back up again. A new witness account or new information that was previously withheld or unknown."

Blood roared in her ears, and Violet gripped the edge of the display table to keep herself grounded in the here and now. "It was a long time ago."

"You're right."

"My memory isn't the best." It was a lie—her memory was impeccable, especially when it came to the events surrounding Jay Malone.

"I understand," Justin said. "And I'm sorry to trouble you with what is I'm sure a difficult memory for both you and your sister. Just one more question for now and I'll be out of your hair." One more glance at the notepad. "Your sister came to live with you after Mr. Malone went missing."

"Is that your question?"

"I guess not. I just wonder. A grieved wife, her husband gone missing." He paused, a finger on his chin. "If there had been anything to—well, to confess, for lack of a better word. I wonder if she would have talked to you about it."

Violet's jaw went hard. "I assure you, Mr. Roby, my sister had nothing to confess, and anything she might have said to me about the state of her heart remains between Trudy and me."

"Of course. I'm sorry to even have to ask."

The strange thing was, he actually did look remorseful, as if his duty to ask the questions had somehow taken something out of him. He clicked his pen one last time and slid it back in his chest pocket. "If I have any other questions for you, may I contact you again?"

"It's a free country, but I can tell you, I won't have any more answers."

He nodded. "I'll be on my way then." He walked out, crossed in front of the large windows, then disappeared. It wasn't any time at all before Trudy and Maya walked in, all smiles and laughter. If they'd been just a few seconds quicker, they would have met Justin in the doorway. Violet forced herself to breathe normally.

"Violet, we had the best idea for our booth at the festival." Maya set her bag behind the counter. "We're going to wrap twinkle lights around tennis balls and hang them from the top of the tent like stars. Don't you think that'll look cool?"

Violet didn't—couldn't—answer. She opened her mouth but nothing came. Then Trudy and Maya were both at her side, having rushed to her when they realized something was wrong.

"What is it?" Maya asked. "Did something happen?" She scanned the room, as if expecting the trouble to be there in the shop. She didn't understand.

Trudy pressed a note in her hand as Maya asked more questions, her lips moving in quick concern, but all Violet could hear was the flutter of a thousand wings as everything she'd built to protect Trudy, all she'd done to keep her safe, everything good they'd built in their lives now, lifted off the ground and flew away.

1982

The departure date for her three-month field study program in the Florida Keys was rapidly approaching, and Violet had yet to pack. Every time she pulled out her suitcase and tried to fill it with her walking shorts, water shoes, binoculars, and visor, something would pull her away and she'd come back hours later to an empty suitcase and clothes strewn all over her room. She kept trying to do it, but it kept not happening, and she couldn't even blame her busy schedule. Yes, the school year was wrapping up in the usual frenzy of tests, report cards, school parties, and phone calls from nervous parents, but it was more than that.

It was Trudy.

Things with Jay were deteriorating, though Trudy hadn't spoken a word of it to Violet. Rather, Violet understood the situation by the streaks and colors on Trudy's skin each time she visited. The fact that Violet had been so fooled by Jay—*Jay's different. He's a good one*—coupled with her inability to do anything about the situation had made Violet restless, irritable, and easily distracted.

But even still, when Frank asked her to meet him at the Sandbar one night after his shift ended—and at the stool where she'd been sitting the night they first met, no less—Violet knew what was coming. She'd seen a small blue box on his bedside table a few weeks before when they'd cooked dinner at his house and she passed his bedroom on her way to the bathroom. Her breath had evaporated in wisps of steam but she kept quiet, not wanting to spoil any surprise he had.

Facing a possible engagement of her own, and in a flash of sisterly affection, Violet wanted nothing more than to talk to Trudy about it. Though she knew it wouldn't happen this way, she couldn't help but imagine she and Trudy sitting shoulder to shoulder on the couch, trading secrets and giggling like the carefree schoolgirls they would have been if they'd been born into a different family, with a different set of circumstances.

Usually Violet called before she visited, a rule Trudy made her swear to abide by, but this particular evening, the night before she was to meet Frank, Violet broke the rule. With her stomach fluttering she raised her hand to knock on the door. Before she touched the polished wood, it opened in a rush and there stood Trudy, wearing the finest dress Violet had ever seen. Short, red, and glittery, with puffed sleeves and a low neckline, it fit her every curve and set off the pink tones in her skin, yet the barely concealed panic in her eyes turned Violet's blood to sand.

"What is it, Tru?" Violet whispered. "What's wrong?"

Tears pooled in Trudy's eyes and she quickly flicked them away. She glanced sideways at something Violet couldn't see. "It's fine," she said brightly. "We were just headed out to dinner."

"Why don't you come home with—" Before Violet could finish, Jay's face appeared around the edge of the door and he snaked his arm around Trudy's slim waist. He was handsome as always, his dark, floppy curls set against his tanned skin, his smile as wide as the sky.

"Everything okay here, love?" He pulled his gaze away from Violet and kissed Trudy's cheek. "You're not upsetting my wife, are you, Violet?" He gave a small chuckle to soften his words, but Violet felt their sting anyway.

"*I'm* not upsetting her." Violet squeezed her hands into fists and shoved them into the pockets of her shorts.

"Well, I'm glad. Trudy and I are just heading out for a dinner party, and I'd hate for her not to have a good time." He opened the door wider and she saw he was dressed in a crisp dark suit. His shirt underneath was bright white, and when he lifted his hand to brush Trudy's hair back off her shoulder, his cuff links caught the light, sparking a flash at his wrist. They were tiny fish bones, shiny silver from head to tail. Such a strange thing to have on cuff links, so macabre, but Violet couldn't tear her eyes away.

"You sure, Trudy?" Violet asked one last time. One last chance for her sister to be strong, to take the step she needed to save her own life. But Trudy just nodded, a quivering smile on her face.

Any hope Violet had had of sitting and talking with her sister, hip to hip, heart to heart, dissipated as anger rolled through her like a thunderhead over the water. She'd done all she could do, short of dragging Trudy by the arm down the driveway and into her car. Jay would surely have something to say about that, and who knew, maybe Trudy would too.

Violet turned and walked back to her car, each step a defiant shout at the deceptively charming cottage behind her, the woman too scared to leave, and the man who'd charmed them both.

In her car she glanced in her rearview mirror before she turned right at the end of the street. Jay stood next to Trudy, his arms crossed, and Violet could have sworn she still saw the shiny, grim bones on his wrist winking in the sun.

Three hours later, she still couldn't get it all out of her mind—Jay's wide, affable smile under those dark, ice-chip eyes. Trudy's obvious discomfort. His fingers pressed tight against her sister's side. And those ominous little cuff links. Such a small thing, but she couldn't stop seeing the flash of them in her mind.

She knew if she went home, she'd just pace and worry, so she just kept driving, windows down, her hair whipping around her neck and against her damp cheeks, her mind working overtime. It was nearly ten o'clock when she made her way back up to Jay and Trudy's street, her foot soft now on the gas, creeping the car to a stop just a little way down the road from their house.

Violet's stomach was a mess now, nervousness swimming with anger and frustration, but when she knocked softly on the door and Trudy opened it, everything else fell away. Blood carved a path on the left side of Trudy's face, from her hairline down to her jaw. Her bottom lip was swollen and split, and she was stooped over, both arms around her middle. Her perfect red dress was ripped at the side.

"Trudy," Violet whispered. "Where is he?"

"He's not here," Trudy mumbled, her lips barely opening as the words slid out. "Showboat."

A curse fell from Violet's lips as she led Trudy to the kitchen for a wet rag. She dabbed the corner of it to Trudy's cheek, but she winced and pulled away. After a few minutes, Violet had cleaned off most of the dried blood and sat Trudy down on the couch with a juice glass of whiskey she found in the pantry. "Drink this, and hold this to your head." Violet pressed the damp cloth into Trudy's hand, but she just stared off into the distance.

"He'll be home soon." Trudy's lips were so puffy, her words were nearly incoherent as they came out.

"Don't worry about him." Violet leaned down and made her sister focus on her. "I'll take care of it. And I'm going to take care of you, Trudy. I promise."

Leaving Trudy on the couch with a promise to return, Violet walked out the back door and down to the dock to wait. Anger and hatred simmered inside her like a soup pot left on a hot eye. She was no stranger to anger or hatred, but this was something altogether different. This sensation had shape, taste, heat. And her guilt was a bitter root through it all.

At least she's safe. The bruises might have been shining even in the dim lamplight, the edges already beginning to darken, but inside the house, her sister was safe. Violet would make sure of that.

With shaking fingers, she caressed the simple gold bracelet around her wrist, the delicate birds engraved on it, the clasp that opened a little too easily. She lifted her chin to face the dark sky, hidden behind thick fog, and thought of the man who'd given it to her. He was so kind, so good. As far as he knew, she was the nice girl he was planning to propose to tomorrow night. He had no idea the volume of hatred that lived inside her right this minute.

She traced the edge of the bracelet over and over like a prayer, until her breathing slowed a beat. Then the tinny whine of an outboard Evinrude made its way up the river toward the dock where she stood. Her heartbeat thudded again in her ears, and she clasped her hands together to stop the nervous tremors.

Jay gazed at Violet as he pulled his boat alongside the dock where she stood, willing her five-foot-one stance to look as imposing as possible. Her resolve wilted only a little when Jay silenced the motor and filled the ensuing quiet with a deep rumble of laughter.

"S'a long way from your classroom, Violet. What'cha doin' out here so late at night?" His words slurred together, lazy and careless. He still wore his suit jacket, the cuff links pulsing faintly at his wrists, but his white shirt was unbuttoned, exposing a stretch of pale skin all the way to the waistband of his pants. His cheek was streaked with a smeared kiss of coral lipstick.

"I came for my sister."

"I thought you were the smart one." Jay looped a coil of rope around a piling and stepped one long leg up onto the dock. "Can't you see she's not down here? She's probably right where I left her." He swung the other leg up, swayed a moment, then came to a stop right in front of her.

She didn't flinch, though she was revolted at the scent wafting off him—cigarette smoke mixed with coconut, sweet and feminine.

"You gonna have a little heart-to-heart with your sister? A little late-night chat?" He leered and leaned toward her. She put a hand up and shoved his shoulder away from her.

"Feisty. I knew there was something about you I liked."

Violet's stomach rolled. "I came for you too. To tell you you're done with Trudy. She's going to leave with me tonight, and you're not going to come after her." Her words were steel, cold and sure.

He raked his hand through his hair, curls in disarray. He chuckled. "Is that so?"

She lifted her head defiantly. "Yeah. It is."

"Go on home, Violet." He pushed past her and started for the house.

As she dragged the thick night air deep into her lungs, she recalled the sight of Trudy's face: her split lip, the bruise swelling her left eye and temple, her hair sticky with blood. If only Violet had done a better job of protecting her sister, if she'd followed her gut, if she'd whisked Trudy away when she had the chance.

It had been her job to protect her little sister, but she'd failed. She'd let Trudy down and neglected to do the one thing her mother had asked of her, her guilt pressing down heavy on her slim shoulders.

She couldn't change what had already happened, but she sure could make a change now. It might have been all Violet's fault—Trudy's broken face and heart, this night, this despicable man—but tonight it would end.

Hot rage erupted inside her at the sight of him lurching up the dock toward the house. Toward Trudy. It was so quick, like she'd been a match just waiting for a flick of the wrist and the spark. She took three long steps toward him and grabbed his arm. Under her fingers, his muscles strained against his shirt, but she didn't let go, instead pulling and flinging him around.

"What the hell?" He stumbled over his feet and one knee came down hard on the weathered wooden boards. "What's wrong with you?" He grunted and swung an arm up blindly. His hand connected with her cheek and a half cry, half groan escaped her mouth. Black spots tunneled her vision, and by the time she regained her footing and sight, he was on his feet again, lips pulled back over his teeth.

"You will *not* hurt my sister again." With each word she pounded on him—his shoulders, his neck, his chest, his head—as waves of anger caused her hands to do things that shocked her.

Outraged, he roared and grabbed her wrists, squeezing tight. Then he shoved her onto the dock, her backbone pressed into the wooden boards, and wrapped his hands around her neck. His clammy, calloused fingers pressed on her windpipe as the black spots crept in again, blurring her sight.

Reaching up, she clawed at his neck, his forehead, his eyes, anywhere she could reach. Blood dripped from his cheeks onto her face, but he didn't stop squeezing. Just as the spots threatened to overtake her vision completely, she gave a final stretch, grabbed his neck, and sent all the strength she could muster into her hands, her fingers.

His eyes bulged and with a muffled groan, he collapsed on top of her, deadweight.

Her cheeks throbbed as the spots receded and the hot, thick night came into focus again. Warm blood trickled down her neck, and she wasn't sure if it was hers or his. She managed to get her hands under his shoulders and push hard enough to get the upper part of his body off her. Then something moved at the edge of her field of vision. She turned, head swimming, and there was Trudy. Her lips were moving but no sound came from them.

A cry escaped as Violet pushed Jay harder and slithered out from under him. With a presence of mind that did not come from her, she squatted and pressed two fingers to the side of his neck, trying to keep her gaze away from the gruesomeness before her.

"There's no pulse," she murmured. "Nothing." Violet was shocked into stillness. All she could hear was the pounding of her own blood in her ears. This repulsive scene wasn't real. *It's not real.* But then she glanced back at her sister, standing frozen, her hands wringing, her mouth moving with silent words.

Violet stepped over Jay's lifeless body and went to Trudy. She wrapped an arm around her sister's shoulders and led her back up to the house. In the kitchen she cleaned Trudy's hands and pushed her hair back from her face. She settled her onto a kitchen chair. "Wait for me. Do not move."

Trudy's gaze was fixed on the far wall.

"Don't move. Do you hear me?"

Trudy's head bobbed, up and down and side to side. Violet took Trudy's face in her hands and looked right in her eyes, trying to convey everything she felt without using words.

Trudy's gaze focused for just a moment, and there she was. Violet's sister, her only family, possessing a strength down deep that Violet had never imagined. She kissed Trudy's cheek. "I'll be right back."

On the way to the dock, she noticed bricks at the side of the yard. She hadn't seen them on her way down the first time. There was a half-built low brick wall, but the project had been abandoned, and now small piles of bricks lay in the humid night air, waiting for a new purpose.

Down on the dock, Jay was crumpled on his side, right at

the edge of the wooden boards. Violet forced herself to put two fingers to his neck again, but it was the same as before. No life, no pulse. She would have known even without checking though. Death was written on his face in his open eyes and gaping mouth.

In her squatted position she drummed her fingers on her knees, thinking. The night was so thick with fog, it rolled and swirled over the river like a living, snarling beast. There were other houses on the river, sleeping homes with sleeping people, but they might as well have been a mile away for all she could see them. There was a sensation of isolation, as if she and Jay and this dock were the only things in all the world that mattered. And for a moment, they were.

The promise to her mother floated back to her again. So long ago, but so acute tonight. *No one can know about this,* Violet thought. *It was my job to protect her. It is my job.*

Violet gave Jay a great shove and rolled him off the edge of the dock, where he landed with a *thud* in the bottom of his boat. Clamping her lips together to ward off nausea, she lifted her head and raked in air through her nose, and her gaze fell on the brick wall. The loose bricks on the ground. She rose quickly and carried the bricks, a few at a time, from the wall to the edge of the dock, just next to the boat.

She didn't even stop to consider what she was doing, only that she had to protect Trudy. She hadn't done it before—she'd been fooled by Jay's charm right along with Trudy, then she'd let Trudy stay with him, taking his fists, his words, his anger. It was Violet's fault. But it wasn't too late. She could protect Trudy now, and this was how she'd do it.

To keep from making too much noise, she stepped down into the boat and laid each brick carefully in the bottom. On Jay and all around him, making a mound in the center of the hull. Violet was sweating, panting, but she kept working. At one point she stumbled and fell back, scraping her wrist on a jagged rope cleat and catching herself on the motor at the back of the boat. The clasp on her bracelet popped open and the delicate gold treasure clattered to the bottom of the boat. When she picked it up she noticed the smear of blood on it. All at once, the magnitude of what she was doing took her by storm.

Two futures rattled against each other—one tucked away safely with Frank and the other always working to move past this awful, dark night.

Two futures, so different from each other, and here she was stacking bricks over a man's dead body.

A sob threatened to break free as she realized she might as well be stacking bricks over her almost-future with Frank. That future was as good as dead.

Violet stared at the bracelet—engraved with birds, given to her by a man who loved her, and smeared with another man's blood. *I can't wear this. Not for something this repulsive.* Instead of fastening the clasp around her wrist again, she set it on a little shelf built into the side of the hull. It had a small door to keep items safe and dry, and she closed it to keep the bracelet out of the way while she worked.

A few minutes later, she was done. He was buried. She now turned to the area behind the motor. She'd seen the drain plugs when she stumbled, and this was how she'd take care of it all.

She remembered from her long-ago morning boat rides with her dad, in a similar type of boat, that if the drain plug was pulled, water would rush in and eventually sink the whole thing. This boat had two plugs, and that equaled an even quicker sinking.

She was right. As soon as she pulled the two plugs, water began to flow in. She quickly climbed out, untied the rope from around the piling, and threw it in the boat. With the extra weight from the mound of bricks, the boat was already sitting low in the water, and under her watchful eye, it slowly began to sink even lower.

Just before it was out of her reach, she leaned down and gave it a great push away from the dock. It crept slowly, almost lazily, toward the center of the river, sinking ever lower as it went.

Sitting back on her heels in the steamy darkness, Violet caught a flash of movement at the end of the dock. A large brown pelican stood on top of the last piling, its small round eye catching light from somewhere and staring right at her. She couldn't tell if its knowing gaze was one of sympathy or accusation, but before she could decide, it stretched its great wings and lifted itself off the wood. With a wide flap it lifted high, sending air currents down and swirling the fog into shadowy tentacles that snaked around the boat until it dipped below the surface and disappeared completely.

A moment later, a few air bubbles rose to the surface, then nothing. The bird was gone, the boat was gone, and all was still. Even the fog seemed to quiet down. It was like nothing at all had happened.

Later, in the car on the way to her house, with Trudy in the passenger seat next to her and a hastily thrown together suitcase in the back seat, Violet rubbed her scraped wrist and realized the bracelet was gone.

Frank.

In those final moments she'd forgotten the bracelet, and Violet knew then she could never go back to him. He was too good, too true for the ugliness that had taken place this night. She could never tell him. She could never tell anyone. It was too late to run to Frank, too late to go back and keep Trudy away from Jay in the first place, too late to keep the promise to their mother, but not too late for everything. As far as anyone else would think, Jay Malone disappeared. He never came home from the Showboat. And if the question ever came up of what happened?

I did it. Violet's answer was immediate. *I finally took care of it. I owe her that much. I owe them both.*

The car was full of pounding silence as neither sister talked on the way home. At Violet's house, her small cottage tucked back from the river among trees and climbing vines and bird feeders, safe from the violence that had taken place upriver, Violet tucked Trudy into bed, then climbed in next to her.

"Trudy?" Violet whispered in the dark, but Trudy's gaze remained on the ceiling. There was no answer.

PART THREE

—————————— land ——————————

fourteen

On the day of Sugar Bend's annual River Days Art Festival, Maya woke up to something clanging outside. When she pulled back the corner of the curtain, she saw the small silver bird feeder that hung from the dogwood tree outside her window. She loved to watch the cardinals bicker and squabble over the birdseed in the tray, but at the moment the feeder was free of birds as it swung back and forth in the wind.

The television was on in the den, so she followed the sound and spotted Trudy at the dining table, working on a light and airy driftwood wind chime she was trying to finish before the festival started. Violet was in the kitchen with a hip leaned against the counter, her arms crossed, staring out at the river.

Violet had been acting so strange lately. She'd been jumpy and irritable, furiously flipping through issues of the newspaper and switching off the evening news as soon as it changed to local coverage. And she stared out toward the river a lot, as if expecting something or someone to rise out of it.

A news reporter had knocked on their door the week before,

asking strange questions about the boat that had washed ashore upriver. Maya didn't know why people were worked up about this random rusty boat, but she answered the man's questions as well as she could—no, Violet and Trudy weren't home. No, she didn't know anything about the boat. No, she'd never heard of Jay Malone. Later, when she had told Violet about the man and the questions, Violet walked straight out the door and down to the river. She sat at the edge, her toes in the water, her gaze on some unseen thing out in the middle.

In the kitchen Violet stirred to life and grabbed a dish towel from the oven door handle as the Channel 10 meteorologist gestured wildly at the map behind him.

"This wind is something else, y'all," he said with a giddy grin. "Out of the east at twenty miles per hour with gusts up to thirty. All you festivalgoers and shop owners better hang on to your tent poles and shopping bags today. Winds like this typically mean a storm is blowing in, but as you can see here on the radar, our entire viewing area is crystal clear. Not a cloud in sight. But the strange wind sure is blowing."

When Maya left a little later with Trudy to go to the shop—Violet left early to do her morning bird survey before heading to Two Sisters—the breeze crept under her shirt hem, wound around her hair, and lifted the edges of the tablecloth she toted to the car. Trudy tried to pass a note to Maya, but the wind caught it and carried it out to the river.

Trudy laughed and threw her hands up, but Maya didn't like it. The wind bothered her, made her feel like things were shifting and unsteady. Her grandmother used to say that anytime the wind picked up, it brought change with it. With her long, jewel-colored skirts rustling in the breeze, changing colors as the layers moved and twirled, she'd laugh into the wind, saying, *"Bring it! Bring on the change! I'm not scared!"*

But Maya was scared. Wind meant change and that was exactly what she didn't want. She'd had enough change in the last ten years to last a lifetime, and she was determined that nothing would take these women or this place from her.

On festival days Maya had learned the shops on Water Street and all through downtown were closed so everyone would visit the booths set up by the river and shop owners would only have to worry about customers at one place. Even still, customers kept showing up at the Two Sisters storefront, tapping on the window and hoping to be let in to browse through the items the women hadn't carried down to their booth.

Maya, Trudy, and Violet trotted back and forth all day, ringing up customers in both places, keeping a firm hand on their merchandise as the wind picked up, and holding down the tent poles so the whole thing wouldn't blow into the river.

Shouldn't we make them follow the rules? Trudy wrote in a note after another customer asked to be let in the shop up the street. *Why should we run ourselves ragged?*

"Because a sale is a sale." Violet's red glasses caught the sunlight and reflected pink shards of light onto the white tent. "And we don't turn down sales of any kind."

Trudy *humphed*, and Maya laid a calming hand on Violet's shoulder. "I'll stay up in the shop, if you want, to take care of the customers there."

"That'd be wonderful," Violet said, her hands busy fussing and refolding and straightening. "Thank you."

Later in the day, Maya was wrapping a glass paperweight in the shape of a starfish when the door to the shop opened. Maya knew it was Tyler before she even lifted her head. The air around her quivered and the tender skin below her ears pulsed in time with her heartbeat.

"The sisters told me I'd find you here." He was wearing his work pants with all the loops and zips and pockets and a perfectly faded blue Holt Feed and Seed T-shirt.

"You found me." Maya handed the wrapped gift to the customer at the register and watched as the woman tucked it in her bag and walked out. The rest of the shop was blessedly empty for the moment.

"How are things going?" A new smile eased onto his face—slight but intense, tempting and teasing.

"Pretty good, I guess." She swallowed hard as a breeze curled around the edge of the door. "We're selling everything in the booth. I keep having to bring more merchandise down there."

"That's great. Think you could sneak away with me for a little bit?"

From the moment he'd entered the shop, Tyler had been slowly moving toward her, a footstep here, then another one. Now he stood just a couple feet away, the space between them pink with heat.

What is happening?

"I—I don't think so. If I leave, there's no one else to watch the shop. Violet and Trudy are down at the booth."

"Okay." He took another step forward. He smelled like hay and grass and soil and life. Maya fought the urge to press her face against his neck and breathe him in.

"Can I come back and see you later, then?"

She nodded. He reached out and took her hand. He ran his thumb over the tips of her knuckles, sending a shiver from her fingers up to her shoulders. Just as he leaned down toward her—closer, a little closer—the door jangled again and a trio of women flocked through the doorway.

"Oh!" One of them giggled. "So sorry to interrupt!"

Maya took a step back and lifted her hair from her damp neck. "It's no problem. Let me know if I can help you ladies with anything."

"We'll be just fine, dear. You continue on with your . . ." The woman flapped her hands toward Maya and Tyler.

Tyler cleared his throat and grinned. "So I'll see you a little later?"

Maya yanked her hair up into a high ponytail and fanned her face as she watched him leave, the muscles under his T-shirt shifting and releasing as he rounded the corner and walked toward the river.

It wasn't until much later, when she locked eyes with a woman in a skirt suit and heels, that she realized the change had come. It was here.

f i f t e e n

Violet was slipping a customer's purchase—a small canvas print of a heron flying over marshy sand and grass—into a bag when a gust of wind funneled down Water Street and pressed her shirt flat against her skin. She turned her face in the direction of the wind, relishing its cool edges, and caught sight of Maya and Tyler by the food truck at the corner of Water and Maple. Their cheeks were flushed, as if they'd been sitting in the sun or running a race. They stood close together, not touching exactly, but the space between them shimmered with desire.

She sighed. *Young love.* She'd been there once and only once. She'd tasted its fruit, imagined its future, and wept when she lost it.

1982

Violet imagined Frank sitting on the stool at the bar, music in the background, whispers and laughter floating in the smoky air.

One elbow propped on the sticky wood surface, his body turned toward the door, waiting for her to walk in. She imagined him fingering the small blue box in his pocket, then standing and pacing nervously, maybe confiding to the bartender that he was about to propose to his girlfriend. She imagined his mouth and the shape of his lips as he formed the words. He had no doubt that she'd come. He trusted that she wanted the same things he did: a life together, full of love and adventure and the sharing of hearts and futures. And oh, how she wanted that too.

But the events of the night before, on that desolate, fog-shrouded dock, had changed everything. She'd never be able to look at him again with innocent eyes, never *not* worry that he'd learn the truth and find his sense of duty and responsibility outweighing his love and devotion to her.

She was supposed to meet him at eight, and as that time came and went, she rocked. Back and forth in the rocker on the back porch overlooking the river. At eight fifteen the phone rang. Five rings, then six, then silence. Violet rubbed the skin of her wrist where the bracelet should have been. Minutes later, the phone rang again, and for longer. A little later, it rang yet again—thirteen times—then nothing. Violet pressed her fingertips against her closed eyelids, blotting out images of his sweet face, his confusion, his concern.

Over the next few days, he called, he showed up at school, he found her on the beach—*What's wrong, Vi? What did I do? Why won't you see me? What happened?*

What could she say that would fix things? Nothing. It was all too far past fixing. And she couldn't bear to hear his broken voice, see the worry and agony plain on his face knowing she'd caused it, so she did her best to avoid him. It wasn't like she didn't have other things to occupy her mind, one of which was figuring out what she and Trudy would do when people realized Jay was gone, and for longer than one of his sporadic, unannounced trips out of town. When people started asking questions.

She was supposed to be on a flight to Florida in another forty-eight hours. She let him think she'd be on that plane, then gone for three months. But she wasn't going to Florida. Trudy was still in such a fragile state—not speaking, not eating, not doing much more than lying in bed and staring at the wall or sitting in front of the window, staring at the trees and the river beyond. Violet couldn't leave her.

She talked to Emmajean about it, telling her only that Jay had disappeared, probably with one of the floozies at the Showboat, and Trudy was devastated.

"Give her time." Emmajean often channeled her brilliant psychiatrist husband when doling out advice. "Silence can be a form of self-preservation, you know."

The night before her now-canceled flight, there was a knock on the door. Violet froze, then remembered Jay wasn't coming back. He couldn't hurt Trudy again. He couldn't hurt either one of them.

"I know you're leaving tomorrow," Frank said as soon as she opened the door. His eyes were weary, as if he hadn't slept in days, his hair pushed in a dozen directions. He wore his dress pants with a bright white undershirt, a state of dishevelment he never would have allowed if things hadn't spiraled out of control. "I just wanted to see you one last time."

There was that pull again on her midsection, the same one she felt every time she saw him. The one that spoke of need, of hunger, of tenderness and dreams. He took a step closer to her, but she put her hand on the edge of the door and held it tight. His gaze went to her wrist.

"You're not wearing your bracelet."

She'd worn it every day since he gave it to her. She even slept with it, wanting a piece of him near her when he wasn't. Its absence since the night on the dock was crushing. "I lost it." So many untruths, but at least that one piece was true.

He pressed his forehead to the door frame and exhaled. "Violet, I don't understand this." His chin quivered and he shifted his jaw. "You have to tell me. Is there someone else? It's the only thing I can come up with that makes sense." His voice broke and he put his chin to his shoulder a moment. When he faced her, his eyes were damp, but his gaze was firm. "Tell me. Is there someone else?"

Violet thought of Trudy sitting in the window seat in the back bedroom overlooking the river. Day in, day out, not saying a word, her future cracked because of a man Violet should have protected her from.

"Yes." Her fingers tightened on the door and she willed herself not to cry. Not yet. "There's someone else."

Frank's eyes opened wide. He swallowed and took a step back. Nodded. "Okay then. Thanks for telling me the truth. Good-bye, Violet."

She closed the door, slid to the floor, and put her face in her hands. Finally, she wept.

⁓

Roll call for the morning shift had just ended when Sergeant Webb rounded the corner from the kitchen and rapped his knuckles on the wall next to Frank. "Hey, Roby. My office, three minutes." He was gone before Frank could answer.

Stopping by the restroom, Frank splashed a handful of cold water on his face. He pressed his hands against the cracked porcelain sink and looked up at himself in the mirror: haggard cheeks and red-rimmed eyes that spoke of lack of sleep. Hair badly in need of a close cut. A red splotch on his jaw where he'd cut himself while racing through his morning shave.

As water dripped off his chin, the door opened and two officers entered, full of rowdy laughter that made Frank's head pound.

"Roby, you look like hell." One of them approached the urinal on the wall.

"Thanks." Frank dried his hands on a scratchy paper towel, tossed it in the garbage, then left the restroom and walked to the kitchen for a Styrofoam cup of bad coffee.

With nine seconds to spare, Frank knocked on Sergeant Webb's door. The man looked up from his papers and nodded toward the chair in front of his desk. The chair was notoriously rickety, and Webb was well known for asking new guys to come into his office for a chat, then laughing when the chair didn't hold up its end of the bargain. Frank eyed the folding metal chair, then sat gingerly on its front edge. The chair held, much to Frank's relief and Webb's obvious disappointment.

"Roby." Webb licked the pad of his finger and flipped a paper over. "I got a cousin on the force over in Pensacola. He tells me they're looking for new guys to join up. Seems they had a lean year. You interested?"

"Interested? In Pensacola?"

Webb shrugged as he flipped another piece of paper. "It's a good place. Bigger, so there's more going on. You'd be busy. And it might be a good chance for you to, ah, you know, start fresh."

"Start fresh?" He'd only been on the force in Sugar Bend for six months. Hardly long enough to need to start over.

Webb finally raised his head and met Frank's gaze. "Yeah. After the Showboat incident . . . well, when Mike asked if I had any guys who might want to work with them, I thought of you."

"Huh." Frank crossed his arms and sat back in the chair, then sat up straight again when the metal squeaked. Things had been strained after "the Showboat incident," as Webb called it— when Frank had reported on the two cops who'd been enjoying themselves there when they should have been cracking down— but tensions from that had mostly simmered down.

But then there was Violet. It had been a week since she told him she was moving on—with someone else. A week since he'd left the best parts of himself clinging to the other side of her door while his shell walked away. A full week of sleepless nights, frustration and anguish seeping from every inch of his skin and bones.

She'd be back at the end of the summer. He could either be here waiting . . . or not.

"I'll go."

Webb looked up in surprise. "Yeah?"

"Yeah. When do I start?"

Two weeks later he stood in the center of his new apartment, trying to get his bearings after his first full shift at the Pensacola precinct. Sergeant Webb was right—he was going to be busy, but busy was good. Busy meant less time for remembering. For hurting.

The move from Sugar Bend had happened so fast, he'd hardly stopped to think about what he was doing. He'd yet to unpack all his things, and one wall of the small den was still lined with boxes. Books, a spatula, two pairs of shoes, and a toolbox covered the surface of the kitchen table, and takeout food containers filled the meager linoleum counter space. All around him, his new, unfamiliar life lay scattered, stacked, and strewn. This was what he wanted—that fresh start Webb had talked about. A way to forget, to move on. But it didn't mean he liked it. Or that he thought it would work.

He swiped his hand across his face and then, pulled by a force too strong for him to resist, he crossed the room to where a shoebox sat on the table by the telephone and pressed his fingers gently on top. He didn't need to open the box to feel what was there. Tucked away underneath layers of papers and pens, receipts and old checkbooks, was a small broken shell wrapped in a paper towel.

"It looks like a bird just about to take flight." Frank could

still hear her bright, clear voice in his mind, as comforting as a sunrise, as close as his own heartbeat.

He pressed his hand flat against the lid of the box, as if the shell's presence in the bottom of the box could summon more of her back to him. But all he felt was rough cardboard against his palm, spongy carpet under his bare feet, and a vast emptiness pulsing in his chest.

"Get it together, Roby," he muttered. "She's moved on. Now it's your turn."

Reaching for his running shoes by the sliding glass door, he pulled them on and headed outside, into the evening's soft rays.

⁓

They showed up in the morning, while the sisters were both still in their pajamas on the back porch. Trudy hadn't progressed much from a silent apparition watching the river day after day, but at least she left her bedroom now for portions of the day. She still hadn't said a word, though, in the almost three weeks since the night on the dock.

Violet had just made some tea and toast when they heard the knock. They both froze, Trudy's mug halfway to her mouth, Violet's mouth full of buttery toast. Then in what felt like slow motion, Violet set her plate on the table next to her and rose from her chair. As she turned to walk back through the house to the front door, she paused with her hand on Trudy's shoulder. Tried to infuse her sister with some measure of strength Violet wasn't even sure she herself possessed.

She doubted that strength again when she saw through the front window the police cruiser sitting on the curb outside the house. Her knees nearly buckled and she grabbed the back of the couch to steady herself as the knock came again. Short, rapid bursts on the wood. A soft murmur of male voices. Violet smoothed her unbrushed morning hair and tightened the belt of her thin robe around her waist—*I have to protect her*—then opened the door.

Two male officers, one near to her own age, one much older. She recognized the older one as the officer she'd spoken to the day she'd gone to the police for help, well over a year ago. She pressed her lips together in a firm line. It was hard not to think about how things might have been different now if he'd listened to her that day. If he'd believed her.

"Good morning, Ms. Figg," the younger one said. "I'm Officer Lawson and this is Officer Hutchins. Are you Trudy Malone's sister?"

Violet hesitated. "Trudy is my sister, yes."

"Is she here? We need to ask her some questions."

At a rustle behind her, Violet peeked over her shoulder. Trudy was standing just inside the door from the back porch. Facing the officers again, Violet asked, "What is this in regard to?"

"Her husband," Officer Hutchins said. "Jay Malone." His gaze bored into hers, then slipped over her shoulder. He'd spotted Trudy. "If you can just spare a few minutes to answer some questions. We won't take up too much of your time."

Violet asked them to wait while she and Trudy changed

clothes, and moments later the four of them sat at the round table in the kitchen. Trudy's hands worried the hem of her shirt, while Violet pressed hers together under the table.

"Mrs. Malone, we've received word that your husband hasn't shown up at work for nearly three weeks," Officer Lawson said. "A few of his employees grew concerned when they weren't able to track him down. No one answered the phone at his—at your—house. Do you know where he is?"

Trudy shook her head.

"Are you not concerned about his absence?"

When Trudy didn't answer, he looked at Violet, then back at Trudy. "Ma'am?"

"Of course she's concerned," Violet answered. "We both are. Trudy's been so worried, she can't even speak. But this is what Jay does. He disappears without warning. Days at a time, occasionally weeks. He never tells my sister when he's leaving or where he's going."

"So neither of you have seen him?"

"No, sir. Not in weeks."

Lawson checked a note in his pad. "We asked around and it seems the last place anyone saw him was at the Showboat the evening of May sixth. He participated in illegal gambling on the lower deck of the boat, then was seen leaving later that night with a woman. I understand that woman was not you." He eyed Trudy, an eyebrow raised.

Trudy reached for his pad and pen, raised her own eyebrows in question.

"She needs to write a note," Violet said.

"She needs—? Okay. Sure." He turned a page and handed it to Trudy along with his pen.

I was not with Jay that night. He left and never came home, she wrote in a shaky slant, then slid the pad back to the officer.

He read her words and nodded. "When we spoke with the owner of the Showboat, he did tell us Jay had gotten himself into some debt with a few regulars there. Do you know anything about that?"

"I don't think my sister had much to do with their finances," Violet said quietly. "Jay took care of all that."

"If you didn't know anything about the finances, then you may not know he sold his ice cream shops shortly before his disappearance. Is that a correct assumption?"

Violet and Trudy exchanged a glance. A delicate line marred the space between Trudy's brows.

"No, we didn't know that."

Officer Hutchins had sat back in his chair, arms crossed, watching the exchange. Now he narrowed his eyes at Violet. "I remember you."

Violet held his gaze.

"You came to talk to us about Jay Malone."

Next to her Trudy shifted, and Violet could feel her sister's eyes on her cheek. "I did. You told me all about how good a man Jay is. How upstanding. Gambling, debt, leaving his wife— doesn't sound too upstanding to me."

Hutchins was the first to break eye contact. He clenched his jaw and uncrossed his arms, then leaned forward. "Regardless of all that, is there anything more either of you can tell us about where Jay could be? You have to admit, it's unusual for someone to disappear into thin air like this. There's usually an answer."

Violet thought of that night. The dark, dank air, Jay's lurching steps on the wooden boards, his angry, slurred words. The thought of claiming self-defense had crossed her mind, many times actually. But too much had happened. The bricks, the boat. There was no coming back from it.

Under the table Violet reached for Trudy's hand. "You probably know the answer as well as we do. He was in debt. He'd been with another woman. He sold his business. He had no other family to speak of." She shrugged. "Sounds to me like he walked away."

Later, after the officers had gone and Trudy had retreated to her bedroom, Violet walked out to the dock behind her house and watched the water for hours. The easy flow of it was mesmerizing—life coming and going, rising and sinking with every tide. If she squinted and held her head the right way, it was even possible to forget for a moment all that the river had witnessed.

At a footstep on the dock, Violet turned to see Trudy walking toward her, her bare feet skimming over the wood, the air around her shimmering in silence. She lowered herself onto the dock next to Violet, and there they remained as the day slipped away, the two of them bound together in a strange mixture of mystery, guilt, and rebirth. They stayed until the sun set in the west, lighting the sky on fire. Only then did they rise and make their way back inside, the falling darkness hovering around them, vast and quiet.

s i x t e e n

Daylight was fading fast, but the wind was still strong. It rushed around the corners of downtown shops, flattened tablecloths against table legs, and sent napkins and children's balloons soaring into the sky. The art show portion of the festival officially ended at seven o'clock, and as merchants closed their booths and took down their tents, the street party began. Two different bands—one bluegrass, one country—set up at opposite ends of Water Street, the middle of the road was cleared for dancing, and a few rickety carnival rides sat in a grassy field overlooking the river. Children ran free, their cheeks sunburned and sticky from cotton candy. Parents trailed behind, carrying shopping bags, half-eaten hot dogs, and cans of beer.

Customers still milled around, winding between the remaining tent booths, though merchants were quickly packing things up to carry back to their respective shops. Violet's eye was on the crowd as she nestled a few unsold candleholders and small notebooks with pressed-flower pages into boxes. She spied Trudy's old friend Billy Olsen with a baby girl in his arms, standing near a man making balloon animals. Across the street a police officer stood at the booth selling local grits and goat cheese. She only saw him from behind, but from the set of his shoulders and his light blond hair, she knew he was the same one who'd visited her at the shop. *Justin Roby.* Maya and Tyler were at that same booth, chatting with a woman who'd taken several of Maya and Trudy's art classes.

And a few booths down, there was Frank, wearing a red shirt and holding his cane. He'd yet to come by her booth to say hello. In fact, he hadn't even looked her way. She sensed hurt rising from his heart in sharp rays, making the air around him spark and rattle.

Violet's stomach flipped and her breath came in rapid bursts, causing her heart to stutter. Everything was closing in around her—the people, the sticky heat, and the music that caused the air to throb against her temples and the base of her neck. As she absorbed the sight of Frank, her memories of long-ago nights mixing with this windswept one, Justin turned, spotted Frank, and called to him. Frank waved and a moment later the two embraced.

Then a woman Violet had never seen approached Frank. She wore a crisp skirt suit and heels and her red hair was pulled back in a tight, smooth ponytail. She put a hand on Frank's shoulder, and when he took a step back from his nephew, she handed him something.

In the exchange Violet saw a flash of gold between their hands. He covered the item with his other hand, and like a marionette controlled by an unseen hand, his head rose and he looked right at Violet.

⁓

Liza hadn't been able to get away from the dream. It always started with the sound of the boat—that bug-like whine of a motor as it skimmed across the water. Then the images associated with the boat—fists and whimpers, damp cheeks and broken glass. Since finding the bracelet and sliding it into her pocket, the dreams had only gotten stronger, and stranger. Then just last night, she'd dreamed she gave the bracelet to a gentleman wearing red and holding a cane.

Once she woke this morning, she put the dream out of her mind and didn't think about it again, until she saw the man at the festival. His face was so kind, and he was wearing a red shirt with a black bird stitched on the chest pocket. His left hand rested on the head of a cane. And even stranger was who he stood next to—the handsome, clean-cut police officer she'd spoken with when she visited the police department. The officer who said he was looking into the mystery surrounding the boat and that she could call with any more information or questions. She'd never called him back.

As she stared at the man with the cane, a little voice in her mind told her to give him the bracelet. She felt the pressure of it—such a tiny, nearly weightless thing—in her purse. With her gaze locked on the gentleman, she unzipped her purse and reached in. Her fingers closed around the cool metal and she pulled it out, the wings of each tiny bird fluttering against her skin. A moment later, she tapped him on the shoulder.

"I know this is strange, but I think I need to give this to you."

Opening her hand, she caught his quick gasp when he saw the bracelet. The careful, almost reverent way he picked it up and set it in his palm told her all she needed to know: He had a history with it. This small gold circle engraved with birds meant something to him. He stared at it, looked over his shoulder, then walked straight toward an older woman in the Two Sisters booth wearing red glasses on a chain around her neck and a short-sleeved denim shirt.

Standing next to the older woman was one much younger, with long dark hair and beautiful tawny skin. As soon as her eyes locked onto Liza's, Liza knew her time there was done. Not just at the festival, but at the newspaper. In Sugar Bend. She'd write her final article, then she'd be gone.

Liza found herself walking back to her car, parked at the edge of the festival, her heart lighter than it had been in months. Maybe years. As she walked she tipped her face up and inhaled the salty-sweet breeze. Even if she didn't yet know where she did belong, it was nice to know where she didn't.

⁓

Violet stood stock-still as Frank walked toward her, but before he reached her, Justin touched his elbow and spoke to him. Next to Violet, Maya stood close, hovering, her gaze heavy on Violet's cheek. She asked Violet something, but all Violet heard was a hum, like the split second before the power goes out. In her peripheral vision she saw Maya speak to Trudy, who then turned toward Violet.

Before they could stop her, Violet grabbed two half-empty boxes and hurried out of the tent and down the street toward Two Sisters. The street party was in full swing now, with food trucks parked haphazardly on sidewalks and curbs, dancers twirling in couples and small groups, and both bands throwing their chords and harmonies into the wind, which whipped signs and posters and banners to bits.

When she finally made it through the crowd and back to the shop, she paused and took a deep, steadying breath. For a minute she busied herself, unloading and stacking and neatening, as she tried to quiet her stampeding heart.

Breaking down the now-empty boxes, she caught a reflection in the front window. Frank stood in the doorway, the golden glint of the bracelet in his hand. "It was Jay Malone."

"What?" Her voice wobbled in her throat.

"You told me there was someone else." It wasn't anger in his voice or hatred or pain. Just a breath of sadness that nearly crushed her. "It was Jay Malone, wasn't it?"

She raked her teeth over her bottom lip, unable to speak.

"Your bracelet was in his boat. This bracelet." He held out his hand. "The one I gave you. You loved him, didn't you?"

Sadness creased his brow just as a hot spark of anger flared in Violet's chest. But it died away quickly. The time for anger was gone. "Do you know what kind of man he was?"

"Do you?"

She put a hand to her chest when her words stalled.

"I went to his house once, on a domestic disturbance call. It was before I met you. But the bracelet . . ." He slid it back and forth between his hands. "It couldn't have gotten there unless you'd been there, in his boat. And that could only mean you'd been with him. You'd been *with* him."

"You don't know what you're talking about." She turned to hide her cheeks that flamed.

"Violet," he pressed, his tone one of need, plain and simple. Need and love, even still. "Did you love him? Was he why you left me? After all these years, you could at least tell me the truth."

The truth. It was what she'd been hiding for so long. She'd built her life around hiding it, and now the tidal wave in her chest—the overwhelming urge to let it all go—crashed down hard on her.

"I didn't love Jay Malone," she said, her back still to him. "I didn't love him; I killed him."

There was a sound of movement at the door. Trudy, Maya, and Tyler were crowded into the doorway, their faces painted with shock and alarm.

As the weight of a thousand pounds slid down her arms and to the floor, Violet exhaled. *It's time,* she thought. *These are my people and they deserve to know. Come what may.*

Behind them came another voice. "Uncle Frank?" The police officer, Justin, stuck his head through the open doorway. "Everything okay in here?"

"You may as well come on in too." Violet motioned with her hand. "Sit down, all of you. I have a story to tell."

When everyone was settled, she perched on a chair by the register and clasped her hands together over her knees. She exhaled a long, thin stream of years, then began.

"A long time ago Jay Malone was known as the friendliest guy in town." Violet swallowed a lump of disgust that crept up the back of her throat. "But he wasn't who everyone thought he was."

seventeen

It took forty years, but Trudy Figg finally woke up. It had something to do with hearing her sister tell the story of that night—*their* story—and something to do with the whirl of wind that snaked through the partially open front door. It was blue and pulsing and alive. When it sensed Trudy, it headed straight for her, curled around her back, and gave her a push. And it wasn't a soft push, either. It was a persuasive shove. *It's time*, the wind said.

Violet had tried so hard to rescue Trudy from Jay's clutches, but he had a vise grip on Trudy's hand and heart, and as hard as Violet tried to break it, he just held tighter. Trudy had never been the strong one—that was always Violet, everyone knew that—so she resigned herself to life with Jay and whatever would come of it.

But one night Violet showed up with a steely determination in her eyes—"You're coming with me, Trudy"—but her determination only fueled Jay's anger.

Trudy never knew where it came from—the roar and

crush of his ire and disappointment. She'd just barely been mature enough back then to know it hadn't started with her—something that forceful and ugly started much earlier and went much deeper—but she also knew she didn't have the power to fight it. The prey always knew when it'd been caught in the web. Fighting only made it worse.

When Violet had left that night, disappointed and resigned that Trudy wouldn't stand up to him, Jay took his anger and embarrassment out on his wife. His fists were like hammers, his mocking voice like a dagger. When he finished he gently smoothed her hair back from her forehead, kissed her damp skin, and said he'd be home later. Then he walked out. She heard his boat motor crank and knew he was headed to the Showboat.

Time crept by—it could have been one hour, it could have been five—then a knock sounded at the door. With her head wrapped in a fuzzy gauze of fear and pain, she crept to the door and opened it, and there stood Violet. Trudy crumpled like an empty grocery sack, then all she knew was Violet's soft hands, her warm fingertips, her strong arms carrying her to the couch. A warm cloth on her head, a glass at her elbow, then, next to her feet, a suitcase. "I'll take care of it," her sister said. "I promise."

In her stupor Trudy nodded off, and when she came to, Violet was gone but there was a sound. A shout or some kind of mangled scream. She rose from the couch and wobbled out the back door, moving toward the sound coming from the dock. Her head was still fuzzy, but a small pinhole of clarity opened in the fuzz and through it she saw her husband on top of Violet, his hands around her neck.

Trudy quickened her pace and as she approached the dock, she stumbled over the bricks Jay had been using to build a terrace at the edge of their property. That pinhole of clarity opened wider. The world around her became clearer.

Her fingers closed around the edge of a brick, the hard red clay biting into the skin of her fingers. Her feet on the warm wooden boards were silent. As she got closer she could feel the steamy, red heat rising from his back and head. Desperate to save Violet—and yes, herself too—Trudy raised her arm high in the air, the brick clasped tight. Just before she brought it down, Violet reached up from under Jay, her hands scrabbling for Jay's neck.

"Then he collapsed." Violet flicked her thumbnails together. "I don't know how hard I squeezed, but somehow it was hard enough. I did it. I killed him."

"It's not true," Trudy said.

Violet's head snapped up so hard she felt a crick in her neck. It was Trudy's voice, but not. It was scratchy and raw, more sandpaper than smooth vocal cords, but it was so sweet—the sweetest thing Violet had ever heard.

Though the door was barely cracked open, the wind had somehow filled the shop. The seashell and driftwood wind chimes hanging from the ceiling fluttered, paintings clattered on the wall, and the breeze across the tops of etched wineglasses zipped and sang. The shop was alive, but Violet's gaze was centered on her sister and that sweet sound she'd heard.

Then, like a sharp ray of sun breaking out from behind a cloud, Violet realized what hearing Trudy's voice meant. She had a sudden urge to jump up and cover everyone's ears before Trudy could continue, to keep them from hearing the words that would indict Trudy.

In a flash she was out of her chair and on her knees in front of her sister. "Don't do it," she whispered. "You don't have to. It's fine this way."

Trudy rubbed her throat as if trying to coax life back into it. "It's okay, Violet." She cupped Violet's cheek with her rough hand. "For all these years," she whispered, "anytime I'd close my eyes, I'd see his hands around your neck. But I'm awake now. It's time for the truth." Her voice was dry and raspy, but she gazed out at the group with conviction. "I picked up the brick. I hit him with it. I killed him."

The room went silent. The wind was gone, and in its place was a stillness that sank deep. The faces of the people in the room registered a range of shock, disbelief, and confusion. As Violet knelt on the floor at Trudy's feet, she felt the cool metal kiss of the bracelet in her right hand. She didn't remember Frank giving it back to her.

"Is it true, Violet?" he asked.

She bit down hard on the inside of her cheek, then met Frank's gaze. "It's true. I didn't have enough strength left in my hands to hurt him. I knew that. Trudy saved me. She killed Jay to save me. But it was my intention to hurt him—that's why I went to the dock in the first place. I wanted to hurt him for all he'd done to my sister. For all the ways he'd hurt her. Trudy just got to him first. She did what I couldn't do." She ran a fingertip around the bracelet. "It fell off in the boat that night. The clasp was loose. Do you remember that?"

Frank nodded.

"When I realized later that it had likely gone down with the boat, I took it as a sign of what I already knew. You were too good a man for everything that had happened. I worried if you found out what Trudy had done—what *we* had done—you'd feel the need to turn her in, and I'd promised my mother I'd take care of her. It was my job and I'd already let her down so many times."

Tears spilled over her bottom lashes and dropped onto her hands. She blotted her cheeks with the backs of her wrists and looked out at the room. "Now you know our story. Finally." She let out a gust of air. "It's up to you all what happens now. You can leave or you can stay."

Silence again. Maya and Tyler were pressed together at the shoulders, and Frank had one hand on his cane while the fingers of his other hand covered his lips. Justin leaned forward, elbows pressed to his knees, and rubbed his hands together. He cast a glance toward Frank, then stood.

"I know this was a long time ago, but . . ." He rubbed his forehead. "Regardless of the circumstances around it, technically a crime has just been confessed, so I'll have to bring you both in and get everything—all the details—on record. And I need to talk to my lieutenant."

"Justin." Frank's voice was quiet, and he spoke without turning toward his nephew. "Is that necessary?"

"I'm sorry, but it is." Justin was firm.

"It's okay," Trudy said, her voice still ragged. "We'll go. We don't have anything to hide." She stood and held her hand down to Violet. Violet grasped her sister's hand and let Trudy pull her to her feet. She gave Violet's hand a tender squeeze, and Violet's heart swelled.

"You're not going to handcuff us, are you?" she asked Justin.

His eyes grew wide. "No. No, that won't be necessary. But if you don't mind . . ." He gestured with his hand out toward the street. "I'll drive you on down to the station."

The bracelet in her hand tingled against her skin, and she turned toward Frank. "I'd like Frank to come too."

Frank sat still, his gaze fixed on some unseen image on the floor in front of him. Violet stared at him, trying to fill every air molecule between them with the fullness and sincerity of her heart. When he finally lifted his head and returned her gaze, she saw it for what it was. A second chance. She breathed in and felt the corners of her mouth rise a bit.

Justin glanced back and forth between the two of them. "I think that'd be fine. You can follow in your car, Uncle Frank."

Frank used his cane to pull himself up, then waited by Justin as Violet and Trudy walked through the doorway, hand in hand.

⌒

"I understand you're both here to confess to a murder," Lieutenant Delaney said. "Is that correct?"

"Not both of us," Trudy said. "Just me."

"No, that's not—" Violet began.

"Hang on a minute." Delaney wrote something down in a notebook. "Let's start at the beginning, why don't we?"

When they'd arrived at the police station half an hour ago, the place had been nearly deserted, with a single cruiser in the parking lot, a bunch of empty desks, and the scent of stale coffee in the air. Within minutes of their arrival, though, the activity level skyrocketed. The lieutenant and a few other officers—all higher ranking than Justin, by the looks of them—strode through the door as if ready for battle, laptops opened, pens poised, faces alert.

With every minute, Violet's heart beat faster, as memories of the last time she was in the police station came back to her: Men gathered round. Muffled laughter and disbelief. Grating disregard.

"Trudy, this is not going to go well," she whispered as they waited in chairs by a paper-strewn desk. "I buried him with the bricks, I sunk the boat, I—"

"It's okay, Vi," Trudy said.

"I don't think it will be." She let out a gasp of mirthless laughter, her heart beating in her throat. "There's no way they're going to believe me. It's one thing to have killed a man, but quite another to have hidden his—"

"Okay, ladies," Delaney said loudly, sitting down behind the desk and clicking his pen. "I'm ready when you are." He tipped his head toward Violet. "Why don't we start with you?"

"Just tell your truth," Trudy whispered in her ear.

Violet took a shaky, bracing breath, then began. She told the entire story, everything she knew to be true. How she'd been tasked with taking care of her sister, but she'd been fooled right along with Trudy, thinking Jay was a kind man, a good man. How she'd watched bruises bloom on her sister's lovely skin, watched Jay turn her into a fearful, nervous, jittery shell of herself. How Violet had gone to their house to do whatever was necessary to make Jay stop hurting her sister. Then she told them of the boat, the bricks, and the bubbles on the surface of the water.

When Violet finished, it was Trudy's turn. She spoke in fits and starts, her voice quiet and raspy, occasionally barely more than a breath, but she didn't stop. She told them of her life with Jay, his warm public charisma paired with his cold cruelty behind the doors of their home. Of how her strength and grit returned just in time to save her sister from a broken man intent on killing her. Probably killing both of them.

As they both spoke, the other officers in the room were rapt, their eyes trained on the two women, absorbing every word. No interruptions, no mocking glances, no casual brushing away of the truth.

"Is that everything?" Delaney scribbled down a couple more words, then glanced up at them. "Have you told us everything?"

Violet took Trudy's hand again. "It's the whole story. Our whole truth. I only ask that if you need to punish someone for this, I'm the one who takes the fall. It comes down to me."

"No." Trudy's voice was firm, but she had to clear her throat before she could continue. "I didn't tell the truth to cover it right back up again. I'm not proud of what I did, exactly, but I'm not sad about it either. Not then or now. The fall is mine to take."

Delaney clicked his pen closed and set it carefully on top of his notebook. He sat back in his chair, the flimsy metal groaning in protest. "Our records show the police came to your house after Mr. Malone was discovered to be missing. They spoke to you, Violet, because your sister wasn't talking. Why didn't you come clean then? Why didn't you tell them about his abuse and about your attempt to protect your sister? Why carry the secret all these years?"

"I didn't think they'd believe us. I'd tried once—I came here, to this very station, to talk to the police about Jay when I first realized he was hurting her. I didn't know what else to do. But no one believed me. They told me all about how Jay was a model citizen, one of Sugar Bend's best, and how I must have misunderstood the situation. So forgive me if I didn't feel confident in telling those same police officers what had happened in the span of that one awful night."

"Except that you wouldn't have told them what really happened. You would have lied to them. Told them you did it. That it was you who'd killed him."

Violet swallowed. "You're right. I would have lied."

He exhaled. "I have to say, this is not how it usually goes. People argue all the time over who's going to take the fall for a crime, but it's usually because no one wants to take it at all. Rare to have two people choosing to take on punishment themselves." He gestured between Trudy and Violet. "You two must have a special relationship. I've got a sister, but I have to say, I'm not sure she'd take a murder confession on her own shoulders to keep me from paying the price."

Violet bit her lip. "I'd do anything for Trudy." Over Delaney's shoulder, she could see Frank sitting at the back of the room, in the shadows. He held her gaze.

"I can see that," Delaney said. "And it's clear your sister would do the same." He leaned forward, propped his elbows on top of the desk, and rubbed his hands together. "I'm very glad Officer Roby brought this to my attention. Anytime a crime is confessed, we take it very seriously, from a kid stealing a stick of gum right up to two women admitting to killing a man." He eyed the two of them, his face unreadable. "The circumstances around a crime always play a big part in how we respond. In this particular situation, from all you've told me, it sounds like a clear case of self-defense. Nothing more."

Violet felt her mouth drop open. "But . . . I hid it all. I hid him."

"Here's what I think. I think in the heat of the moment, after nearly losing your own life and desperate to protect your sister from further harm, you did what you felt like you had to do. There's no penance to be paid here. Further, I think that if you, Trudy, hadn't taken definitive action that night, the two of you very well may not have survived the night. Now, it never should have gotten as far as it did. Police officers are sworn to serve and protect, and it sounds like they did neither of those things for you." He shifted his jaw. "And for that, I offer you both my sincerest apology."

Violet lifted her chin. "Thank you."

Delaney placed his palms on the desk. "I've been on the police force a long time. Long enough to learn sometimes the law doesn't fulfill its obligations and good people have to step in and take care of matters. That's off the record, of course."

He glanced behind him to where an officer was typing. His fingers stilled on the keyboard. "You two have my utmost respect. We may have some further questions for you down the line as we make sure our records are in order, but as for now, you're free to go on your way." Delaney stood from his desk and looked behind him, nodded at Frank, and walked back down the hallway and out of sight.

As the rest of the officers stood and murmured softly to each other, Frank approached Trudy, his cane thudding gently with each step. When he reached her, he lifted his head, the lines around his eyes deeper and more pronounced. "I have a confession of my own to make, Ms. Figg. I met your husband back then. I had a . . . well, a strange feeling when I was around him. I couldn't quite put my finger on it, but he was so convincing. So likable."

"I know," Trudy said, her voice a bare rasp now. "I'm the one who married him."

"I came to the house once. I saw you in the window. Did you see me?"

Trudy nodded.

"I always wondered about you. Wondered if you were okay."

"I wasn't okay then, but things got better. Because of Violet.

She took care of me." Trudy shrugged. "I guess we saved each other." She rose and pulled her bag out from under her chair and looked up as Justin rounded the corner from the back of the office. "I'm ready to go home."

"Yes, ma'am." Justin glanced at Violet. "How about you?"

Before she could answer, Frank spoke up. "Justin, if you don't mind, I'd like to take Violet in my car. If that's okay with you, Violet."

Unable to read the expression on Frank's face, Violet just nodded, then turned to Trudy and wrapped her arms around her. "It's over," she whispered. "Finally."

"Yes," Trudy whispered back. "But it's also just beginning." She winked at her sister, then slipped her arm through Justin's and walked with him out the door.

A moment later, Violet and Frank walked out of the police station into the now-still night air. Violet paused in the glow of a lamppost near the parking lot and closed her eyes. The damp air was fragrant with sweet night blossoms, silt, and river brine. When she opened her eyes, her gaze settled on Frank. He stood a few paces away, his back to her. She clasped her hands together to slow the nervous tremors.

"When you said there was someone else," he said without turning around, "you meant Trudy."

"Yes."

He sighed. "For years I thought about the woman in the window. I had no idea it was your sister. I wish you'd told me." When he finally turned and looked at her, his face was streaked with sadness. "Why didn't you tell me? I could have helped."

"You said it yourself. You always had the urge to tell the truth. Even before you joined the force. You held yourself and everyone else to a high standard when it came to truth and honesty. As you should have. I knew if I told you what had happened, you wouldn't have been able to stay quiet about it."

"Violet, you have no idea—"

"As a man you may have wanted to protect us," she said gently. "But as a police officer your oath would have propelled you to take action. And I couldn't let that happen to Trudy. I did what I had to that night—Trudy and I both did—and afterward, I figured it was better if I just disappeared from your life, if we never told anyone what happened. It was easy for me because Trudy wasn't talking, and I just never spoke of it. Eventually she and I went on with our lives as if it hadn't happened. Other than the fact that Trudy no longer spoke."

"Until tonight."

"Until tonight. Now it's out in the open, and I suppose you have a decision to make."

"Violet, I'm not a police officer anymore. My nephew has taken on that role, but you and Trudy both have been cleared. There's no price to pay."

"But you, Frank. You have a decision. You might not be a police officer anymore, but you're still the only good, honest man I've ever known. I wouldn't blame you in the least if you drove away and I never saw you again." Her chin quivered and she shifted her jaw to hide it. "What happens next is up to you."

Frank stared at her long enough to cause prickles of

perspiration to bloom at her hairline and in the crooks of her elbows. She wiped her damp palms on her shorts and lifted her head. She waited.

Finally he took a step toward her, then another, until he stood a breath away. He propped his cane against the side of his leg, put his hands on her cheeks, and lowered his head to look her full in the face. "You seem to think I'm some sort of perfect man, but I'm not. I wouldn't have turned you away back then, and I'm surely not going to turn you away now. Not when I've just found you again."

Her eyes filled. When they spilled over, he caught the tears with his thumbs. "Violet Figg, you're the bravest woman I've ever met. And you've been strong for so long."

"I've had to be. There was no one else."

"I know. But now there is. What do you say you let me be the strong one for you now?"

Not trusting herself to speak, she only nodded.

"I've wanted to do nothing but hold you since the moment I saw you on the beach with your clipboard and green hat. Is it okay if I do that now?"

Violet let a small laugh escape. A whisper of breeze twirled around them, and the space between them grew a little smaller. "It's okay," she whispered.

Frank pulled her toward him, his arms thinner than they'd once been, softer, but just as sure, just as steady. And her body responded, her arms lifting and wrapping around him, her face burrowing into the hollow of his neck. His firm chest buoyed her, enveloped her, and the years floated away.

~

The Sugar Bend Observer, Sugar Bend's Community News Source
Letter from the Editor, Liza Bullock
August 2022 | Volume 11, Issue 8

For those of you who have been following our reports on the boat that washed ashore upriver back in May, you know the boat was discovered to have been owned by Jay Malone, former owner of the Friendly's Ice Cream establishments. You also know Mr. Malone went missing in 1982 and was never heard from again. Many people hoped the reappearance of the boat would cast new light on Mr. Malone's whereabouts or reveal what actually happened to him. A bracelet was found in the boat, in surprisingly good condition, and we were hopeful that would give a new angle to follow.

However, the bracelet has been handed over to its rightful owner, and that's where the trail stops. As of last week the boat has been hauled to the dump, according to Carl Waters, the contractor working on the house where the boat was found.

"It was never going to run again," Mr. Waters said. "It was rusted through on the bottom and covered in barnacles and decay. Anyway, hauling it off seemed to fit, since we decided to tear the house down too."

Mr. Waters originally planned to renovate the house, along with several others in the surrounding area, but he said the house had turned into a nightmare project.

"I'm used to working on difficult houses, but this one was something different. Absolutely everything was harder than it should have been, and it felt like we were working under a dark cloud. Once we made the decision to tear it down, everything just moved like clockwork."

And so it seems that the mystery of Jay Malone will go unsolved, at least as far as it's up to this editor, as this will be my last issue with *The Observer*. However, regardless of whoever the next editor is, I have a strong suspicion the truth about Mr. Malone will stay just beyond our reach. It seems some secrets are determined to remain in the past.

Fondly,
Liza Bullock

eighteen

Violet was on the beach again, her eyes following the birds arcing through the sky and flying lazy loops over the water. She'd left her clipboard at home though, along with her binoculars and her data sheets. This time she was content to soak it all in—the feel of the sun on her shoulders, the squeak of sand underfoot, the scent of salt and time and memory on every breeze. She didn't need to document each wing and song and trace every flying arc through the sky because today she was with Trudy. It felt good to be here with her sister, in this place where Violet had walked so many miles and recounted so many regrets and fallen dreams. Now was the time to trace over those miles with something else. Hope, maybe. Or possibility.

As a slow wave receded, Trudy reached down and picked up a quarter-sized pair of coquina shells, pale blue and still connected at the hinge. She inspected them, then set them carefully in the bottom of her bucket.

Violet had one more training session with Frank before he

was ready to take on the bird surveys on his own, but Violet had asked him if they could postpone today's survey. "I'm going to take Trudy with me this time," she'd said to him this morning.

Of course he'd been okay with it. "The birds will wait. And I will too."

Again Violet marveled at the constancy of the man, the absolute steadfastness that the years hadn't diminished or changed. Somehow, despite all the intervening time and the secrets and revelations, he was still here.

"I know what Mom wrote in her letter all those years ago," Trudy said suddenly.

"What?"

"The letter she wrote you. I found it one day when I was searching for something in your room."

Violet had never had the courage to throw away the letter, though she'd wanted to.

"She made it your job to keep me safe," Trudy continued. "To protect me. Even back then when I knew nothing but boys and clothes and lipstick, I knew it was too much for her to have asked you. You were just a girl. We both were. You shouldn't have had to shoulder the responsibility of keeping me safe." Trudy spoke quickly, as if afraid the words would stop again if she didn't get them all out. A cloud passed in front of the sun, blotting out the harshness of the rays and raking shadows up the beach.

"That's why I never wanted to talk to you about what was happening with Jay," Trudy continued. "It wasn't your fault and it wasn't your job to fix it." She paused. "Even when it was really bad, I knew there was nothing you could have done to change things. It wasn't until you came back for me that night, until I saw you out there on the dock, with his big, ugly hands on your neck . . ." Her voice broke and her chin quivered.

Violet touched her arm. "It's okay, Trudy."

But Trudy shook her head. "When I saw him on you, I realized I could take care of it. I could be the one to do something about it. I knew I at least had to try." Her voice dropped to a whisper. "I wanted to hurt him. I hit him so hard, Violet. Everything he'd done to me, all his cruelty and manipulation, I put it all into that brick and I hit him so hard." She squeezed her eyes closed a moment, clearly remembering. "I wasn't even scared. I knew it was going to be either him or you, and I'd choose you a thousand times over him. Over anyone."

They'd stopped walking by now and stood close together by the water's edge. An incoming wave washed in, then receded, dragging bits of tiny shells and sand over their feet.

"But in all the years since that night, all these quiet years, your life has been on hold. I tried so many times to drag myself out of that silence, but I couldn't do it. Finally I guess I stopped trying. I knew you were missing out on so much, and I just let it happen. Violet, I'm so sorry."

Violet reached up and brushed the tears from her sister's cheek. "But Trudy, seeing you like this? You're finally free. You're using your voice and your whole heart. You're finally living the way you were meant to live. I'd do it all again, the same way, if it meant I got to see you like this."

Trudy nodded. "I do feel free, finally. But Violet . . ." She leaned her head toward Violet and held her gaze. "You're free now too."

Their arms around each other was the kind of comfort that could only come when two people knew each other all the way down to the core. Trudy and Violet had faced life together, they'd even faced death together, and that kind of connection was impossible to destroy.

From down the beach they heard someone call, "You're the art lady, aren't you?" A woman in a turquoise bathing suit and flip-flops was making her way toward them, her arms pumping, her hair piled on top of her head. "The one who makes all those sculptures from found things? I read that article about you in the newspaper."

"That's me," Trudy replied.

The woman's eyes grew wide. "I thought you didn't talk."

Trudy grinned. "I do now."

"Well, good." The woman fanned her face with her hand. "I want to come to one of your classes. I've been collecting shells on this beach for years, and I've never known what to do with them. Think you could help me?"

The sun broke out again, soaking everything in its white-hot brilliance, and Violet took a step back as Trudy and her student-to-be dove into a conversation about shells and twine and imagination and patience.

It had taken Trudy some time to get used to the speed at which spoken conversations took place—she was so used to the slow back-and-forth of writing her words, then waiting for the other person to read them—but she now seemed eager to try out her newly remembered skill on anyone who would listen.

Violet chuckled a few minutes later when the woman glanced at her watch, then down the beach behind her, as if searching for an escape route from Trudy, who'd been talking without even seeming to take a breath.

That woman has a whole world of words to unload, Violet thought. And she intended to provide time and space for her sister to say every single one of them.

A moment later, the woman was gone and the two sisters were walking again, their gaze on the sand in search of just the right treasures for Trudy's bucket.

"Would you look at that," Trudy murmured as she approached a small, pale skeleton.

Violet's breath caught as she spied the slivers of rib bones, the wispy tail bones, the gaping hole where the eye had been. She opened her mouth to caution Trudy, to warn her, but before she could speak, a brown pelican swooped in from behind them and landed with quiet grace on the sand right next to the bones. The bird pivoted so its small, round eye gazed right at the two women, then it leaned its smooth, feathered head down and scooped the bones into its pouch.

Violet pinched her lips together, her fingers tight on Trudy's arm. They watched as the bird took flight, soaring over the blue-green water, its wings flapping once or twice to keep it aloft. They watched until the bird and the bones faded, then disappeared over the horizon.

Tyler was moving bags of potting soil to make room for a few pallets of canning tomatoes a farmer had brought in that morning. He'd been at the store since six, and he was hot and dirty. So when Maya walked in the front door, he stepped behind a rack of spades and shovels and brushed the dirt from his pants and tried to smooth his hair as best as he could.

Peeking out from behind the rack, he saw her approach the counter and say hello to his dad. His dad gave her a small smile and a nervous tug on his cap, then went back to his logbook, where he'd been writing down each day's transactions for decades. He'd probably be doing the very same thing for years to come.

Tyler thought back to the conversation he'd had with his dad the day after the art festival. The wind that had made such strange things happen that night seemed to follow him home, and over breakfast the next morning, he found himself admitting he wanted to be a teacher.

His dad had tugged on his cap, much like he'd done just now, and studied his son. "You don't want the store." It wasn't a question.

"No, sir, I don't. I'm sorry."

His dad took off his glasses and rubbed his eyes with the back of his wrist. "Son, you don't have to apologize. I've known for a while you didn't want this life. I guess I was waiting for . . . I don't know what. But I shouldn't have made you feel like you didn't have a choice." He replaced his glasses and popped a piece of bacon in his mouth. "This is my life, the only thing I've ever wanted to do, but you have yours. I won't get in the way of that."

Tyler sat back in his seat and exhaled. "But what happens when you retire? Who'll take over the store?"

His dad laughed. "I'm forty-nine years old, Ty. I don't plan to retire anytime soon, but when I do, I'll figure it out. You do what you need to do, and I'll take care of the rest."

Tyler wasn't sure what his dad would do—bring on someone else who could take over the business one day, talk to his sister about possibly coming in to help, or something else Tyler couldn't think of because deep down, he wasn't a businessman. But Dixon Holt had always figured his way out of tight spots. It was what good business owners did. And Tyler had no doubt his dad would figure his way out of this one too.

As Maya stepped away from the front counter and scanned the store for Tyler, he stepped out from behind the shovels. Her dimpled cheeks made the blood run faster in his veins.

They hadn't seen each other since the night of the festival, when he dropped her off at the Figgs' house. He'd kissed her there on the porch as the night's strange wind fluttered the edges of his clothes, slid down his arms, and stole his words.

Standing in front of her now, he still felt like that wind was carrying away his words as fast as he could think them. She tucked a strand of hair behind her ear, and he reached out and caught her hand in his. "I've missed you."

"It's only been a few days."

"I know. And I've missed you for all of them."

She squeezed his fingers.

"That was a crazy night. I still can't believe everything that happened with Ms. Violet and Ms. Trudy." He frowned. "I've known them a long time. I had no idea they'd been through something so terrible."

"I know. They're pretty strong women. And I think they're going to be okay," Maya said. "There was something about that wind—"

"Right?" He took a step toward her. "I felt it too. It did some crazy things." His cheeks heated, remembering their kiss and standing so close to her on the porch that night, like there'd been a magnet in the center of her chest, pulling hard on the center of his.

"Hello there, Tyler," came a man's voice from behind Maya. Tyler blinked and looked over her shoulder. Billy Olsen walked toward him with his granddaughter propped on his hip. Mr. Olsen raised horses on a farm nearby, and he was one of the store's best customers. He was also a widower helping to raise his new granddaughter.

"Hi, Mr. Olsen. How you doing?"

"Oh, pretty good. I came in for a couple of your chicks. I figure Maisie would like to have some chickens running around the farm. I can teach her how to collect the eggs one day."

"I'm sure she'll like that." Tyler put his hand on Maya's back. "Mr. Olsen, this is my . . ." He trailed to a stop. Thankfully, Maya stepped in.

"I'm Maya." She extended her hand. "Is Maisie your granddaughter?"

"Sure is. I'm watching her a couple days a week while her mama works in town."

"I bet she'll love learning about the farm as she gets older."

Tyler watched as Maya chatted easily with Mr. Olsen. She was a different person now from the pensive, closed-off girl she'd been when he first met her. He couldn't have imagined that when she finally opened up, he'd be there to see it.

"I'm trying to put together a bedroom for her at my house," Mr. Olsen said. "I have a crib set up, but I can't find the mobile we used to have for our girls when they were babies. I thought it might be in the attic, but I think Barbara probably got rid of it years ago."

"You want a mobile?" Maya asked. "I know just the thing. It's in our shop downtown, Two Sisters. Do you know it?"

Mr. Olsen sighed. "That's Trudy Figg's shop, isn't it?"

Maya nodded. "And her sister, Violet. Trudy makes beautiful things, and she just finished a wind chime made from driftwood and little pink and white shells. She didn't intend for it to be a mobile, but I think it'd be perfect over a baby bed."

"It's been years since I've seen Trudy."

"You should come by the shop then. Trudy's there every day."

Billy smiled, and for a quick moment, Tyler could see what Billy must have looked like as a young man. Hopeful and handsome. "Thank you very much, young lady. I just might do that."

Tyler showed Mr. Olsen to the enclosure where they kept the chicks, and a little while later, he left the store with three fuzzy yellow chicks in a shallow box.

Tyler took Maya through to the loading dock in the back where they sat on folding chairs in front of a big box fan.

"I have to tell you something." He leaned forward onto his elbows as the warm breeze from the fan swirled around them.

"That sounds serious."

"It's not bad." He squeezed his hands into fists, then stretched his fingers out straight. "I just . . . I told my dad I want to go to college. And that I can't take over the store."

She leaned toward him. "You did?"

"Yeah. It sounds weird, but I think hearing the Figg sisters tell their truth gave me courage to tell mine."

She reached forward and wrapped her warm hands around his. "It doesn't sound weird at all. How'd your dad take the news?"

Tyler shrugged. "Fine, I guess. He said he'd had a feeling I didn't want to stay with the store." He rubbed a hand across his forehead. "I applied to Auburn last fall, just to see what would happen. Turns out I got in, and with a partial scholarship, too, but I turned it down. I didn't have the nerve to tell my dad I wanted more than what this place could give me."

"But you got in." Maya grinned. "And you got a scholarship? That's amazing."

"I'll have to call and see if there's even still a spot for me. If there's not, I'll reapply for January."

"But you're going to college."

"I guess so. As long as I can still get in. And as long as the scholarship still stands."

She gave his hands a squeeze. "You'll be great. Any kid would be lucky to have you as a teacher."

She didn't get it. "But I'll be in Auburn. It's four hours away."

"Okay," she murmured, still not understanding the problem. She leaned forward a little closer.

"And you'll be here."

"I will." She lifted a shoulder. "This is where I belong."

He ran his thumb over the tops of her fingers. "I hate that we've only just started and now I'll be leaving."

"It's okay. Because you know what?" She leaned in and kissed him, long and sweet, then whispered in his ear. "You belong here too. But take your time. I'll be here when you get back."

Violet found Maya sitting on the dock behind their house, her legs dangling over the edge of the wooden boards, the river moving beneath her feet in sun-dappled swirls. Lying next to her was a shoebox filled with odds and ends. Instead of turning around and leaving Maya to her reverie, she followed an impulse—the barest hint of a nudge in her spirit—and continued down to the dock.

"What's going on out here?" she called as she approached.

Maya craned her head. "Hey there." She turned back to the river. "Not much. Just thinking."

"Mind if I think with you?"

Maya tilted her head toward the space next to her, on the other side of the box. Violet slipped off her sandals, folded her body down, and, ignoring a squeeze in her knee, sat.

It was early afternoon, and the sun perched high in the sky with only a thin scrape of clouds marring the blue. Not wanting to push, Violet waited for Maya to speak first, and finally she did.

"I guess you're waiting for me to tell you about this box." Maya nudged it with the tip of a finger.

Violet glanced down at it for the first time, noting a fork and a small shoe before she lifted her gaze. "Only if you want to tell me about it."

Maya reached in and grazed her fingers across the items almost lovingly. "Remember the little shell box? The one I took from the shop the first day I came in?"

"Mm-hmm."

"I used to take things from the places where I lived. They were just silly little things, things that didn't even matter." She picked up the fork from the box and twirled it in her hand before dropping it back in. "They just made me feel, even if just for a minute, like I belonged there in that house. I guess it felt like taking a little piece of each place made me more real. More permanent." She tightened her ponytail at the back of her head. "It sounds so stupid when I say it out loud."

"It's not stupid. Nothing that comes from your heart is going to be stupid." Violet paused, considering her words carefully. "But you kept all these things, all this time. And you gave the shell box back. Why is that?"

A corner of Maya's mouth lifted. "I don't know. I think I knew this place was going to be different. Or maybe I just hoped it would be. Everywhere else I lived . . ." She pressed her lips together. "Even though I wanted something real, I knew those places weren't right for me. I think I gave the box back because I realized I wouldn't need it. Because eventually I'd have you. You and Trudy." A rosy pink spread across Maya's cheeks.

She reached down and snapped the lid of the shoebox closed. "Anyway, I don't need this box anymore. I don't need the stuff in it. I feel like I'm finally home. In myself and in this place. With all of you."

Maya slid the box behind her, away from the edge of the dock, and in the empty space left behind, Violet covered Maya's hand with her own. They sat, each looking out onto the quiet, unhurried river and the tide flowing in, breathing out.

Later, as the three women moved around each other in the kitchen putting things together for lunch, then as they sat around the table, passing plates of pimento-cheese sandwiches and glasses of tea, Violet marveled at the emotions swimming in her heart as she looked out into the wide-open future.

She thought back to another time when she'd seen the years unspool before her. Back then it had just been Trudy and her, and the unknown that lay ahead felt like a stark, scary void. But from where she sat now, everything was different. It was beautiful. Unknown, yes, but so full of possibility and promise, it nearly overflowed into the air around them.

It wouldn't be these three together forever though. Of course not. Maya would choose her own road, and she and Trudy would as well. Maybe the two sisters would stay right where they were, or maybe they wouldn't. The point was, they all had a choice. Life was theirs for the choosing, and for the taking.

It was evening. Trudy and Maya were at the shop putting the finishing touches on their shared project, which they'd decided to call "Gathering." The piece seemed to change each time Violet saw it, but what it most resembled was a nest—driftwood and sea oats carefully twined together to create a safe place for eggs made from delicate shells and sturdy tumbled glass.

The piece was a triumph and they'd originally wanted to keep it as a reminder of how good it could feel to land in the right place. But a customer had seen them working on it in the shop and inquired about purchasing it when they finished. After some deliberation, Trudy and Maya both decided they were okay with letting it go. The customer was coming in the morning to pick it up, and they wanted to make sure it was as perfect as possible before it went to its new home.

Tyler was picking Maya up and taking her out to dinner when she and Trudy finished. They'd been spending as much time together as they could before he left for college in a few weeks.

Violet and Frank had finished their last survey of the summer birding season that morning, and afterward he'd accompanied her back home. They'd spent the day's long, leisurely hours together, and she found herself slipping back into that long-ago place where she wondered what it would be like to spend all her hours with him. All the rest of her days. There were fewer of them now than when they first met, but she figured she'd still be around for a while yet.

He'd just gone inside to retrieve a bag of seed to refill a couple of the bird feeders. She waited for him, staring at the scene before her. To the west the sun had dropped below the horizon, but the sky still glowed fuchsia and purple, casting the river in pinky corals. A bright, thin strip of gold streaked through the sky over the water, like a fancy woman casting one last glance over her shoulder. Overhead, a light breeze sent the tree canopy into whispery waves and cooled the flush of her skin.

Back at the beginning of the summer, before the first set of fish bones appeared, before Frank picked up his binoculars and met her on the beach, before Maya walked into their shop and stirred Trudy to life, Violet had had a dream. Somehow she'd had the presence of mind to know she was dreaming, but it was so pleasant she tried to keep herself from waking up.

In that hazy place between asleep and awake, she'd seen two pairs of hands, one young and one old, rummaging through bits of wood and shells and dried things. She saw a key sitting in the middle of a strong, small hand. There were coffee mugs with steam rising from the tops and plates of cookies. She saw birds flying high over the river, then a hand roughened by age taking hers and holding tight.

Separately the collage of images hadn't meant much, but seen together, one after another like an old viewfinder camera, they seemed to stitch together a life she didn't understand and never thought she could be a part of. And now, finally, she was beginning to understand.

Footsteps in the grass behind her were followed by a warm hand on her elbow, then Frank's sturdy presence by her side. After tipping the bag of seed into the last empty feeder, he led her to the glider swing down by the edge of the water. They settled onto the swing, stretching their legs out in front of them. Frank laid his cane down in the grass, then reached for Violet's hand. It was such a natural movement, his rough hand taking hers, as if it had happened every day for the last forty years. But they were just starting.

With his free hand he traced the edges of the bracelet around her wrist. Where his skin touched hers, she felt the tiny flutter of the golden bird wings. "I sure am glad to see this on your arm again."

"I still can't believe it survived that awful night."

"I can't believe you and Trudy survived that awful night. And that you're here, next to me, after all these years." He chuckled. "It feels like a dream I hadn't even had the heart to hope for."

Violet nodded, her mind still reeling with all that had changed over the course of the summer. "I got used to my life with Trudy. Then with my students and later, the birds and the shop. It was enough, it had to be, because I never thought there could be more."

"And now?"

"Well, it's different now, isn't it? There's so much possibility. At this age it almost feels like too much of a luxury."

"Not too much. I think it's just enough. Though I would like to suggest one more thing to you."

He reached into his back pocket and pulled out a square of paper and handed it to her.

She unfolded it and smoothed the creases. It was a flyer and splashed across the top were birds in a rainbow of colors— frigate birds and wood storks, pink flamingos and roseate spoonbills, white pelicans and purple gallinules—along with the words *Birding Tours to the Florida Keys*.

"What's this?" Violet's stoic whisper belied her suddenly thrumming heart.

"Just something I stumbled across online." He shrugged. "The first time you tried to go, it didn't work out. I thought you might like to try again."

Violet put her fingers to her lips and scanned the page, reading each detail regarding the weeklong trip to the Florida Keys to study tropical birds in their natural habitats and migration patterns. There'd be boat rides and nice hotels, seaside dining and time to sightsee.

"I know it's not the same as your field study, but I thought this would at least get you to the Keys. I remember you saying it was somewhere you'd always wanted to go but never thought you'd have a chance to visit."

Violet lifted her eyes to Frank's smiling face. "You know why I couldn't go on that trip, don't you? I wanted to go so bad, but I couldn't leave Trudy. She was so fragile then. So broken."

"My dear, so were you. But you're not anymore."

"I'm not. I feel stronger than ever."

Frank grinned, his whiskery cheeks lifting and reminding Violet of long-ago, sun-soaked days. He took her hand again and pressed the back of her fingers to his soft mouth, setting her skin on fire. "I was thinking I might come along too. If you think that's a good idea."

Violet laughed. "I'd like that very much."

He put a finger under her chin. "I'm so very glad you walked back into my life."

She leaned forward and gently pressed her lips to his. Past met present in a shower of memories and old dreams. She put a hand on his chest and felt his beating heart under her fingertips. "Actually, you walked back into mine," she whispered against his lips.

For much of her life Violet thought she'd never be free—from her duty-bound promise to her mother, from Jay's menace and tyranny, from the memories that were like shackles on her wrists. But now, with her sister's courage, her own surprising sturdiness, and this man's persistent devotion, freedom danced along her skin like a kiss, warming the blood in her veins.

Violet sat back against the swing and leaned her head against Frank's shoulder, his arm holding her close. He sighed, a gentle rumble that passed through his body and into hers, settling her like feet on firm sand. She gazed out at the water, the place that held both secrets and salvation, mystery and mercy. Then she closed her eyes and breathed the mild, river-scented air deep into her soul.

Acknowledgments

Thank you to everyone at Harper Muse, including Amanda Bostic, Jodi Hughes, Becky Monds, Nekasha Pratt, Margaret Kercher, Taylor Ward, Halie Cotton, Savannah Summers, Laura Wheeler, and Kimberly Carlton, for your help in bringing this book to life. An extra thank-you to Kim for so carefully and thoughtfully reading this story and offering feedback that helped me strengthen it even more. Thank you to the sales team for your hard work getting books into the hands of readers, and to Julee Schwarzburg for your editing prowess, for making me a better writer, and for helping me figure my way out of all those timeline knots. Thank you to Karen Solem for always being willing to jump on the phone to help me brainstorm and work my way out of sticky corners.

Thank you to Erik I. Johnson, Director of Bird Conservation for Louisiana Audubon, and to Nicole Love, Coastal Coordinator for Alabama Audubon, for answering my questions about bird-watching along the coast and for giving me information that helped me create Violet's passion for coastal birds.

This book was a hot messy mess (Lindsey, I think you helped me coin that perfectly appropriate term!), and I had a lot of help transforming it into what you're holding now. Thank you to Anna Gresham and Holly Mackle for the brainstorming and for helping me get the characters out of the parking lot (even if that parking lot scene is nowhere to be found in the final version!). Thanks for being my partners in writing and life. Thanks also to Lindsey Brackett for the Voxer commiseration, encouragement, and laughter. Thank you to my sweet husband, Matt Denton, and our girls, Kate and Sela, for sharing in this writing life with me and reminding me to close the computer and have some fun sometimes! Thank you to all the Kofflers and Dentons and friends who message me to tell me when they've read my books or passed them on to others.

To all the booksellers and librarians who introduce readers to my books, thank you, thank you. And a special thank-you to my favorite local bookstores, Little Professor in Homewood, Alabama, and Page & Palette in Fairhope, Alabama, for being so supportive, welcoming, and fun! Thanks to the entire Bookstagram community, a tireless and enthusiastic group of book champions who give so much support to authors like me. And thanks to all you readers who read my stories then tell your friends and daughters and babysitters and tennis partners and strangers at the pool about them. I appreciate you so much and wouldn't be putting these stories out into the world if it weren't for you!

Discussion Questions

1. Was there a character you resonated with more than the others? A character you didn't understand? A character who reminded you of someone from your own life?

2. Maya stole things from the places she lived as a way to remember what didn't belong to her, as she hoped for a life that actually was hers. Did you understand her desire to have something of her own to hang on to? Why did she so quickly know she needed to return the shell box to Violet?

3. When Maya left her last foster home, she drove south and looked for a sign pointing her in some direction. Her grandmother Maria had frequently talked about signs and had taught Maya to look and wait for them. What do you think about signs? Have you ever experienced some sort of sign showing you the way to go?

4. Neither Trudy, Violet, nor Maya had a mother who stayed. Discuss the impact of Trudy and Violet on

Maya's life and why the two sisters felt so strongly about helping Maya. Why do you think Maya felt so drawn to the sisters?

5. One of the ways people may deal with a difficult situation is to avoid talking about it. After the night on the dock, the sisters didn't talk much about Jay. Do you think their intention was to pretend all was just fine? How might their lives have been different (or better or worse) if they'd been willing to talk about Jay all those years ago?

6. Violet gave up her chance at love and her wished-for life in ornithology to stay close to home and watch over Trudy. That's a huge sacrifice for a sister—or anyone—to make. Do you know anyone who has made a similar choice?

7. As the story tells us, "Trudy and Violet both navigated life the best way they knew how—for Trudy it was working with her materials and setting the pieces just right, while for Violet it was through the birds, savoring their ease of flight, identifying their needs, helping them on their way." Do you have something that serves as a way to navigate through your life? Or a way to relieve stress or anxiety?

8. After the night on the dock, Violet said she would never *not* worry that Frank would learn the truth about what had happened and that his sense of responsibility and duty to his job would outweigh his love and devotion to

her. Did you understand Violet's decision to leave Frank after what happened on the dock?

9. Toward the end of the story, Trudy admits to Violet that she knew her silence and pain after Jay's death kept Violet from living her own life and caused her to miss out on so much. She tells Violet she's free now. Has there been anything in your own life that has caused you to put your life on hold? If you found freedom from it, what form did that freedom take?

10. If the book were made into a movie, who should the cast be?

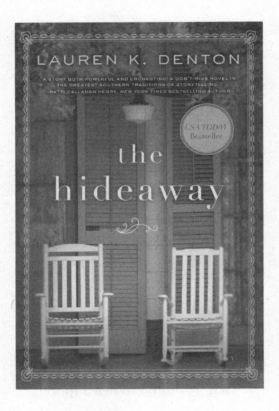

Also available from the author of the *USA TODAY* bestseller *The Hideaway*—two stories about two very different Southern families and the second chances they embrace.

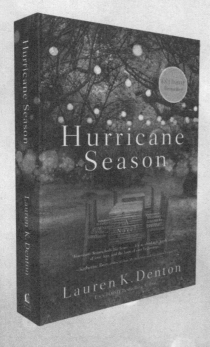

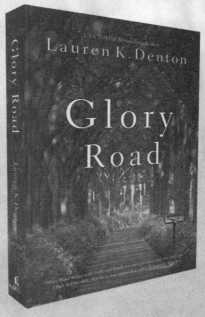

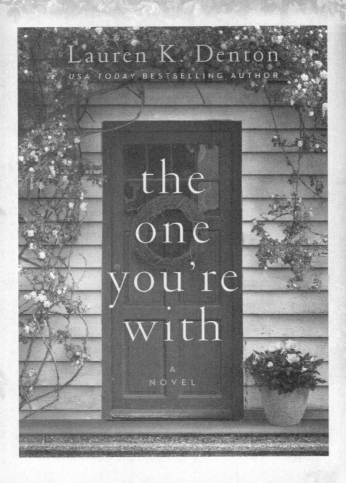

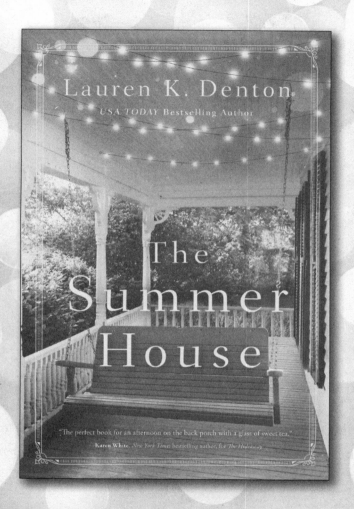

About the Author

Angie Davis Photography

Lauren K. Denton is the author of the *USA TODAY* best-selling novels *The Hideaway* and *Hurricane Season*. She was born and raised in Mobile, Alabama, and now lives with her husband and two daughters in Homewood, just outside Birmingham. Though her husband tries valiantly to turn her into a mountain girl, she'd still rather be at the beach.

LaurenKDenton.com
Instagram: @LaurenKDentonBooks
Facebook: @LaurenKDentonAuthor
Twitter: @LaurenKDenton